# WITCHIN' USA

## A MOONSTONE BAY COZY MYSTERY

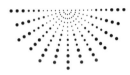

## AMANDA M. LEE

WINCHESTERSHAW PUBLICATIONS

# Last Will and Testament

I, May Belladonna Potter, resident in the City of Moonstone Bay, County of Shadow Lark, Island of Moonstone Bay, being of sound mind and disposing memory and not acting under duress or undue influence, and fully understanding the nature and extent of all my property and of this disposition thereof, do hereby make, publish, and declare this document to be my Last Will and Testament, and do hereby revoke any and all other wills and codicils heretofore made by me.

I direct that all my debts, and expenses of my last illness, funeral, and burial, be paid as soon after my death as may be reasonably convenient, and I hereby authorize my Personal Representative Ned Baxter, hereinafter appointed, to settle and discharge, in his or her absolute discretion, any claims made against my estate. I am to be buried in the Moonstone Bay Cemetery, no embalming, with a statue of my choosing to be put in place within six weeks of my death. If I should be seen after my death, my final resting place is to be moved accordingly.

The entire residue of the property owned by me at my death, real and personal and wherever situate, I devise and bequeath to Hadley Hunter, of Clinton Township, County of Macomb, State of Michigan should (she) survive me by thirty (30) days, otherwise to Moonstone Bay Historical Preservation Team, of Moonstone Bay, County of Shadow Lark, Island of Moonstone Bay. If both Hadley Hunter and Moonstone Bay Historical Preservation Team fail to survive me by thirty (30) days then I give and devise the residue of my estate to my Personal Representative Ned Baxter as well as the Moonstone Bay Downtown Development Authority to distribute to a variety of charities he/they sees fit.

If Ned Baxter fails or ceases to so serve, then I nominate Wesley Dunham of Moonstone Bay, County of Shadow Lark, Island of Moonstone Bay to serve.

I, the undersigned May Belladonna Potter, do hereby declare that I sign and execute this instrument as my last Will, that I sign it willingly in the presence of each of the undersigned witnesses, and that I execute it as my free and voluntary act for the purposes herein expressed, on this 5TH day of May, 2015.

May Belladonna Potter

1

# ONE

"**W**elcome to Moonstone Bay. We have eight hotels, fifteen bars and hundreds of shopping destinations. Where can I take you?"

I arched an eyebrow as I stared at the man standing next to what could loosely be described as a taxicab. He was handsome – in a work out four hours a day, five days a week sort of way – and his brown hair was a tad unkempt. Given the cut of his cheekbones and broad shoulders, the messy hair made him all the more appealing. Sure, the Hawaiian shirt and chinos tempered his sex appeal, but not by much.

Unfortunately for him I wasn't in the mood for hot guys and flirty banter. All I really wanted was a bottle of Pepto-Bismol and a cold cloth for my forehead. The choppy ride to Moonstone Bay – my new island home – on the world's smallest and most turbulence-prone airplane ever designed had been nothing short of vomit inducing.

"I'm going to the Moonstone Bay Lighthouse." I shifted my bag so it rested on my larger suitcase, which thankfully rolled on wheels. If I had to lift it I knew I'd throw up … or maybe pass out due to the heat and humidity. That wasn't the way I wanted to say "hello" to my new home.

"Really?" An eyebrow winged up on the taxi driver's handsome face. "You're Hadley Hunter, huh?"

I wasn't sure if I should be surprised or impressed. "Am I your only recent transplant?"

The man shrugged. "We're a tourist destination. That means we see a lot of new faces. Very few of those faces are permanent."

I spared a glance for the sunny sky, sandy beach and lush foliage that filled the area surrounding Moonstone Bay's small airport. It wasn't an airport like the one I'd left from in Detroit. That had been a metropolitan airport, packed with stores, restaurants and terminals. No, the Moonstone Bay airport had only one terminal and two stores. You were either coming to or going from Moonstone Bay. There were no connecting flights.

"I see." I forced a smile as I tucked a strand of my long black hair behind my ear. I could already tell the humidity was going to be murder on my tresses. It would soon become wider than it was long if I didn't get a hand on decent hair care products. I didn't give that due thought before rushing headlong into lunacy and uprooting my entire life to move to a place I'd never heard of and surrounding myself with people I'd never met.

Maybe I should go back. No one wants to deal with permanent summer hair, right?

"You seem a bit overwhelmed." The man smiled as he grabbed my suitcase and loaded it into the back of the cab. The vehicle in question was actually a small bus, one of those you see in movies from the sixties and think are cute on first inspection – until you're forced to sit on cracked vinyl seats and realize the air conditioning no longer works.

"I'm not overwhelmed." Even though the words came easily to my lips I didn't believe them. I hoped the man would be a different story. I was determined to meet this new adventure with a bold heart and open mind. I'm naturally snarky and prone to bouts of rampant complaining, so I wasn't sure that was possible. I was going to give it my best shot, though. "I'm simply a bit sick to my stomach."

"Ah." The man nodded, recognition dawning. "You were on the

morning flight, which means you were on the smallest plane that stops here. If I remember correctly, that plane makes the ride a bit ... rocky."

That was putting it mildly. "I think I'll take the ferry next time."

"If you have a weak stomach, that won't help. The waters are choppy when you come in through the bay."

"Well, great." I meant the exact opposite. I'm the only person I know who'd pick a new home that promised continuous vomiting whenever I traveled to and from it. That was so ... me.

"Yeah, you're overwhelmed." The man grinned as he extended his hand. "I'm Booker, by the way."

I slowly accepted his hand. "Booker? Is that a first or last name?"

Booker bobbed his head and grinned. "Yes."

Huh. Given the way he looked – half hot, half schlub – I guess I could expect nothing less. "It's nice to meet you. I take it you're the island taxi driver."

"Among other things." Booker ushered me to the passenger side of the small bus and opened the door. "Hop in. I'll give you the ten-cent tour of our fine island on the way to the lighthouse."

"I can't wait."

Booker was the chatty sort, which seemed to go with his outfit rather than his chiseled facial features. He didn't bother looking both ways before pulling into non-existent traffic as he began his running commentary.

"You'll find there're very few vehicles on the island," Booker explained, waving at an elderly woman on the sidewalk. "The island is only fifty square miles and the bulk of the population resides in the main city."

"The island and the city are both named the same thing, right?"

Booker nodded. "Moonstone Bay."

"It's a unique name."

"It's a unique place."

I'd landed only an hour before, so I could hardly argue with that. "So, I'm guessing the main industry is tourism." I kept my eyes on the scenery flashing past the window. "Does that sustain the entire island?"

"Pretty much." Booker's smile was enigmatic. "There are farms on the far side of the island, so we have our own fresh produce and meat. Other than that, almost everything we do is in the name of tourism."

"You don't sound particularly happy about that."

Booker pursed his lips. "I'm not unhappy with it. I'm merely … used to it. This is a new experience for you so it will probably take a bit of time to get used to island living. It's not something most people embrace overnight."

That was a strange statement. "Isn't island living the same as living anyplace else … just on an island?"

Instead of agreeing, Booker barked out a laugh. "You're cute."

"Thanks … I think."

"Island living isn't like anything else you've ever experienced, I can promise you that."

"You don't even know me," I pointed out. "I could be a wild person who jumps from island to island for all you know."

Booker slid an appraising look in my direction. "I think you're probably wild, but I doubt very much you've ever lived on an island."

"Why is that?"

"Because you're whiter than Maddie Park's new bikini."

"Maddie Park?"

"She owns a store on the main drag. That's not important."

"Then why did you say it?"

"Because I talk a lot and sometimes I simply say things to fill uncomfortable silences."

"We've yet to have an uncomfortable silence."

"Give it time. I always seem to find them." Booker lifted his chin as we hit a busy part of town. "This is the main drag. It's where you'll find all the stores and restaurants. Even though we're taking the scenic route, you'll find that when we get to the lighthouse that you're within walking distance of all of it."

"I guess it's good that I don't have a car, huh?"

"You won't need one. And they limit how many vehicles are

allowed on the island," Booker supplied. "I recommend getting a bicycle. It makes things easier. Maybe one with a little basket so you can transport groceries."

That sounded nothing like me. "I'm pretty sure you'll never see me on a bicycle with a basket."

"Oh, come on," Booker prodded. "I think you look exactly the type to have a basket, a pink bike helmet and one of those little horns to make sure people stay out of your way when you illegally ride on the sidewalks. By the way, that's a big no-no. The Moonstone Bay Downtown Development Authority will fine you if you're caught riding a bicycle on the sidewalks. That's only allowed on the roads."

"Good to know."

"I can see you're trying not to laugh, but I'm not exaggerating," Booker said. "The fines are like five hundred bucks so ... just keep it in mind."

That sounded absolutely absurd given the state of the world today – you know, real crime and stuff – but he appeared serious enough that I filed away the tidbit for later. "I'll remember what you said. I promise."

"Good." Booker was back to smiling. "So, this is the main drag, and pretty much everything you'll need is here. That includes grocery and hardware stores. The bars are great and friendly to everyone. The same goes for the restaurants."

"It looks so ... colorful." That was the only word I could think to describe it. From the kitschy T-shirt store with the pink awning to the tiki bar with colored surfboards dotting the walls, the entire main drag was a nuclear bomb of pastels. "Do you have regular seasons?"

"We're an island in the Atlantic Ocean off the southern coast of Florida," Booker noted. "We only have two seasons. Hot and hotter."

"I guess that means your schedule is busy and busier."

Booker nodded without hesitation. "That's exactly right. Maybe you are geared toward island life after all."

Somehow that sounded like an insult. "Give me the rundown," I instructed, resting my hand on my stomach in an effort to settle it as I leaned forward. "Are there any crazy politicians? Eccentric residents? Overenthusiastic cops?"

Booker nodded. "Yes."

"Which?"

"I didn't realize I had to make a choice."

"Good grief." I heaved out a sigh. "I guess living on an island is like living in a fish bowl, huh? Everyone knows everyone's business and all of those little things that drive you nuts about other people in big cities are magnified."

"Or maybe people are the same everywhere – at least deep down – and you find those sorts of things wherever you go," Booker suggested. "You, for example."

My eyebrows flew up my forehead. "Me?"

"Word on the street is that you come to us from Detroit," Booker explained. "I'm guessing you've seen your fair share of crime. That's the stereotype, at least. Island folk deal with that all the time. People think we're simple and quaint. People probably think you've witnessed a few murders and had your hubcaps stolen. How does that make you feel?"

"I've only seen one murder after a botched robbery outside of a casino and my hubcaps have been stolen three times."

Booker merely shrugged. "Were they nice hubcaps?"

I ignored the question. "I think stereotypes are often wrong, but they exist for a reason."

"Perhaps you're right." Booker flicked his turn signal and steered the bus toward the beach. "I knew your grandmother well. May was ... interesting."

I wasn't sure what to make of the statement. "I never met her."

Instead of being surprised, Booker merely pressed his lips together. "I know. She told me."

"She told you?" I couldn't contain my curiosity. "I've been trying to sort my way through this situation since I first got notification of her death three months ago. I had no idea she existed."

"She knew about you." Booker's expression was hard to read as he

7

remained focused on the road. "She told me about you before she died."

"You were with her when she died?"

"Not at that exact moment," Booker clarified. "May was a favorite daughter of the island. When she got sick – when we realized that she might not be able to fight off the cancer as easily as she did the old biddies at the senior center – we all made it a point to spend time with her."

"Because you thought she needed help?"

"Because we didn't want her to be alone," Booker corrected. "No one should be alone at the end."

"I guess." I tugged a restless hand through my hair as I shifted on the seat. "I'm confused how she knew about me and yet I never knew about her."

"Perhaps you should ask your mother."

"She's dead."

"Oh, that's too bad." Booker's expression reflected remorse. "May mentioned that Emma died when she was close to crossing over, but I was hopeful that she was merely delirious. She didn't talk about Emma much after she left the island."

"I don't know anything about her," I said, licking my lips. It wasn't in my nature to volunteer sensitive information to a guy I didn't even know, but there was something about Booker's quirky personality that appealed to me ... and not in a *Sex and the City* way. More of a *Friends* way. I'm talking about *Friends* before they all started pairing off. Wait, what were we talking about again?

"You didn't know your mother?" Booker furrowed his brow. "But ... I don't understand."

That made two of us. "My mother died giving birth to me."

"Oh." Booker's expressive face flooded with sympathy. "I didn't know that. I always thought Emma ran off and lived happily ever after ... or at least as much as was possible. It makes me sad to realize she's been gone all these years and I didn't even know it."

I took a moment to give Booker another probing stare. He looked to be my age, maybe a few years older. He certainly wasn't old enough to have hung around with my mother when she lived on Moonstone Bay. "Did you know my mother?"

"Of course not." Booker answered almost immediately. He seemed sincere, yet there was something off about the response, something I couldn't quite identify. "She and my mother were friends."

"Really?" I forced myself to relax a bit. "Maybe I could talk to her once I'm settled. I don't know anything about my mother except that she was married to my father and they were looking forward to having me. That's what my father told me, anyway."

"I wish that was possible, but my mother passed on some time ago."

"Oh, I'm sorry."

"I was sorry, too." Booker forced a smile for my benefit. "As for your mother, I'm sure I can come up with names of a few people who knew her. They'll want to meet you because … well … just because."

"Because of my grandmother?"

"She was beloved around here."

"And my mother?"

Booker shrugged as he pulled into a long driveway. I saw the lighthouse, white brick walls with red accents and a fancy blue roof reaching into the sky offsetting the lovely beach tableau stretching out behind it. "Your mother was before my time, but I believe she was beloved, too."

"Then why did she leave?"

"Island life isn't for everyone." Booker flashed a toothy grin. "But it's the only way for some people. I have a feeling you might be one of them."

Even though I found him a bit odd, I couldn't help but return the smile. "What makes you say that?"

"Because you're here." Booker stopped the bus in front of the lighthouse. "This was your grandmother's home for her entire life. It was your mother's home for the first nineteen years of her life. Now it's your home."

"You seem to know a lot about my mother despite the fact that she was older than you."

"It's a small island. Gossip spreads like mustard on a ham sandwich."

I tilted my head to the side, dumbfounded. "I don't believe I've ever heard that saying before."

"Then you haven't been hanging with the cool kids." Booker put the bus into park and killed the engine, his eyes bright as they caressed the lighthouse's bright façade. "I'm glad you'll be staying here. It's been sad to see the place so dark and quiet the past three months."

"Yeah, well, I wasn't sure I was going to come at all," I admitted. "When I got the letter ... well, let's just say I wasn't sure what to make of it. I had no idea I had a grandmother. For some reason I always thought my mother was alone in the world."

"Why did you think that?"

"My father knew very little about her, and apparently she never volunteered information."

"Maybe she thought she would have more time."

"Maybe." I pressed the heel of my hand to my forehead as I reached for the door handle. "Well, thanks for the ride. I appreciate the tour."

Booker snorted. "You're a poor actress, but I appreciate the effort." Instead of waiting for me to collect my luggage and head toward the lighthouse, Booker pocketed his keys as he exited the vehicle. "Would you like some help?"

Of course I would. I didn't want to get a reputation for being needy, though. "I'm sure I can manage."

"That's not what I asked."

"I ... can figure it out." I struggled with the answer, but managed to muster a smile. "It's just a lighthouse, right?"

Booker snorted, legitimately amused. "Yeah. How about I give you a tour and we'll see if you still feel the same way? How's that sound?"

It sounded like the best offer I'd had all day. "It sounds like you can carry the big suitcase."

"It would be my pleasure."

# TWO

The lighthouse wasn't what I expected. Actually, I wasn't sure what to expect. I'd seen my fair share of lighthouses in Michigan – it is the Great Lakes State, after all – but they were nothing like what I found when I walked through the front door of my new home.

Booker seemed at ease, as if he knew the layout and where May Potter (I was still having trouble referring to her as "my grandmother") put everything. The main floor consisted of a homey living room and kitchen, a metal spiral staircase cropping up out of the middle of the floor, and kitschy wall decorations that made me smile even as I internally cringed at some of them.

I left my luggage in the middle of the living room and gave the kitchen a cursory glance – I'm more of a takeout person – before heading up the staircase. The lighthouse boasted a tall tower but the secondary structure was more of a square. The staircase went all the way to the top, but I stopped for a brief sojourn on the second floor – the top of the square – and found a beautiful bedroom waiting for me.

The floors were hardwood; the bed frame made of reclaimed wood and covered in a homemade quilt. There was a blue settee in the corner and an ornate makeup station against one wall. There were windows on three sides, and I immediately fell in love with the illumination the sun offered.

"You'll get used to the sun," Booker explained, appearing in the doorway behind me. "You'll want to close the blinds on the ocean side during the morning hours and the other side during the evening hours. Otherwise it will be steaming hot in here."

"No air conditioning?"

"Yes and no," Booker shrugged. "The building has air conditioning, but it's a big building and it will cost an unbelievable amount of money to cool it. I'm not sure how you're set for funds, but ... you might not want to risk running the central air system twenty-four hours a day. It's better to leave the windows open. The proximity of the water makes for a nice cross breeze."

"That's a good tip." Speaking of my finances ... I shifted a bit so I could look Booker in the eye when I continued. "Did you know that May – I mean, my grandmother – was going to leave me ... um ... what she left me?" I wasn't comfortable talking about money, but I had to talk to someone. I knew exactly one person. "Does everyone else know?"

Booker scratched the side of his nose as he considered the question. "It was well known that May's family was, well, I guess the term would be 'independently wealthy.'"

"Did you also know that her will had a stipulation that I had to move here to inherit?"

Booker cracked a smile. "No, but that sounds just like her. I'm sure she didn't mean it as a source of blackmail. She probably only wanted you to get a gander at your heritage before making an important decision ... like abandoning it. She was big on family history."

"So why didn't she get in touch with me when I was growing up? I mean, to hear you tell it, she knew she was sick and probably not long for this world. Why didn't she contact me so we could talk before it was too late?"

"Are you sure she didn't?"

"My father would've told me." I was certain that was true. "He's an attorney. The will notification came to his office. He was as surprised as me."

Booker held his hands palms up. "I don't know what to tell you. I do know that May mentioned you over the years, although in a vague sort of way. She'd say things like, 'I'm leaving this for my granddaughter' or 'Maybe someone will spruce up the flowerbeds when my granddaughter arrives.' I really don't know why she didn't contact you."

"That makes two of us," I muttered, rubbing the back of my neck as I glanced around. "The house looks clean, but ... cluttered."

"She had a lot of stuff. She liked stuff. A lot of people are like that."

"A lot of people have hoarder tendencies, too," I noted. "I guess I'll have my hands full sorting through things over the next few days."

"And then what will you do?"

The question caught me off guard. "What do you mean?"

"Well, you're independently wealthy as long as you stay here," Booker pointed out. "You just told me that yourself. Once you get the place fixed up to your specifications, what do you plan to do with your time?"

That was a very good question. It was something my father asked before I left Michigan. He kept trying to get me to stay, insisting that knowing the history of a dead family wasn't important. I considered the argument and ultimately disagreed. I was doing nothing but treading water at a dead-end job in corporate website design anyway. If I really wanted to pick up where I left off professionally, I could do it anywhere – including here.

"I haven't decided," I replied, opting for honesty. "I want to look around and get a feel for the place first. After that ... I'm not sure what will happen."

"You're staying, though, right?"

"I ... for now." I didn't have a better answer than that. I didn't know if I could stay here. I only knew I wanted to investigate, perhaps get a feel for the roots I didn't know I had. Other than the next few weeks, the future was cloudy. It had always been that way for me. I could never see next year when tomorrow was murky. "I don't know what will happen a month from now, but for the time being, I will be here."

"Well, I'm sure you'll figure it out." Booker awkwardly patted my shoulder. "If you need help or someone to give you a walking tour, give me a call." He pulled a business card from his pocket and rested it in the palm of my hand. "I know you'll be busy for a bit, but make sure you take a look around town. I promise you'll like it here."

"I'll get right on that." I offered up a mock salute as Booker moved toward the staircase.

"Just out of curiosity ... ." Booker stilled with his hand on the railing. "Did you only come for the money?"

I expected the question. It would've been the first one I asked, too. "No. I came because I always felt as if something was missing from my life. I grew up with, like, ten photographs of my mother, an old quilt that looks a lot like this one and thousands of questions. I might not stay, but I have to know."

"That makes sense." Booker's shoulders relaxed as he offered up a heartfelt smile. "I'm glad to hear that."

"I'd be lying if I said the money wasn't a bonus," I added. "I wouldn't be able to do things this way if I didn't have access to money."

"That makes sense, too." Booker held two fingers up in a peace sign. "I'll be around if you need anything."

I smiled as I watched him go, thankful for the offer even though I wasn't sure if that was a comforting or disturbing thought.

I DIDN'T SLEEP well. The sun was nice to wake up to, the sound of the water soothing as the waves slapped the beach, but my muscles ached from moving stacked boxes and looking through closets.

Instead of risking a trip to town yesterday when I wasn't ready to answer questions, I'd found a can of Campbell's soup in the pantry and heated that up for dinner. I'd have to go shopping – and soon – but I was more interested in sifting through a life left behind. May Potter's life, that is. It was sort of my life, too, but it wasn't something I left behind. It was something I didn't even know existed.

There was coffee in the cupboard, but it belonged to one of those old-school drip coffee machines. A day without caffeine is akin to a day without oxygen, so I suffered through and made a mental note to find a place to buy a Keurig. A coffee shop that offered something with a gourmet twist to drink would be a nice find, too. I carried my coffee mug to the back patio and settled on one of the loungers there, thankful that the area was so quiet. I'd taken enough time to wipe down the furniture before the sun set the previous day, but I'd had very little time to explore outside.

Even though it was early, the sun barely drifting above the water's edge, the temperature was already in the high seventies and I could tell it was going to be a stifling sort of day. I sipped the coffee as I leaned back in the lounger, inhaling the salty air as my lips curved. I wasn't used to living on the beach. Heck, this was the beach to end all beaches. I would never get used to living like this. It was my first morning in a new and exotic locale, so I saw no reason not to enjoy it.

So far I'd found nothing in the house to hint at a reason, and a reason was what I was looking for. I needed a reason why my grand-mother knew about my existence and did nothing to contact me. I needed a reason why my mother had another life and never told my father. I needed a reason for living a half-life for twenty-seven years and having nothing to show for it.

Er, well, I had something to show for it now. I had a lighthouse … and money. Sure, it wasn't "let's buy a yacht" money, but it was certainly "rent a boat on alternating weekends" money. I couldn't complain about that – and because I can complain about anything, that's saying something.

I exhaled heavily, thoughts of continuing my cleanup forcing their way to the forefront of my brain. It wasn't as if I was on a timetable, yet putting it off didn't hold much appeal. I needed something to do with my time until I settled in, and organizing was the easiest option.

I drained the rest of my coffee before standing, a dark chunk of beach debris catching my eye about fifty feet down the sand. Initially I moved to return to the house, but something about the misshapen form bothered me. On a whim, I descended the steps and moved toward the lump.

My heart started thumping as I approached, even though I wasn't sure what I was looking at, and I cocked my head. I'm sure I resembled a curious dog rather than a muddled woman, but I was drawn toward the dark item and couldn't force myself to turn around.

With each step my heart pounded louder, my stomach twisted harder and my mind rebelled further. I couldn't be seeing what I was seeing. It simply wasn't possible. This was paradise, after all.

It couldn't be what it looked like.

It shouldn't be what it looked like.

It was, though, and paradise was suddenly lost.


"**WHEN DID** you find the body?"

Galen Blackwood, Moonstone Bay's top cop, was six feet of hard muscle and luscious black hair surrounding a face that would've made angels weep. No, I'm not being dramatic. The man was a fine specimen of the male form. In fact, he was the finest specimen I'd seen outside of a television show revolving around hot biker dudes. That's what he reminded me of, a biker dude. Not a dirty one who sold drugs or anything, of course, but a more sanitized version.

Wait, that made me sound like a special snowflake, didn't it? I hate that.

Galen yanked me back to reality by snapping his fingers in front of my face. He may have been hot, but the gesture was unbelievably annoying. "Are you listening to me?"

I offered up a scowl as I shoved my girly thoughts about his hot body and sinful face out of my mind. Looks have nothing to do with personality, and I was starting to think in this case that the only thing Galen had going for him was on a superficial level. "I was listening," I gritted out, fighting to maintain my temper. "I was just trying to decide what time it was."

"You do know how to tell time, right?" Galen asked dryly.

I narrowed my eyes. "I must've missed that lesson. Bummer."

Galen's lips curled but otherwise he didn't react. "So when did you find the body?"

"Right before I called 911."

"You didn't do anything else?"

"Like what? A rain dance?"

"Like touch the body or try to think up an alibi to cover your actions for the past twelve hours," Galen answered, not missing a beat.

"You think I did this?" My eyebrows flew up my forehead as I gestured toward the body. Galen had brought two individuals dressed in paramedic garb when he arrived. They were busy poking at the woman – who looked to be in her sixties and really, really dead – while pretending they weren't eavesdropping on our conversation. They weren't doing a very good job. "I didn't do this. Why would I do this?"

Galen wore khaki shorts and a black shirt that showed off a pair of impressively buff arms, so when he shrugged things rippled in odd places. I couldn't stop myself from staring.

"I'm not saying you did this," Galen clarified. "I'm merely trying to understand what happened."

"What happened is that I woke up this morning, made some really bad coffee in a machine I'm not sure how to use because I thought they only existed in museums these days, and then I saw something on the beach," I supplied. "I decided to look closer, realized it was a body, and called you. That's the extent of my knowledge on this situation."

"And where were you during the overnight hours?"

"In bed."

"In the lighthouse?" Galen inclined his chin in that direction. "You're Hadley Hunter, right? You're May Potter's granddaughter. I heard you hit town yesterday."

"Yes, and I'm so thankful for my welcome party," I drawled, refusing to tamp down my irritation. "Yes, I was asleep in the lighthouse. I didn't want to risk sleeping on the beach until I knew the

Moonstone Bay Downtown Development Authority's position on that."

Instead of being offended, or even a bit annoyed, Galen merely smirked. "I see you've been talking to Booker."

"He drove me from the airport to the lighthouse."

"He also hates the DDA. He thinks they're evil and out to get the unsuspecting Moonstone Bay populace."

"Are they? I mean, just because you're paranoid, that doesn't mean they're not out to get you."

Galen shrugged. "Anything is possible."

"So I should refrain from riding a bicycle on the sidewalk, right?"

Galen bobbed his head. "Most definitely. He wasn't exaggerating about that."

"Awesome." I flashed a sarcastic thumbs-up and rolled my neck until it cracked. It was only after glancing down at my feet, which were growing hot in the baking sand, that I realized I was still dressed in pajamas. Sure, nothing was on display, but the cotton sleep shorts rode low on my hips and the tank top didn't have a shelf bra, so very little was left to the imagination. Son of a blistering headache!

I did my best to cross my arms over my chest without drawing attention to that particular area. "This place just keeps getting better and better," I muttered under my breath.

"Did you say something?" Galen arched a challenging eyebrow.

"I said that I have nothing to do with the dead body on the beach," I replied, changing course. "I mean ... why would I kill someone my first night in town? That seems a little reckless, doesn't it? Wouldn't a smart person feel out the area before committing murder?"

"You're assuming you're a smart criminal," Galen pointed out. "I'm not yet sure that's the case."

Oh, well, screw him. He may be hot, but he's a complete and total tool. Tool quotient trumps temptation. "Do you have any other questions you want to ask me?"

"Surprisingly enough, I do," Galen replied. "They're not germane to this case, though, so they'll have to wait. As for murdering the woman on the beach, I'm fairly certain you're innocent. I can't rule you out completely, but you're not on the top of my list of suspects."

"How reassuring." I mustered as much mock enthusiasm as I could manage. "That's such a relief."

"The deceased is a local," Galen explained, ignoring my sarcasm. "Her name is Bonnie Wakefield."

"You knew her?" I swallowed hard, sympathy rising. "I'm sorry."

"I knew her. That doesn't mean I liked her."

"Oh, then I'm not sorry."

Despite the tense situation, Galen snickered. "I like your attitude. I can see a lot of May in you."

"I didn't know her, so I'll have to take your word for it."

"That's a shame." Galen planted his hands on his narrow hips. "As I said, you're not a suspect, but I need to make sure I've covered all my bases if I want to track down the real killer."

"And who is that?"

"I have no idea, but we've officially gone from two victims to three in as many months, so I'm pretty sure this case is going to get the bulk of my attention from here on out."

I was determined to remain strong and unfazed, but the admission was enough to knock the air out of me. "Three victims?"

"In three months," Galen confirmed. "The thing is ... your grand-mother was the first victim."

It was as if he took a stick and used it to knock my legs out from under me.

"Oh, yeah." Galen was seemingly unbothered. "We have a serial killer on the loose." He clapped his hand to my bare shoulder. "Welcome to Moonstone Bay."

And I thought the worst thing to happen to me today would be figuring out how to use the strange coffee pot.

3

# THREE

"That can't be right."

My mind revolted even as my heart skipped a beat. The hot police officer wouldn't stop staring, and my brain apparently didn't want to fire on all cylinders. It wasn't an attractive combination.

"Well, last time I checked, I know how to read a coroner's report correctly," Galen argued, clearly missing my distress. "I'm pretty sure I'm right. Now, I know that women like to be right above all else, but this time I think you're wrong."

"But … ." I tripped over my tongue as I tried to center my thoughts. "She had cancer. Booker said that. He said that she was sick and everyone on the island was spending time with her so she wouldn't be alone."

Galen's expression shifted as he pinned me with an unreadable look. "That is true," he confirmed. "May had cancer. She was fighting it. In fact, she was putting up a brave fight before it happened."

"Before what happened?"

"You don't know any of this, do you?" Galen shook his head as he rested his hand on my shoulder, the warmth associated with the gesture centering me. "Sit down." He gestured toward a spot in the shade under an oversized palm tree.

I'm not one for doing as others instruct for no apparent reason, but I didn't put up an argument. Galen waited until I was settled before continuing.

"May was sick for a long time," Galen started. "She didn't have an easy fight – not that anyone with cancer can ever say that – but she was very weak. She had unbelievable strength of character, though, so she wasn't about to lie down and let something bad happen to her.

"She was going through chemotherapy and the doctors were hopeful," he continued. "She didn't have a firm prognosis, but the doctors thought they could extend her life – and not in a way that would've made one question the wisdom associated with the decision."

"Meaning she would've had good quality of life," I surmised. "So … what happened?"

"First, let me ask you something," Galen prodded. "Didn't you ever ask the people who informed you of May's death how she died? She wasn't a young woman by any stretch of the imagination, but she wasn't old and decrepit either."

"I didn't think about it," I admitted, rubbing my sweaty palms over my bare knees. "I didn't know her. She was an ideal more than anything else. I wondered about my mother's mother, but since I didn't know my own mother it wasn't something I dwelled on."

"I didn't know that." Galen's voice gentled. "I assumed you got to spend some time with her."

"You know what they say about people who assume things, right?"

"Yes, that we make wonderful cops." Galen let loose a lopsided smile as his dimple came out to play. "I'm sorry I made the wrong assumption. I'm also sorry you never got a chance to get to know May. She was a treasure.

"As for her death, she wasn't winning, but she wasn't losing either," he continued. "A woman who was spending time with May – Bonnie, in fact – arrived at the house to check on her one morning. She was dead, cold in the bed.

"At first we thought she died of complications from the cancer.

Still, we had the medical examiner run a few tests just to be on the safe side. It turns out May's death didn't have anything to do with cancer and everything to do with poison."

My unsettled stomach flipped. "Poison?"

"Hemlock, to be exact."

"I'm not sure what that is, but I'm sure you know better than me." I ran a hand through my morning tousled hair and rested my chin on my knees. "So you don't have a suspect?"

"Not at present," Galen replied. "However, the deceased – three women, all in the same age group, all prominent property owners here on the island – give me the idea that this is bigger than I initially thought."

"You didn't think it was a big deal when May Potter died?"

"I did, but I also thought it might've been something like a mercy killing," Galen answered. "I thought maybe someone close to her believed May was in pain and tried to ease her suffering."

"What about the second victim?"

"Winifred Chase. She was sick, too. Her son found her dead in bed, and I almost let it go. She looked as if she was at death's door for twenty years, so it wouldn't have surprised me at all if she'd slipped away in the dead of night.

"Still, I decided to gather a blood sample, and it just came back from the lab about a week ago," Galen continued. "She was poisoned, too."

"Hemlock?"

"Nightshade."

"What does that tell you?"

"That someone is hunting senior citizens on my island and I don't like it." Galen shifted his position so he could lock gazes with me. "I really am sorry for telling you the way I did. I thought you knew."

"It seems I don't know much of anything."

"This hasn't been much of a welcome for you."

"I used to live in a suburb of Detroit. I'm used to worse."

"That makes me inexplicably sad." Galen gripped my forearm and tugged me to a standing position, automatically dusting off the bottom of my shorts as if I were a child before catching himself. "Um ... sorry. You can probably do that yourself, huh?"

"Yeah." I finished the task while searching his face for clues. "So what happens now?"

"Now the medical examiner takes photos and collects the body," Galen replied. "Then two of my men will spend the day on the beach combing for evidence."

"Do you expect to find any?"

"Probably not."

"You still have to do it, right?"

"Pretty much," Galen confirmed. "Technically we don't have any evidence tying Bonnie's death to that of your grandmother and Winifred."

"You believe otherwise."

"I think the odds of three women in the same age group dying in a way that's not connected – especially in such a short time frame – have to be long."

I couldn't argue with that. "When will you know for sure?"

"Hopefully by tomorrow. I'll have the coroner put a rush on the labs."

"Will you call me when you know?" I felt a bit needy, even some-what whiny, asking the question. That didn't stop me from yearning for a response.

"I'll call you," Galen promised. "As soon as I have answers of any kind, you'll be the first to know."


"**YOU MUST BE** Hadley Hunter."

It seemed my arrival was common knowledge and apparently everyone knew I was not only in town but also what I looked like. That's exactly what I found when I took a break from the lighthouse – and watching law enforcement tirelessly scour the beach – and headed into town.

Moonstone Bay was full of kitsch and cheese, and I made it only a few blocks before I needed a break. I popped my head into the nearest tiki bar – there were four as far as I could tell – and grabbed a stool at the bar.

The woman behind the bar, a perky blonde with a set of the brightest blue eyes I'd ever seen, immediately headed in my direction when she saw me. She was already speaking before I had a chance to order.

"I'm Hadley," I confirmed, doing my best to keep from scowling. I didn't want to get off on the wrong foot with the residents, after all. It wasn't the bartender's fault that I found a dead body on my property less than twenty-four hours after hitting town. "I take it there's been some sort of memo sent out about me or something, huh?"

"The library board put together a newsletter." The bartender beamed as my smile slipped. "And I'm kidding. I'm Lilac Meadows. This is my bar."

My mouth dropped open, myriad thoughts vying for top billing in my busy brain. "Your name is Lilac Meadows?"

Lilac nodded. "It is."

"Is that your real name?"

"As opposed to what, my stripper name?"

I didn't want to admit that was the first thing that popped into my head. "It's just ... I'm from Detroit. People don't have fun names like that in Detroit. It must be an island thing."

"Yeah, that must be it," Lilac said dryly, shaking her head. "Still, despite the laughing I'm sure you're hiding so I don't yank out your hair, I get it. What can I get you?"

"I'll just have an iced tea with lemon if you have it."

"Coming right up."

I watched Lilac work, taking the occasional glance around the empty bar before speaking. "Is it normal for things to be this dead?"

"We're between tourist groups right now," Lilac explained, sliding the iced tea in front of me. "Basically our busy period is Wednesday through Sunday. Then, on Mondays and Tuesdays we have quiet days before starting all over again."

"So no one ever stays more than five days?" That sounded odd. If I were going to fly to a tropical island for a vacation I'd want to stay a lot longer than five days.

"They do," Lilac answered. "Mondays and Tuesdays are simply quiet by comparison."

She said the words, but I wasn't sure I believed them. Still, arguing about busy days on a tourist island was pretty low on my to-do list. "I'm still learning my way around," I offered. "In fact, this is my first trip downtown."

"I thought Booker gave you a tour." Lilac wrinkled her nose. "He said he gave you a tour. If he dropped you in the middle of island madness without a tour ... ."

I cut her off with a shake of my head. "He drove me around. He even carried my luggage inside. It's not the same as exploring on your own, though."

"Did he take you in the bus?"

I nodded. "I didn't think buses like that still existed."

"They shouldn't, but Booker refuses to give it up. He's a bit traditional that way."

"Traditional?" I rolled the word through my head. "That's not the word I'd use to describe him."

"What word would you use? Wait, let me guess ... hot. You thought he was hot, didn't you?" Lilac's eyes lit with mirth. "Don't worry about it. Everyone thinks he's hot."

"He's definitely hot." I wasn't embarrassed to admit it, especially with Lilac's personality so bubbly and warm. "In fact, I've decided you guys must have something in the water because I've met exactly two guys and they've both been freakishly hot."

Lilac was intrigued. "Who else did you meet?"

"Galen Blackwood."

Lilac snorted. "Oh, you have had a busy two days. You crossed paths with our two most eligible bachelors. They always earn a lot of female attention."

"I'm not interested," I cautioned. "I'm simply commenting on the fact that they're hot. Their personalities leave a bit to be desired."

"They're men, honey. They can't stop themselves from being total turds when they open their mouths."

"Not all men are like that."

"You're right," Lilac conceded. "The gay ones are better." She seemed distracted when she tapped on the bar. "You know what? You haven't had a proper tour of town yet and this place is dead, how about I show you around?"

It was a nice offer, but I didn't want to be responsible for tearing Lilac away from her work. "Oh, you don't have to."

"I want to." Lilac untied her apron and placed it on the bar. "Come on. We haven't had a new resident for a long time. You need a tour if you're going to understand."

That was an odd thing to say, even odder than the other weird things I'd heard since arriving on the world's quirkiest island. "What do I need to understand?"

Lilac's smile was enigmatic. "Just about everything."

**"SO, WE'VE BEEN** through the stores, restaurants and government offices," Lilac said two hours later. "What else do you want to see?"

Being a Michigan transplant, I had trouble focusing on Lilac's voice at a certain point due to the heat. I was at a point where I struggled to pretend the oven-like temperature and the wall of humidity didn't bother me. It was a bona fide theatrical extravaganza, but Lilac barely broke a sweat. I didn't want her to think I was some sort of weakling. "I don't know. Is there anything else to see?"

Lilac shrugged as we turned down a side street. "I don't think so, but ... let me give it a second and really think about it. We'll walk around the block while I'm doing that. There's a great view of the dock at the end of this street."

Great. More walking. That was the last thing I wanted. I heaved a sigh and wiped my forearm against my forehead as I forced a smile. "I love a good view."

Lilac cast me a sidelong look as she slowed her pace and handed me the oversized bottle of water she carried. "I forgot that it takes some folks time to acclimate to the weather. I'm so used to it that I don't even notice."

I'm fussy about sharing drinks with people – you know, that whole backwash thing is gross – but I was so desperate for hydration that I would've shared a bottle of water with the entire island at this point. I wouldn't even turn down the water if Lilac was a drooler, which thankfully she didn't appear to be. I unscrewed the cap, guzzled a quarter of the bottle down without blinking, and then wiped the overflow from the corners of my mouth before speaking again. "Thanks. That hit the spot."

Lilac snorted as she trailed her fingers over a pretty flowered hedge. "You need to learn to voice your opinion, honey. If you're thirsty, ask for water."

The smile I offered up was rueful. "I didn't realize I was that thirsty until I had the bottle in my hand. It's just so ... freaking hot."

"It is, but it's an island. You'll get used to the heat."

I wasn't sure, but I kept that concern to myself. "This entire thing is new to me," I admitted after a beat. "I never fancied myself living on an island. It was never even a consideration. Okay, maybe Harsens Island. That's not really an island, though. It's kind of an island, but it's so close to the mainland that you can swim there in five minutes flat."

Lilac arched an eyebrow as I babbled. "I've never heard of Harsens Island. Is that in the gulf?"

We were from two different worlds. I should've expected that. "Never mind." I handed back the water bottle. "It's not important. Show me the nice view. I'm getting my second wind."

Lilac pursed her lips as she looked over my red face and sweaty brow. "I'm starting to think you need a third wind."

I was pretty sure that wasn't a compliment. Instead of picking a fight and ruining a potential friendship, I turned my attention to the plot of land in front of me. It looked like a normal residential street except for the huge ten-foot-tall fence at the far end. "What's that?"

Lilac followed my gaze. "Oh, that's the cemetery."

It didn't look like any cemetery I'd ever seen. "Why are the walls like that?"

"Oh, well ... ." Lilac chewed her bottom lip. "Aren't all cemeteries like that?"

She had to be joking. That was all I could think. "Not the cemeteries where I'm from."

"Maybe it's because of the inclement weather," Lilac suggested. "We get a lot of bad storms in these parts, so maybe the town founders were worried the caskets would float away."

"Oh, is it an above-ground cemetery?" I'd never visited one in person but I'd seen photographs. "That sounds cool." I picked up my pace and hurried to the gate, frowning when I found it locked. "What's the deal?"

"The cemetery is only open for residents," Lilac explained. "No one wants tourists wandering around and disturbing the ... um ... environment."

"But what would the tourists do?" I honestly didn't understand.

"Who knows? They're tourists, right?" Lilac made a face as she gestured toward the sidewalk. "We should continue our walk."

"But what about the cemetery?"

"I'm not morbid, so I don't pay the cemetery a lot of attention," Lilac replied. "It's not my thing."

"But ... ."

Lilac held up a hand to still me. "Listen, the cemetery is one of those things people ignore because it's dark and depressing. No one wants to think about death on an island."

I wasn't quite ready to let it go. "So no one ever visits? No one ever hosts séances around Halloween or anything?"

Lilac was appalled. "Why would anyone do that?"

"It's a big thing in Detroit. They have ghost walks and everything."

"Well, that's not what we do here." Lilac spared a quick glance for the cemetery gate and sighed. "No one goes into the cemetery unless they're never coming out. Do you understand what I'm saying?"

"No." I honestly didn't.

"I'm saying that you should never go into the cemetery because it's private and people like to keep private things … um … private," Lilac pressed. She started to move down the street and then stopped, grabbing my arm before I moved too far away from the gate. "Whatever you do, never go into the cemetery at night."

That had to be the oddest warning I'd ever heard. "What will happen if I do?"

"People will be upset."

"The DDA?"

"Very possibly."

"Will I get fined?"

"Most definitely."

Lilac was so earnest I couldn't help but give in and ease off the questions. "Okay. I won't go into the cemetery. I was only mildly curious. Given this morning's adventure, I've had enough death for the foreseeable future."

Lilac searched my face, as if looking for subterfuge, and then ultimately released me. "Great. I'm glad you understand." The bright smile was back as she pointed toward the beach. "That great view I told you about is right over there."

I was over the tour but I didn't want to hurt her feelings, so I continued to pretend I was interested in the remainder of the day's version of Show and Tell. "I can't wait."

# FOUR

Galen was still in my yard when I returned to the lighthouse. He smiled as I approached, taking in my red face and sweaty hair while handing me the bottle of water he held.

"I take it one of the things that everyone learns pretty quickly about island life is that you should always carry a bottle of water," I grumbled, accepting the container and guzzling a bit before returning it. "I think I might be dying. I thought I was in good shape until I spent the past few hours participating in an island tour."

Galen's smile widened. "You were on a tour? With who?"

"Lilac Meadows. Is that her real name, by the way? She says it is, but I'm afraid to be insulting and call her on it."

Galen gestured toward the shady part of the patio and followed so we could sit. "That is her real name," he confirmed. "I know, because I've issued her a few tickets."

"Oh, really?" I arched a challenging eyebrow. "What for, jaywalking?"

Galen snorted. "You'll have to ask her about that. I make it a point to never ticket and tell."

"So … you could tell me, but then you'd have to kill me?"

"Something like that."

I sighed and turned my attention to the activity on the beach. Things seemed to be wrapping up, and I couldn't help being grateful. "How much longer?"

"No more than an hour," Galen replied, extending his long legs in front of him as he got comfortable. "For what it's worth, we didn't find any footprints on your property – at least none that didn't belong to you. We believe Bonnie's body was dumped into the water at a different spot and washed up here."

"I know you probably think that makes me feel better, but it really doesn't."

"I understand, but I didn't want you to feel afraid in your new home," Galen supplied. "The island is generally a very safe place – and that's not something we simply slap on brochures to appease the tourists – so I don't want you to worry."

"Do I look worried?"

Galen smiled as he looked me up and down. "You look like you're learning a hard lesson about wearing black on an island. There's a reason most people wear breathable fabrics and light colors."

"You're wearing a black shirt," I pointed out.

"Yes, but I'm manly and I'm supposed to sweat." Galen puffed out his chest, amusement lighting his features. "You're supposed to glisten, not sweat."

"I'll keep that in mind." My tone was dry as I tugged my hair away from my face. "Seriously, this humidity is murder. How do you stand it?"

"You'll get used to it."

"I hope so." I honestly did. Despite my odd tour of the island with the sometimes-spastic Lilac leading the way, I found I liked the serenity of Moonstone Bay. I wanted to make this work. I wasn't sure until this very moment ... but I did. A life left floating wasn't much of a life, and that's how I felt I'd spent the better part of my adult years.

We lapsed into amiable silence for a bit, Galen finally stirring. "Tell me about your tour."

"I'm not sure how much there is to tell. I needed a break from watching you guys work on the beach, so I headed into town. Thankfully, even though the lighthouse feels isolated, it took me less than five minutes to hit the main drag."

"The island is good that way."

"Definitely." I bobbed my head in confirmation. "Then I decided I wanted iced tea, but there were about thirty bars and restaurants to choose from. Do you know that you have four tiki bars? Four! Who needs that many tiki bars?"

"We actually have seven tiki bars," Galen corrected, grinning at my discomfort. "But you ended up in Lilac's bar. In a way, that's a good thing."

"Why is that?"

"She's gregarious and easy to get along with."

"She's definitely that," I agreed. "She explained how Mondays and Tuesdays are slow on the island, and then insisted on giving me a walking tour because she believes Booker fell down on the job."

"Booker has many fine qualities," Galen said. "One of them is not serving as a tour guide."

"Yes, I'm a big fan of his bus and the fact that he dresses like a reject from *Magnum, P.I.*"

Galen's chuckle was so loud it caused me to jolt. "It's been forever since I've heard a good *Magnum, P.I.* reference."

"Netflix has opened my eyes to a whole new world of television."

"Good to know." Galen must've realized I was staring at his water bottle, because he handed it back to me with zero comment. "Where did Lilac take you?"

"Up and down the main drag," I replied, gulping some of the water before continuing. "She told me where to get the best produce, which deli will rip me off when ordering lunchmeat and which liquor store has the best rum."

"All important things to know ... especially about the rum. We take our rum very seriously on Moonstone Bay."

"Are you pirates?"

"Only on Devil's Night."

I didn't know what to make of that statement – perhaps it was a joke I didn't get – so I let it slide. "Tell me about Bonnie. Do you think her death is tied to May Potter's?"

"I think it's a definite possibility, but I won't know until I get the coroner's report," Galen replied, his eyes lit with interest as they locked with mine. "Why do you call her by her full name instead of referring to her as your grandmother?"

I shrugged, noncommittal. "She was never my grandmother."

"But she was."

"I never knew her," I argued. "She never called me on my birthday or sent a Christmas card. She apparently knew where I was but never visited … or called … or even sent a 'wish you were here' postcard."

"I hate to keep harping on this, but are you certain?"

The way he phrased the question caused my stomach to perform an unbalanced somersault. "What are you asking?"

"I'm merely asking if you're certain that May never tried to contact you," Galen replied, his voice calm. "The May I knew would've moved heaven and earth to get to know her only granddaughter."

"And yet I didn't know her."

"I realize that, but … are you sure something else didn't happen?" Galen pressed. "Maybe your father didn't want May to know you and he kept it from happening."

My father was many things – a renowned criminal attorney, a poor tipper, a snazzy dresser and a total jerkwad when it came to dating women younger than me – but he wasn't a liar. "You don't know my father. You don't know what he's like. He loves me."

Galen held up his hands, signifying surrender. "I didn't mean to upset you."

"My father knew I wanted to know more about my mother," I snapped. "He wouldn't have kept that from me."

"I'm sorry." Galen's expression was difficult to read, but I felt he was sincere. I also felt that he was backing off only because he didn't want to upset me. It wasn't that he believed my father was a good guy as much as he didn't want to deal with an emotional female. "I shouldn't have said that."

"It doesn't matter." I shook my head and looked to the surf. "I know my father. Nothing you can say will make me think he's a bad man."

"I'm not trying to make you think he's a bad man." Galen's tone was earnest. "I just … I knew May well. She was a cool lady. She was one of those crazy old ladies you want to hang around with because she always said whatever came to her mind. Do you know what I mean?"

"Not about May, but in general." I nodded. "I didn't mean to snap at you."

"It's okay. You're getting used to a new place. I keep trying to put myself in your shoes, but I can't quite seem to come to terms with what you must be feeling. Three months ago you didn't even know you had a grandmother. Then, overnight, you found out you did and that she was dead.

"The good part is that you have a new home on a tropical island," he continued. "The bad is that your last tie to your mother is gone. For some reason I assumed you knew your mother while growing up. This has to have been difficult for you."

"I don't know how to explain it," I admitted, rubbing the back of my neck. "It's just weird. I still shouldn't have snapped at you that way. You're trying to help. I didn't sleep well last night. That's not an excuse, but … I don't do well when I'm running on fumes."

"I don't either." Galen flashed a charming smile. "I like my eight hours as much as the next person."

"Thanks for understanding."

"Don't mention it." Galen waved off my concerns. "You said you didn't sleep well. Is there a reason? Did you have nightmares or something?"

"Nightmares?" That was an odd question. "No, I didn't have nightmares. I think it was the fact that I was sleeping in a strange place. The bed belonged to someone else, which is always weird, and I kept thinking I heard things."

Galen knit his eyebrows as he leaned closer. "Someone was in the lighthouse?"

"No, it's just … I'm not used to living on the water," I explained. "I kept hearing noises that were strange to me because I'm from the suburbs. I don't believe the noises were strange to the house, just to me."

"Oh." Galen visibly relaxed, releasing his grip on the arms of the chair. "I'm sure you'll get used to it."

"I'm sure I will, too. The sound of the ocean is soothing. I love walking at night, so I'm looking forward to spending time on the beach after sunset. That probably won't happen tonight – or maybe even this week, given the dead body – but I'm looking forward to it."

Galen's smile was back. "A nighttime walk is divine."

"Just so long as I don't go into the cemetery, right?" The question was pointed for a reason. Lilac was firm on the warning, and even though I tried bringing it up during the remainder of our tour she wouldn't go into specifics. I hoped Galen would.

"No, you should definitely avoid the cemetery after dark." Galen turned his attention to the driveway, refusing to expand on the statement.

"But why?"

"Cemeteries are a place for the dead, not the living."

"I thought cemeteries were a place for the living to visit the dead."

"Not on Moonstone Bay." Galen inclined his chin toward the driveway before I could dig deeper. "You have a visitor."

I knew exactly three people on the island so that seemed unlikely. I turned to find an older gentleman in a peach-colored suit picking his way up the driveway.

"That's Ned Baxter," Galen supplied, getting to his feet. "He's a local attorney."

"Why would he be coming here?" I couldn't stop the rising stem of panic. "Did you call him because you're going to arrest me for murder?"

Galen's expression shifted from curious to amused as he slid me a sidelong glance. "I already told you that you're not a suspect."

"Then why do I need a lawyer?"

"Ned is a family law attorney," Galen replied, laughter lacing his

35

words. "He handles child custody arrangements and probate issues. I believe he was May's attorney."

"Oh." I sucked in a calming breath. "Now that you mention it, I think I did see his name on the documents my father showed me."

Galen didn't bother hiding his surprise. "So May's will went straight to your father?"

I nodded, distracted by the peach suit. "Does he know that color is ... weird?"

"It's an island, honey," Galen replied. "That color is only weird when you hit the mainland."

"Good to know." I pasted a bright smile on my face as Ned hit the edge of the patio. "Hi."

"Hello." Ned's voice was warm and welcoming as his eyes bounced between Galen and me. "Am I interrupting?"

"It's not a date or anything," I answered hurriedly. Galen's snicker caused me to scald him with a dark look. "What?"

"I think he was referring to something else," Galen answered, jerking his thumb toward the beach activity over his shoulder. "Ms. Hunter discovered a body on the beach this morning. Bonnie Wakefield, in fact."

"Oh." Ned's face drained of color. "That's horrible. How did she die?"

"We're not sure yet," Galen replied.

I opened my mouth to mention the poison, but the expression on Galen's face told me that he'd rather keep the information private for the time being, so I changed course. "Your name was on the will I received a few months ago."

"Yes, that's why I'm here." Ned recovered quickly, shaking his head to dislodge the body conversation so he could focus on the real reason for his visit. "I heard through the coconut vine that you arrived yesterday – Moonstone Bay is a small community – and I wanted to check in and see how you're doing."

"I've been better." I forced a wide-eyed smile. "Even when visiting Detroit I didn't often stumble across bodies. It's been a somewhat jarring move."

"I can see that." Ned made a clucking sound with his tongue. "I'm sorry. You must be rethinking your decision to move to Moonstone Bay."

"I haven't given much thought to that either way," I countered. "So far I've simply been getting the lay of the land and going through some of the stuff inside."

"Well, if you decide you don't want to stay I can help you with matters of property transfer and the like," Ned offered.

I opened my mouth to respond, but Galen did it for me.

"Why wouldn't she want to stay?" Galen asked. "She's barely given the island a chance."

"I understand that, but this is all new to her," Ned explained. "In fact, I had no idea May even had a granddaughter until she asked me to establish the will a few months before her death. I was ... surprised, to say the least."

"I don't know why you would be surprised," Galen argued. "May mentioned Hadley numerous times over the years. Still, it's good you handled the will. Hadley wouldn't have any idea what she was entitled to if you hadn't."

"Yes, well, that's my job." Ned wrinkled his nose. "The lighthouse is an important historical property. I want to make sure its future is secure. I was actually relieved when I found out that May had a viable heir. Otherwise, I'm not sure what would've happened to the property."

"Thankfully we don't have to worry about that," Galen said.

"Yes, thankfully."

I could sense a bit of unease between the two men, so I attempted to distract them. "Do you know why May didn't contact me before her death, Mr. Baxter?" I asked, drawing his contemplative eyes to me. "I had no idea she existed until the will showed up, but clearly she knew about me."

"I don't have an answer for you, my dear." Baxter's expression was rueful. "As I said, I didn't know you even existed until a good six months ago. I was shocked, but didn't feel it was my place to question her. She was a client. We were definitely on friendly terms, but I wouldn't call her a lifelong friend or anything. I'm sorry."

"I'd call her a lifelong friend because I knew her my entire life," Galen offered. "I knew about Hadley years ago."

"You did?" I couldn't help being surprised. "What did she say about me?"

"Just that she had a granddaughter," Galen replied, his expression softening. "She didn't share much more than that. Of course, I was a kid for a lot of that time. She mostly just gave me lemonade when I was playing on the beach."

"Oh." I was understandably disappointed. "I thought maybe … ." I caught myself before I slipped into melancholy. "It doesn't matter. It's in the past. We can't change the past."

"Not unless it's Memorial Day," Galen agreed, causing me to tilt my head. "As for the rest, I can't comment. I can get out of your hair, though. I know you have things to do."

Galen flashed a charming smile before sidestepping Ned and heading toward the driveway. "Take care of yourself, Hadley. I'll be in touch when I know more about Bonnie's death."

I watched him go with a mixture of dread and relief. "Okay. Um, thanks." I forced my attention back to Ned. "Did you need anything else?"

Ned shook his head. "No. I only came to see if you were settling in okay. I'll get out of your way, too. If you need anything, or have any questions, don't hesitate to call."

"I will. Thank you."

And just like that I was on my own in a strange place. Again. Seriously, could Moonstone Bay get any weirder?

5

# FIVE

I woke to noises.

I bolted upright in the bed – a bed that didn't feel like it would ever be mine – and tilted my head to the side as I tried to identify the unfamiliar sounds.

The bedroom window was open and I could hear the waves caressing the sandy shoreline. That wasn't it, though. I'd already grown accustomed to the ocean sounds. I liked them. They were soothing and muted, not something that would cause me to jerk out of a pleasant dream that involved a shirtless Galen rubbing suntan lotion on my ... wait, that was hardly the thing to focus on given the circumstances.

I rubbed my eyes and debated whether or not I should search the lighthouse. I didn't know the layout well enough to attempt to do it in the dark, but if I flicked on a light and someone was inside it would tip them off that I was awake. That might trigger a fight or flight response – the fight being the worst possible choice in that scenario – and I wasn't sure how I would react.

Of course, this was an island, not Detroit. The noise I'd heard could've been some sort of beach animal on the patio for all I knew.

I sucked in a steadying breath to calm myself and tossed off the sheets, quietly getting to my feet and padding toward the doorway. I listened hard, hoping for the sound of muted whispers or animal claws on the hardwood floors, because that would mean I wasn't imagining things. Sure, that would mean I was in a house with intruders or man-eating monsters, but at least I wouldn't be crazy. Dead is better than crazy, right?

I blew out a sigh, my tousled bangs fluttering, and forced myself to step into the hallway. I heard a light clinking sound, as if dishes were being emptied from the dishwasher, and squared my shoulders before determinedly walking in the direction of the kitchen.

The metal staircase was narrow enough that I didn't risk sliding to one side or tripping as I descended. The lighthouse was mostly dark, but the moon over the water was bright enough that it offered occasional bursts of illumination through the multitude of lighthouse windows.

I'd just about convinced myself that I imagined everything when I heard a noise in the kitchen a second time. It was completely dark and I couldn't see any movement in the murkiness, but this time I was sure I heard something. I had a few options, although none of them particularly called to me, and I was unsure how to proceed.

I could run out the front door and scream for help. I could run out the front door and hide behind a bush before calling 911 and requesting help. I could go back upstairs and hide underneath the covers until morning. Or, and this was the dumbest idea of all, I could walk into the kitchen and confront whoever broke in.

I did the latter. No joke. Here's the thing about me: I'm braver than I am smart. When I was a kid, all anyone needed to do was dare me and I would do the most asinine things. You know all those memes that say "This is why women live longer than men?" I was in those – except I was the woman making the stupid decisions. I can't seem to help myself.

Despite my rampant idiocy coming out to play, I didn't walk into the kitchen without a backup plan. I expected to turn on the light and scare off an intruder. But if the intruder didn't run I didn't want to be caught without a weapon. With that in mind, I grabbed one of the heavy metal bookends from the cabinet near the hallway wall, gripping it tightly before moving to the kitchen.

I ran my hand over the wall to the left, feeling for the light switch, my heart pounding so loudly I thought the noise would overwhelm me. It was only after thirty seconds of searching that I remembered the light switch was on the other side of the doorframe.

I heaved a sigh, shifted the bookend from one hand to the other, and flicked the switch. For better or worse, I'd made my decision. Standing in the dark and trying to talk myself out of it wasn't going to work. It never worked.

I blinked rapidly when the room flooded with light, taking a moment to get my bearings. At first I felt sheepish, as if I'd imagined everything. There was no scary man standing on the other side of the island counter waiting to pounce. There was no dark and scary female searching through the drawers for the family silver.

There was absolutely nothing. I'd imagined it all. The kitchen was empty and safe and ... hmm. I know I didn't leave the dishwasher open.

"You're up late, dear!"

I screeched at the female voice, jerking out with the hand that gripped the bookend and swiping it in the direction of the unexpected visitor. The woman – a tiny old lady with long silver hair and amused green eyes – didn't flinch as the bookend went through her. No, you read that right. The bookend went through her. It didn't bounce off her. It simply passed through her.

"What the ... ?" My mouth dropped open as I tried to register the phenomenon.

"You need to put that down." The woman inclined her head toward the bookend. "It's old, turn of the century. I mean the turn of the previous century, for the record. It's iron."

I managed to find my voice, although it was squeaky. "Does that mean it's fragile?"

"No, it's iron, dear." The woman's grin was mischievous. "It simply means that it's heavy and you'll start feeling the strain in your muscles if you're not careful."

She wasn't wrong. My shoulder was beginning to ache. I grimaced as I cradled the bookend to my chest and glared at the woman moving toward the dishwasher. I was dumbfounded when she removed the dishes I'd put in for washing earlier and carried them to the cupboard.

That's when my righteous indignation flooded forward. "What do you think you're doing?"

"Putting the dishes away."

"I can see that, but ... why?"

"Because I know where they go, and I thought I would save you some time."

That sounded perfectly reasonable – except for the fact that I was fairly certain I was talking to a ghost and she shouldn't be able to carry dishes. "Who are you?"

The woman's eyes twinkled as she flicked them in my direction. "Don't you know, Hadley?"

"I ... ." I worked my jaw and forced myself to calm, carefully resting the bookend on the counter as I struggled to make my brain work. "You're May Potter."

"No."

"You're not May Potter?" I'd seen photographs. There were at least forty snapshots in frames around the house and most of them contained some version of this woman over the course of her life. I was certain I was right. "You must be."

"I am May Potter," the woman confirmed. "But you should call me 'grandmother.' I've waited decades to hear it, after all. I think I deserve it."

I pressed the heel of my hand to my forehead, part of me convinced I was dreaming. "Uh-huh."

"You look a bit pinched, dear." May's ghostly hand mimicked patting my cheek. I could feel a brief flutter but no actual contact, which only served to weird me out even more. "Sit down. I'll make you some tea."

Sit down? She had to be joking. "I'm dreaming, right? That's the only explanation."

"You're not dreaming."

"Then how do you explain this?" I sounded shriller than I was comfortable with, but because I was talking to a dream vision of the grandmother I'd never met I wasn't overly worried about sounding like a loon.

May fixed me with a calm but pointed look. "I've been watching you since you arrived and I figured now was the time to make my presence known. I didn't want to let things go too long, because I thought you might freak out if I did."

"What do you think is happening now?"

"I think you're shocked and taking a moment to come to your senses," May replied, seemingly unbothered by my tone. "I think that's perfectly reasonable. Sit."

I watched her move toward the pantry, my stomach tightening with each ghostly step.

"I think you need something without caffeine," May mused, tapping her bottom lip as she perused the tea selection. "Chamomile sounds good, right?"

"Actually, I'd prefer some whiskey," I gritted out as I sat at the small kitchen table and watched the ghost bustle in the direction of the stove.

"I think liquor will make matters worse," May countered. "You're already confused. Alcohol will merely give you the option of believing you imagined all of this tomorrow morning, and then we'll have to start over."

"And that would be a travesty, huh?"

"It certainly would." May set the kettle to boil and then moved in my direction. She didn't walk so much as float. "I'm so glad you finally made your way to Moonstone Bay, dear. I can't tell you how good that makes me feel."

"Uh-huh." I flicked my eyes to the back door, briefly wondering if I somehow managed to make it there and screamed for help if anyone would hear me. "I was curious and wanted to see."

"I don't blame you. The will must've come as a complete and total shock."

"It did." I dragged my eyes back to May, curiosity getting the better of me. "Why didn't you contact me before you died?"

"I thought about it," May replied, refusing to make eye contact as she flitted around the counter. "I thought I had more time."

The simple statement was enough to tug at my heartstrings. "Galen said that you were sick but not dying. He said that you were poisoned. Is that true?"

"Galen, huh?" May's eyes lit with mirth. "I didn't realize you were already on a first-name basis with our esteemed sheriff."

"Sheriff?" I rolled the title through my mind. "Doesn't Moonstone Bay have only three cops?"

"That doesn't mean he's not the sheriff."

"I guess not. Still ... you didn't answer me. Were you poisoned?"

"I honestly don't know," May replied, removing the kettle from the stove and pouring the steaming water into a mug. "I know I was feeling poorly the last night before I went to sleep. I know I never woke up. I don't know if I was poisoned. If Galen says so, though, I have to believe him. He's not a liar."

"He's weird," I muttered, rolling my neck. "He might not be a liar, but he's weird."

"You're only saying that because he unnerves you." May carried the tea to the table and slid it to the spot in front of me before pulling out the chair across the table and sitting. She looked perfectly normal, a caring grandmother getting to know her daughter's child – other than the fact that I could mostly see through her.

"He definitely unnerves me," I said after a beat, debating the best way to proceed. I remained convinced I was dreaming. In some ways that was better. That meant I didn't have to fear for my life. But I wanted information. Even if my subconscious was providing that information, I still wanted to know. "Why didn't I ever meet you? Why didn't my mother ever tell my father about you? Why would someone want to kill you?"

"You have a lot of questions." May chuckled, her voice harsh and dry. "I guess that's fair. Why didn't we ever meet? I wanted to, but your father didn't think it was a good idea."

The admission was simple, but it set my teeth on edge. "What do you mean? My father didn't know about your existence until the will showed up."

"Your father is not a bad man, nor is he guilty of terrible misdeeds, but he's not entirely innocent in this scenario," May replied, her tone calm. "Your father knew I existed from the beginning."

"He would've mentioned you," I protested. "He didn't know."

"Oh, dear, he knew." May made a clucking sound and I could practically feel the sympathy oozing out of her ghostly pores. "Your father met me two weeks before he married your mother. He was charming, kind and furious when I refused to give my blessing to the union."

My heart felt heavy and I gripped the mug because I felt the need to do something with my hands. "I don't understand."

"In case you haven't noticed, Moonstone Bay is not a normal place," May volunteered. "It's ... different."

"You mean because of this 'island life' nonsense?"

"Island life is real, but that's not what I'm referring to," May replied. "The island itself is different. It's a ... different world, so to speak. We'll get into that later. It's a conversation that takes more than a night, and we have more important things to focus on."

"Like the fact that you're a ghost yet you can still make tea?"

"No, that would be something that falls under island life." May was blasé. "Tonight, I think you need to know the family story. The other information can wait a bit. I expect you'll find out most of it on your own."

"Oh, joy."

May snorted. "You have your mother's sense of humor. I'm glad to see that."

"I wouldn't know."

May's smile slipped, something I couldn't quite identify flitting through her eyes. "I'm sorry about that. I really am. You'll never know how sorry."

I steeled myself against the myriad of emotions passing over May's face. "I don't really care about that. You were about to tell me why my father lied about knowing you." I wasn't sure I believed the charge, yet part of me – a very small, cold part – knew it was possible. My father was a pragmatic soul, after all. If he convinced himself it was in my best interests to hide information, he would do so.

"Your mother left Moonstone Bay when she was eighteen," May explained. "She wanted to go to college on the mainland. Moonstone Bay is a United States territory, which you well know, so allowing her to go to college in Florida wasn't as difficult as you might think."

"I do know. I was surprised to find that I didn't need a passport or anything to move to the island, even though I'd never heard of it before. It seemed so easy."

"That's the easiest thing about living on this island," May confirmed. "But your mother, she wanted to see the rest of the world. I thought it was a fine idea. I thought she would go to college and then return to the island once she got it out of her system. But she met your father."

"And they fell in love," I murmured.

"I believe they fell in lust first – which is common at that age – but essentially, yes," May said. "One day Emma informed me that she was dating a nice young man. The next thing she told me was that she was getting married and never returning to Moonstone Bay.

"I was shocked, to be sure," she continued. "I made the decision to fly to them and put a stop to their plans. This was before they moved to Michigan. Your mother and father were still in Florida at the time. I put my foot down and threatened to disown your mother if she didn't change her mind. I'm not proud of my reaction, but I did it, so I need to own it."

"And what did she say?" I was genuinely curious.

"She said she was pregnant with you and had no intention of walking away from your father."

"I see." And, because I did, I wasn't sure how to proceed. "Was that the last time you talked with her?"

"No." May's answer took me by surprise. "You have to understand that I was feeling pretty sorry for myself around that time. I wasn't a pleasant individual to begin with, so that only made matters worse. When your mother cut off contact for several months, I turned myself into a victim."

"Okay, but ... ."

May held up her hand to silence me. "We don't have much time. I'm still getting used to my new reality, so my strength wanes. I want to get this part out before that happens. I can come back and discuss the rest later."

That sounded like a terrible idea, but I didn't voice my concerns. "Okay."

"Your mother and I didn't talk for months – and months and months – and when she finally called I thought it was because she wanted to apologize," May explained. "But she didn't. She wasn't sorry. Honestly, she had nothing to be sorry about. I was the one in the wrong."

"So ... what happened?"

"Your mother called when she was in labor," May replied, waiting a beat so the realization could wash over me. "She was in a lot of pain, and I think she knew something was about to go terribly wrong."

I swallowed the lump in my throat. "I see."

"I don't think you do," May countered. "She was very excited for your arrival, but she wanted me to know a few things in case ... well, in case she didn't get to tell you certain things herself."

"Which she didn't."

"No, she didn't."

I worked overtime to tamp down my bitterness. "What did she tell you?"

"She said that I should let your father raise you if something happened, make sure you had a normal life and didn't know about your heritage," May answered. "She didn't want you to know what you were. She thought you would be happier being normal."

I had no idea what to make of that. "I'm sorry, but ... what?"

"I wanted to do what Emma thought best, but as the years went on I had more and more trouble letting things be," May said, her eyes clouding. "I tried talking to your father several times. I wanted to meet you. Each time he put me off."

"He would've told me that."

"Are you sure?"

47

"I ... ." I really wasn't sure. I loved my father, but if he thought May would upend the quiet life we shared, he would've had no problem shutting her out.

"It doesn't matter now." May's eyes drifted toward the window. "I don't have much time left right now. I can feel it. I have to get the rest of this out."

"What?"

"I made the mistake of not standing by my daughter when she made a life decision," May said. "I also made the mistake of listening to the orders she gave out of fear. She wanted you to have a normal life, but sometimes being normal isn't the right way to go."

"I don't understand what that means," I pressed. "What's the difference between normal and here?"

May cackled, the question catching her off guard. "Oh, my dear, you have so much to learn. I'm looking forward to watching you learn it."

"That wasn't really an answer," I pressed.

"It wasn't, but it's the only thing I have to give you at present," May said. "I made many mistakes and you'll have to pay for them. I'm sorry for that. Still, you have time to fix the mistakes I've made. I think you're more than capable of that."

"And how will I do that?" I prodded. "How will I fix these so-called mistakes?"

May's eyes sparkled as she lost a bit of her luminosity. She was fading. "You're a witch, dear. We can do anything."

I was convinced I'd heard her wrong. "Excuse me?"

"You're a witch," May repeated, her wizened countenance barely visible as she faded to nothing. "Look around. See what you see. Listen. Keep your ear to the ground. Everything will become obvious if you take the time to learn."

My frustration bubbled up. "What does that mean?"

There was no answer. May was gone and I was back to being alone in a lighthouse that didn't feel as if it belonged to me.

This was all a dream, right?

6

# SIX

I woke feeling more tired than when I fell asleep.

I spent the first hour of wakefulness in bed, debating whether or not what happened the previous evening was real or a result of my overactive imagination. I shoved it off to the imagination side until I arrived in the kitchen and found the dishwasher empty. Then I was back to debating. Of course, I could've emptied the dishwasher myself while in some sort of sleep state. Perhaps I had a brain tumor and didn't realize it. That would explain everything. It was almost comforting to wish for a tumor. Almost.

The sun barely peeked over the horizon as I carried a mug of coffee to the patio and settled in one of the loungers. It was cool – especially by Moonstone Bay's standards – and I predicted that I would have to become something of a morning person if I expected to survive the island.

I had a mountain of work today, yet I was more interested in debating whether or not I'd been dreaming or had a brain tumor. May didn't say much but what she did say was enough to make me question my sanity. A witch? She said I was a witch. That made absolutely no sense. How could I be a witch? Witches are green with warts and stuff, right? Even May, who was advanced in age, didn't look anything like a witch.

Still, even though I wanted to push the idea out of my mind I couldn't quite let it go. Moonstone Bay was unbelievably odd. The cemetery was only one thing that caused me to question the community. I mean ... well ... maybe witches hang out in the cemetery after dark every night and that's what they're trying to hide.

It made sense ... kind of.

Okay, it only made sense if you were willing to embrace the fantastical. I'm a big fan of horror and fantasy movies and books, but that didn't mean I believed either existed in the real world. There was plenty horror of the real variety going around, so much so that no one needed to add supernatural mumbo-jumbo to the mix.

I mean ... come on. It's ludicrous.

I believed that, and yet the witch stuff threatened to overtake my brain. I was furious with myself for even considering following it up. Still, I felt the need to talk to someone about what May had told me. I had no idea who that someone should be.

Could I risk a conversation with Galen? Probably not. He already thought I was loopy and only spent so much time talking with me because he was a sympathetic soul and felt sorry for me.

I could try talking to Lilac, but she clammed up when it came to the cemetery. Whatever she knew – and I was convinced she knew something – she had no intention of sharing it.

Who did that leave?

I could always call my father. The idea left me with a cold sensation in the pit of my stomach. I would call him, ask him about what May said, and then listen to his response. I needed to calm myself before that happened, though. My father wasn't a fan of emotional manipulation, and if I started screaming, yelling and crying he wouldn't take it well.

I was so lost in thought I didn't realize I was focusing on something in the water until it moved. At first I thought it was a bit of ocean debris – you hear stories about floating garbage on the water all of the time – but then I realized the item in question appeared to be small in some instances and larger in others. How was that even possible?

I left my coffee on the small table next to the lounger and squinted as I stared at the ocean. The rising sun was so bright it made focusing difficult and the first thing I thought of was Bonnie Wakefield's body. If another body washed up on shore my second day I'd have no choice but to leave. I couldn't live in a place where this was a regular occurrence.

After staring at the blob for an extended period of time I realized it was not only moving, it appeared to have appendages. They weren't sea creature appendages either, although I almost managed to trick myself into believing I saw a fin at one point. Instead, as the figure took form, I realized I was looking at a woman.

She climbed out of the water and headed for a spot on the beach, lifting her arm in greeting when she caught me staring. She was pretty, long brown hair trailing down her back, and she appeared to be happy to see me.

Oh, yeah, she was also naked.

"What the … ?" I sputtered to myself as I hurried in the woman's direction. My first thought was that she was in some sort of trouble – perhaps running from a rapist or something – and that explained the lack of clothing. As I closed the distance between us, I realized the woman was smiling and she didn't appear to be in a hurry to cover herself.

"I … who are you?" I blurted out the question before I thought better about offering up such a harsh greeting.

The woman didn't appear bothered by my tone. "I'm Aurora King. You're Hadley Hunter, right? I heard you arrived two days ago. I wanted to stop by yesterday and have a sit-down but I got caught up with other stuff. My father is being a real pain in the blowhole, if you know what I mean. I wanted to meet under different circum-stances."

The only thing I was certain about was that I didn't know anything. "Aurora King?"

Aurora's smile was so wide it almost swallowed her entire face as she used a towel to wipe off the dripping water. "I own the pirate bar on Main Street."

I racked my brain. "The Pirate's Booty?" The name stuck out because the decorations grabbed my attention during my tour the previous day.

Aurora nodded. "That's the one. I know the name is a bit schmaltzy, but it really brings in the tourists so I'm not changing it."

"No, of course not." My mouth was unbearably dry as I tried to look anywhere but at Aurora's nakedness. "I … um … will have to check it out."

"You definitely should. We have the best coconut rum on the island."

"Great."

"Uh-huh."

After an interminably long stretch of silence I finally had no choice but to look at Aurora. I was hoping to find her dressed – she'd left a pile of clothing behind on the beach for a reason, after all – but she remained naked as she regarded me with unveiled interest.

"What?" My voice was raspy.

"You're just not what I expected," Aurora replied after a moment. "I thought I'd see more of May in you. You have some May in you, don't get me wrong, but you're your own person."

My temper flared a bit. "Is that a bad thing?"

"Did I say it was a bad thing?"

"No, but … ." I heaved a sigh as I fought to control my temper. "What are you doing here again?"

"I like to swim here," Aurora replied. She seemed amused by my temperamental shifts. "May didn't have a problem with it. That's why I wanted to meet you – to see if you have a problem with it."

"And if I do?"

Aurora shrugged. "Then we'll talk about it."

I couldn't help but notice that she said we would talk about it, not that she would stop doing it. "Uh-huh." I looked at the pile of clothing at Aurora's feet. "Is there a reason you feel the need to swim naked?"

"It's more freeing. I don't like the feeling of nylon against my bits."

"Does that go for underwear, too?" I have no idea why I asked that question, but I was genuinely curious.

"I'll leave that for you to figure out on your own." Aurora winked, causing my stomach to churn as she leaned over and grabbed a pair of knit shorts. I didn't miss the fact that she shimmied into them without putting on panties first. "You're up early. May was that way, too. She was always up before the sun. We used to share a mug of coffee most mornings when I stopped for a visit."

I didn't miss the pointed tone. "Would you like some coffee?"

Aurora beamed. "That would be delightful! Thank you for asking."

I turned on my heel and stalked toward the lighthouse. Aurora took a bit more time, sliding on a pair of flip-flops and tugging a tank top over her head as she trailed in my wake.

"Are you planning on making any changes?" Aurora didn't speak again until we were on the patio, and the question caught me off guard.

"I haven't given it much thought," I replied, shuffling toward the door. "Wait right here. I'll get your coffee."

If Aurora was offended about not being allowed inside, she didn't show it. "No problem." She threw herself in the lounger next to the one I sat in before noticing her playing in the surf. By the time I returned with her coffee she was stretched out and comfortable. "I've always enjoyed this view."

Even though I wasn't sure what to make of Aurora, I couldn't argue with the sentiment. "I like it, too," I admitted, gazing at the gently rolling water. "I didn't think I'd be able to get used to the noise – it's louder here in some ways and quieter in others – but I really like the sound of the water."

"I love the water," Aurora enthused, sipping her coffee. "If I could find a way to live in the ocean and still afford cool shoes and electronics I would totally do it."

"Isn't that what houseboats are for?"

Aurora snorted. "You're funny. May didn't tell me you were so funny."

"That's because she never met me." I didn't mean to get testy – I honestly didn't – but I was getting sick and tired of people mentioning that May Potter talked about me when she couldn't be bothered to ever introduce herself. The realization that she didn't care enough to put herself out, at least in some meaningful way, chafed.

"I guess that's fair." Aurora tossed her damp hair over her shoulder. "I'm sorry you didn't get to meet her. She was a fun lady. When I'm old like her – although she would hate the fact that I'm using the word 'old' while talking about her – I want to be just like her."

I wasn't sure what that meant. "Why?"

"Because she was feisty."

It was a simple answer, yet I sensed Aurora wasn't being entirely truthful. "And because she was a witch, right?"

Instead of being offended – rather than calling me crazy and tossing around the word "loon" – Aurora nodded as if I'd said the most normal thing in the world. "I always wanted her to teach me spells, but she insisted you had to be born into it.

"She said, 'Aurora, girl, you're fun and you're pretty, but you're not witch material,'" she continued. "She was convinced I wasn't patient enough to learn the craft."

I didn't expect Aurora to accept what I said without argument. I didn't expect her to expand on it. I thought she would call me crazy and threaten to call the nice men with straitjackets to pick me up. Of course, I'd just found her swimming naked in the ocean so I guess I shouldn't have been surprised.

"Yes, well, that explains that." I feigned knowing what I was talking about. "The whole island is full of witches, right?"

"I don't know that I would say Moonstone Bay is full of witches," Aurora clarified, her eyes fixed on the water rather than me. "I think there's a nice balance. Still, when I think about everyone here, I'd estimate the witches are on the low end of the population pool. I think shifters are at the top, half-breeds without a real power base would be in the middle and witches would have to be at the bottom." She used her hands to illustrate what she was saying. "There's been a real slow-down in witch births over the past three decades or so – no one wants to be barefoot, pregnant and mixing mugwort these days – so that's only to be expected."

"Right." She was crazy. That was the only reasonable explanation. The woman was batshit crazy. That meant she was capable of anything. I had to be extremely careful when extricating myself from her presence. "So you think witch birth rates are on the decline, huh?"

"I don't think it," Aurora corrected. "The Downtown Development Authority included it in one of the brochures they handed out during the last solstice celebration. It stuck in my head. That's why I remember it."

"And Moonstone Bay is full of shifters, you say?" Shifters. I rolled the word around in my mind. I read a lot, so I was familiar with the term. It was probably best to pretend I believed Aurora rather than to laugh, point and start screaming about restraints. "Do you think wolf or bear shifters are the biggest here?"

"Wolf shifters are big, but we don't have any bear shifters to my knowledge." Aurora was matter-of-fact. "It's an island. Bears don't hang around on islands."

"They did on *Lost*."

"Good point." Aurora paused for a beat. "Of course, *Lost* was a television show and not real. This is the real world. In the real world you don't find bear shifters on islands. Well, I guess there are koala shifters – they're really the lesser of the shifters, though – and they want to hang on Australia all the time. That's technically an island."

"Uh-huh." Oh, dear lord, she really is crazy. She's talking about koala shifters. I mean … what the fuzzy freak is going on here? "So if wolf shifters are popular, what other kinds of shifters should I expect to find?"

I worked as hard as I could to keep my expression placid. I didn't want to tip off Aurora that I thought she was crazy. I didn't want her to realize I thought her brains had probably spilled out of her ears without her knowledge years before. You should never tell crazy people they're crazy. They don't see it that way. They think you're the crazy one and will attack.

No, really. I saw that on a television show one time.

"We have a lot of marine shifters," Aurora answered, seemingly oblivious to my inner struggle. "There're a couple of dolphin shifters. Beware of the crab shifters. They're cads and will try to get in your pants. They say it's not the same kind of crabs, but it itches all the same. Trust me."

"Uh-huh."

"There're also some uncategorized shifters, just so you're aware."

I had no idea what that meant. "Um ... ."

"Tom at the supermarket, for example, can shift into any animal he wants," Aurora continued. "He doesn't get stuck shifting into one thing and one thing only. I'm kind of jealous of him for that. But his kind is rare. They're even rarer than witches these days."

"Great." The notion of running practically overwhelmed me.

"The most important thing is to never believe any of the sharks are shifters," Aurora offered, finally turning her eyes back to me and holding my gaze. "There is no such thing as shark shifters on this island. They died out. I've known a few people who were convinced that they were dealing with shifters in the water and not real sharks. That's not the case. Everything here is a real shark, so you shouldn't try talking to them."

I had news for her. If I saw a shark in the water I would crap myself before trying to talk to it. "I'll keep that in mind. Thanks for the tip."

"You're welcome." Aurora smiled as she stood. "I can put a list of things together for you so you're not caught unaware. I know this is a lot to absorb all at once – I mean, how often do you move to an island that caters to paranormal entities when they want to go on vacation. But it won't take you long to figure things out. I can tell you're smart."

"You can?" That was news to me.

"Oh, definitely." Aurora enthusiastically nodded. "You're May's granddaughter. That naturally means you have to be smart."

Right. Naturally.

7

# SEVEN

I wanted to spend the day at the lighthouse sorting through things, moving furniture around and generally doing anything that would make the space feel like a home. My home, to be exact. I was inside for only five minutes when Aurora's empty coffee mug appeared to move to the dishwasher on its own. I was happy when she left, but now I wished I had company.

I called out to May, hoping she would appear again, but I was alone.

Instead of dwelling on the fact that I seemed to be a magnet for crazy people – and ghosts (something I still couldn't wrap my head around) – I showered and headed for town. I was convinced Moonstone Bay was a large-scale psych experiment. It explained so much. That didn't mean I wanted to hang around with my invisible friend and help the experiment along.

The police department was only two blocks away from the lighthouse and it was the first recognizable building I passed. Galen's truck was in the lot. I considered stopping to ask him about Moonstone Bay's special brand of crazy. I figured he would tell me the truth. I also figured he would lock me up without a second thought if I was imagining things. I recognized that telling one of the only law enforcement representatives on the island that I'd not only seen a ghost but that I'd also willingly listened to a naked woman discuss koala shifters was a terrible idea. He'd have me pumped full of meds so fast I wouldn't be able to call my father and accuse him of lying to me when I finally calmed down enough to do it.

I pointed myself in the direction of Lilac's tiki bar, giving The Pirate's Booty a wide berth in case Aurora decided to continue our earlier conversation, and was relieved to find Lilac behind the counter. Other than her, the rest of the building was empty.

I wanted to broach the subject of my fraying sanity in a tactful manner. There was no sense in alarming her, after all.

"What can you tell me about the extinction of shark shifters?"

Lilac widened her eyes as she met and held my gaze. "What do you mean? Do you want the legend or the truth?"

My mouth went dry. "The truth."

"They're not extinct but their breeding numbers are in the danger zone," Lilac supplied. "They spend most of their time in South Africa because, for some reason, they're more fertile there. It must be something to do with the water. I've never given it much thought."

"That makes two of us." I faked a smile for Lilac's benefit. I'm not sure if she believed it – her expression said the exact opposite – but I gave it my best attempt.

"Just out of curiosity, why are you asking about shark shifters?"

"I met Aurora this morning and she brought it up."

"Oh, well, that makes sense." Lilac wrinkled her nose. "We all agreed to give you time to get used to the island before starting in on the ... um ... other stuff. We had a meeting and everything. Aurora refused to come. She's not much of a joiner. I should've realized she would screw things up for all of us."

"A meeting, huh?" Just when I think things can't get weirder ... they do. "Was it a town hall meeting?"

"Downtown Development Authority."

"Really?" I wasn't expecting that. "Why?"

"Because the lighthouse beach is a big draw and it's important to

Moonstone Bay's bottom line," Lilac replied, not missing a beat. "That's the Downtown Development Authority's biggest priority."

"Yeah, from everything I've heard about them, they're a bunch of jerks." I heaved out a sigh and rubbed the back of my neck as Lilac poured a glass of iced tea and shoved it in my direction. "Do you have anything stronger?"

"Do you want something stronger?"

"Do you have a hammer to hit myself on the head with?"

"I do, but let's start with a shot of bourbon first, shall we?" Lilac's smile was wide. She grabbed a bottle of Jack Daniels from the rail and added a splash of liquor to the top of my drink. "Hopefully that will settle your stomach."

I had my doubts that would ever happen. "Uh-huh." I slammed the entire glass of iced tea and gestured for more. "Hit me again."

"It seems a little bit early," Lilac hedged.

"Are you my mother?"

"No."

"Hit me again," I gritted out. It took everything I had not to explode.

Lilac looked as if she was going against her better instincts, but she did as instructed. Instead of gulping down this drink, I nursed it as I played with my napkin and stared at the smooth wooden bar.

"I'm guessing you need to talk about a few things." Lilac's expression was sympathetic. "We'll take it one question at a time. What's your biggest concern?"

"Oh, I have so many concerns I don't know where to start." That was true. I felt numb, and it had absolutely nothing to do with the alcohol ... at least not yet.

"Start with the first thing that pops into your head."

"Okay." That sounded fair. "Aurora said that witches are low on the population scale here at Moonstone Bay. She also insinuated I'm a witch."

"Oh, I forgot you didn't even know that much." Lilac rubbed her jaw, her expression rueful. "You know what you need?"

"A hammer?"

Lilac waved off my suggestion. "You're very dramatic. I wasn't expecting that. May was always calm. Sure, she liked a good scene when she thought someone was bullying someone else – or whenever people bought a dog instead of rescuing one because she thought that was such a waste – but, in general, she was pretty unflappable. You're the exact opposite."

"I'm not dramatic," I argued. "I'm easygoing."

Lilac snorted. "I love that you said that with a straight face. You know I'm an empath, right? That means I can read your emotions. It's a little gift of mine, along with a few others that aren't important right now. Even if I couldn't, though, I would know that was a gross exaggeration."

"You're an empath?" I wasn't sure what that meant. "Does that mean you can read my mind?"

"No. I'm not psychic. I can simply read your feelings. I try not to be invasive or anything, but when things are on the surface – like they are with you – it's hard to avoid taking a peek. Sorry if that offends you."

Why would that offend me? I'd just found out my grandmother was a ghost, shark shifters were real, I'm apparently a witch and my new friend Lilac can read people's emotions. It was a normal day in my world. Seriously. There's nothing to see here. Move along.

"Hey, are you listening to me?" Lilac snapped her fingers in my face to force me to focus on the here and now. "Do you feel as if your mind is floating? You might be having a stroke or something. I worried your brain might overload when I sensed how closed off you were to the possibility that things might be shifting for you."

"I'm not having a stroke."

"That's good." Lilac brightened considerably. "Listen, I know this is a lot for you to deal with. We'll just tackle it one problem at a time. You seem obsessed with the shark shifters. You really shouldn't worry about them. They've had a good run and they always find a way to survive. I doubt very much this will be any different."

"Oh, well, that's a relief."

Lilac ignored my sarcasm. "I know, right?"

"Uh-huh."

"As for the witch stuff, have you been to the lighthouse's third floor yet?" Lilac was sympathetic, but also serious. "A lot of the answers you're looking for are up there. I got the feeling when we were together yesterday that you hadn't made it up to the observatory yet so I decided to let it go until later. I figured you would come for me when you had questions. I simply didn't think it would be this soon ... or consist of these questions."

"The observatory?" I knit my eyebrows. "I thought the third floor was where the light comes from."

"Have you even been up there?" Lilac's eyebrows shot toward her hairline. "How can you live in a place and not look at every floor before going to sleep? I'd be so worried that a vampire was living in the attic that I wouldn't be able to relax."

I stilled. "Vampire?"

"We have a few, but they're kind of nutters," Lilac explained, mistaking my question for curiosity rather than horrified fear. "An island isn't a great place for a vampire. Only the crazy ones want to stay for more than a week at a time. To be fair, we get quite a few on the vacation circuit."

Huh. I never considered that. "Is that why your bar is always dead in the afternoon?"

"I wasn't lying about Mondays and Tuesdays being slow periods. Things will pick up when this afternoon's flight arrives around three."

"Okay, but ... vampires? Really?"

Lilac nodded. "Yes, but they're not so bad. Forget everything you've ever seen in the movies. None of it is even remotely real."

"So they don't glow really pretty during daylight and moon over taciturn teenagers for no apparent reason?"

"Oh, that's true."

I stilled. "Seriously?" I felt sick to my stomach. "They glow in the sun?"

Lilac snorted, her serious expression slipping. "You have got to learn to develop a sense of humor," she chided. "Life is not a travesty like you seem to believe. I know most of this stuff is hard for you to absorb, but in a few weeks you'll understand everything and it won't seem like such a big deal."

I seriously doubted that. "Vampires?" My voice went squeaky.

"Don't worry about them." Lilac wagged her head. "Vampires aren't nearly as bad as you think."

"Well, that makes me feel so much better." I sucked down a gulp of my drink. "So you think vampires ... and shifters ... and witches ... and probably a hundred other things ... are real." That was a lot to wrap my head around.

"I take it you don't." Lilac's expression took on a kindly edge. "I know this is a lot for you, Hadley, but I swear it's going to be okay. You're only seeing the bad right now. There're a lot of good things that go along with an island like ours."

"Oh, really? Like what?"

"Like every Day of the Dead celebration involves a Mexican food extravaganza."

"That certainly seems worth all the aggravation."

"Hey, don't knock the margaritas." Lilac wagged a chiding finger. "There's nothing better than a pineapple margarita with a little coconut splash to liven things up."

That actually did sound delicious. Maybe I should switch drinks. I shook my head to slough off the distraction. "I don't understand any of this. I mean ... it doesn't make sense. Why would my grandmother live here?"

"I'm not sure I'm the one who should answer that."

"Who do you think should?"

"Your grandmother."

"She's dead."

"I know, but that doesn't mean she's gone."

I pressed the tip of my tongue to the back of my teeth as I debated how far I should push this conversation. Finally, I did the only thing I could do. "If I tell you something, do you promise not to tell anyone else?"

Lilac immediately started shaking her head, taking me by surprise. "No?"

"No," Lilac confirmed. "I have a huge mouth and I gossip when I'm drunk. I've already proven I like my margaritas, so all I can promise is to do my best. Besides, whatever you're about to tell me I probably already know. In fact, odds are that everyone on the island knows. They simply haven't told you yet."

That sounded annoying. "I'll bet that what I'm about to tell you will come as a surprise." At least to a sane person.

"Go for it."

"Okay." I leaned forward, casting a cursory glance over my shoulder to make sure we were still alone, and lowered my voice to a conspiratorial tone. "Last night, I woke up in the middle of the night to find my dead grandmother was in my kitchen. She was unloading the dishwasher."

"Oh, that was quick." Lilac looked excited rather than surprised.

"Quick?"

Lilac nodded. "Usually it takes several weeks for a newbie to see a spirit. You need to be prepared and stuff, because otherwise it could overload your circuits. You must be really strong. What kind of spells can you cast?"

That was the last question I expected. "Spells?"

"Yeah. Curses, spells, group chants. Are you good with your hands or better with words?"

None of these questions made a lick of sense. "I've never cast a spell," I gritted out, hoping I came off as confused instead of suspicious. "I've had a few spells, but they usually accompany PMS."

"Oh, honey, I hear that." Lilac's smile was warm and earnest. "Still, I don't understand. Given your lineage, you should be all kinds of powerful."

I gripped my drink glass tightly as I tamped down my irritation. "I don't know what that means."

"And I don't entirely either," Lilac admitted. "I know a little bit about May's family – she used to love to tell a good story – but I don't know the specifics, and I'm worried about telling you something that I remember wrong."

"And yet you seem to know a lot more than me," I argued. "I know nothing."

"What did May say to you last night?"

"That she made a mistake when my mother announced she was marrying my father. She said she put distance between them because she thought Mom would change her mind and do something else ... or come back. I'm not quite sure what she expected to happen."

"Okay, I guess that makes sense," Lilac rubbed the back of her neck as she shifted from one foot to the other. "May never talked about her daughter very often. You could tell there was a lot of guilt there. I guess that's why we didn't realize she was dead as long as she was. At a certain point I became aware that Emma died, but I thought it was something that happened fairly recently."

"She said that my mother called when she was in labor because she was afraid." It took everything I had not to choke out the words. "She said that she believed my mother realized something bad was about to happen and that she asked May to give me a normal life."

"Oh."

"Oh? That's all you can say?"

Lilac held up her hands and shrugged. "I'm not sure what to say. Everyone's family is different. Perhaps your mother thought she knew something that your grandmother couldn't grasp. Staying away from you doesn't sound like something May would do."

I wasn't in the mood to admit my father's part in all of this, so I decided to skirt the issue. "Apparently she had some sort of fight with my father. That was all vague. She didn't have a lot of time. She said she was still getting used to controlling her visits."

"That's true." Lilac brightened. "She should get stronger the longer she stays."

"I guess that's a good thing."

"It's a great thing," Lilac enthused. "Trust me. I've been looking forward to May's return. Everyone has. We didn't think she was back yet."

That made absolutely no sense. "You knew she would come back?"

"Everyone on the island comes back after ... well, after."

"Everyone who lives on the island comes back as a ghost when they die?" I was horrified. "What about Heaven?"

"I think the people who live on Moonstone Bay think the island is Heaven."

I'd heard a lot of crap in my life, but that was at the head of the bathroom line. "Is that why no one is allowed in the cemetery after dark? Is it full of ghosts?"

"No, the cemetery is something else." Lilac was back to being evasive. "Go back to your conversation with May. Did she tell you what kind of magic manifestations you should start expecting?"

"I ... no." What did that mean? I was being buried under weird questions and fear. I didn't like it. "What do you mean?"

"Now that you're in Moonstone Bay, now that you're on the island and in your ancestral home, you should start manifesting magic," Lilac explained. She was calm, as if this was the most normal conversation in the world. "The island should anchor your powers. That's how it works."

"Does that mean my mother didn't have powers when she was off the island?"

Lilac shrugged. "I'm not familiar with how it works with witches. My powers still work on the mainland."

"Your powers to read people's emotions?"

Lilac shook her head. "All of my powers."

"You have more powers?" That was it. I couldn't take it any longer. I practically screeched the question, and when I did the glass in my hand exploded, the glass flying in a hundred different directions as a brief flame erupted before fizzling out. One of the small shards zipped past my cheek, cutting me deep enough that I felt it. "What the ... ?"

Instead of being upset or yelling about the broken glass, Lilac clapped. "Now that's what I'm talking about. Good job!"

Yeah. Good job. I just exploded a glass with my mind and I was being congratulated. What could possibly be wrong with that?

8

# EIGHT

I walked around Moonstone Bay for most of the day. Only a quarter of that time was on the main drag. After the fourth time someone I'd never laid eyes on called out my name and wanted to stop for a chat I beat a hasty retreat to the side streets.

I don't know what I expected. Lilac said everyone in Moonstone Bay suffered from a shared delusion. I thought the houses would be dark and dreary, cobwebs in the corners and orange twinkle lights on every eave.

They looked normal. In fact, they looked friendly and inviting.

I really hated that.

I didn't recognize the side street I was on when my phone dinged in my pocket. I frantically dug for it, letting loose a relieved sigh when my father's number popped up on the screen. I'd called him the moment I left Lilac's bar – the urge to talk to someone who wasn't crazy so overwhelming I almost curled into a ball and cried when he didn't answer – but I managed to hold it together long enough to leave a message.

I picked up on the second ring. "Dad?"

"Hello, sweetheart." Dad's voice was warm and booming. Even though I was in the middle of a mental breakdown it soothed me.

"How are the new digs? I expected to hear from you when you landed, but all I got was a text."

"You're still number one with the guilt trip, Dad," I said dryly, slowing my pace and clutching my bottle of water with my free hand. I remembered my tour the previous day well enough to stock up on water before setting out. "I've been busy."

"I'll bet. How's the new house?"

"It's ... unique." That was putting it mildly. "It's actually fairly nice, but it needs some work. I'm still sorting through things."

"What kind of things?"

It was an innocent question on its face, but I couldn't help being suspicious. "Well, the house is full of old clothes and shoes," I started. "It has a big library, too. It's on the third floor and there's a bunch of weird stuff."

"Like romance novels?"

"Ha, ha. You're always the comedian."

I could practically see my father's smile through the phone. "There's nothing wrong with romance novels. I know you're partial to them yourself."

"How many times do I have to tell you that *Outlander* is not a romance novel? It's historical fiction."

"With a big, naked Scot," Dad said. "I've seen the television show. I know what the story is about."

"Whatever," I grumbled, rolling my neck until it cracked. "It's not romance novels." I really had no idea what was on the third floor – although I had every intention of checking once I got up the gumption to return to the lighthouse – but Dad didn't know that. "It's witch books."

"Witch books?" Dad's voice was hard to read. "Like spell books?"

"Yes. There're also witch history books and ... um ... wand books." Witches use wands, right? "Apparently May Potter fancied herself a witch."

Instead of being appropriately appalled, Dad barked out a laugh. "Was she still doing that? I knew that was one of her things, but I was under the impression she gave that up at a certain point. You would think it would lose some of its appeal once you hit sixty, wouldn't you?"

That was so not what I was expecting. "You knew?"

"Well, I knew what your mother told me," Dad clarified. "I didn't know your grandmother very well. I'd only met her a few times."

"She told me."

"What?"

I realized I wasn't far gone enough to admit to my father that my dead grandmother stopped by for a conversation in the middle of the night. He'd be on the first flight with a doctor in tow if I did. Things were bad enough without that.

"Nothing," I said hurriedly, shaking my head. "I was just talking to myself."

"I should be used to that." Dad was back to being happy. "Tell me about the people you've met."

Well, one claims to be an empath, while another is a really hot sheriff who only introduced himself because a dead body washed up on my beach. He then told me that my grandmother was poisoned and that was before a naked woman decided to have a really weird conversation with me over my morning coffee. "They seem fairly normal."

"Really?" Dad sounded surprised. "I would've thought island folk were a wee bit different. That's how your mother always made it sound."

Right. Mom would've told him stories about Moonstone Bay. What did he know? "Did Mom ever talk about Grandma's belief that she was a witch?"

"She did." Dad's voice became wary. "She said your grandmother had a very distinct belief system and that she refused to believe anything to the contrary – even if what she believed was absolute nonsense."

"Is that how Mom termed it or did you add the embellishments?"

I wasn't used to questioning my father in this manner, but I figured if I wasn't firm he would skirt around the issue and I'd be right back where I started.

"What's going on, Hadley?"

"What do you think is going on?"

"I think you're already homesick but don't want to admit it," Dad replied. "There's no reason to stay there. I know you wanted an adventure – and to prove that you're strong and brave – but there's no reason to stay there when you want to come home."

Of course he would see things that way. "Dad, I'm not saying I'm never going to come home. Right now, though, it's not going to happen. I'm happy here."

"You don't sound happy."

"It's more that I'm baffled."

"And what is baffling you?"

There was no way around it. I would have to ask the obvious question. "Was Mom a witch?"

He didn't sound offended by the question, merely resigned. "She said she was."

"Did you believe her?"

"I believed that she believed it."

"That wasn't really an answer."

"I'm not sure how you want me to answer it, Hadley," Dad said. "Your mother thought she was a witch. She left all that behind when we got married. She wanted to be normal – so she was."

"You say it like it's a choice."

"Isn't it? Your grandmother chose to believe weird things and she passed that belief system on to your mother. Your mother realized there was a much bigger world than Moonstone Bay when she left to attend college. She didn't want to go back to the weirdness, so we built our life in the real world."

"And cut out May Potter."

"I guess, from her perspective, that would've been a fair conclusion," Dad conceded. "From my perspective we were doing what was best for us. We wanted a normal life."

Nothing was that simple. Dad was so literal he wasn't capable of understanding. "What about after Mom died?"

"After your mother died I was in charge and there was no way I was going to introduce you to that ... stuff."

"Not that." I fought the urge to roll my eyes. "What about when May Potter contacted you after Mom died? She wanted to see me, right? Why didn't you let her?"

I didn't miss the hitch in Dad's breathing. For the first time he was truly uncomfortable with the turn in the conversation. "Who told you that?"

My dead grandmother. Wait, I couldn't admit that. "She wrote it in her diary."

"Well, she did contact me and wanted to see you," Dad confirmed, choosing his words carefully. "You were about seven at the time. I said you were too young ... and I stand by that. She tried again when you were fourteen, but I still thought you were too young."

"What about when I was an adult?"

"She called and wanted your number, but I didn't think it was a good idea to give to her."

That's what I was afraid of. Anger coursed through me as I fought to rein in my fury. "Why would you do that? I was an adult. I should have been able to make my own decisions."

"You might've been an adult, Hadley, but you'll always be my child," Dad argued. "I loved your mother, but I'm not going to lie. She did some strange things. I was young enough not to see her quirks for what they were."

"And what were they?"

"Mental illness."

The simple answer was like a punch in the stomach. "I see."

"Hadley, I loved your mother and I always will," Dad said. "I'm not sorry I kept May Potter out of your life. The woman was unbalanced. I didn't want to tell you about her at all, but I thought that taking your inheritance away from you was somehow unfair."

I knew better than that. "No, you realized that if anyone ever found out you could lose your law license," I corrected, bitterness coming out to play. "I'm not an idiot. I know how it works."

"That's neither here nor there."

"Oh, but it is." I shook my head in an effort to regain control of my emotions. I was about to fly off the handle, and that wouldn't be good for anyone. "I know why you did it. But it doesn't matter now."

"Hadley, come home."

I made up my mind on the spot, even though part of me vehemently argued against it. "I am home. I'll call you in a few days and we'll talk again. I need some time to … absorb … all of this."

"Hadley!"

I didn't wait to listen to the rest of his excuses. I ended the call and slid the phone in my pocket, briefly pressing my eyes shut before my emotions settled enough to allow me to start moving again.

After that I walked.

And walked.

And walked.


**DARKNESS CREPT** up on me and before I realized it I'd walked away most of the day. I was angry with myself, not just for losing an entire day's worth of work but also for being afraid to return to my own home.

It was my home now. Whether it would be a month from now was anyone's guess, but for now it was mine.

I was turned around a bit, although I could see the lighthouse in the sky and knew which way to point myself. After walking another block and turning onto another side street I began recognizing some of the landmarks. The one that caught my attention was the ridiculously tall cemetery wall.

I knew it was a mistake to head in that direction, especially because almost all traces of light had fled the sky. That didn't stop me. The cemetery was a curiosity, after all. Despite the fact that everyone in Moonstone Bay showed signs of clinical delusions on a grand scale, I couldn't help but believe that the cemetery warnings were part of the show. If they branded themselves as a paranormal destination – I mean, who does that? – the cemetery threats had to be part of it.

That was the only thing that made sense, right?

Right?

The cemetery gate was chained, a huge padlock holding it in place. That didn't stop me from yanking on it. I knew it wouldn't give, but I figured I was due for a shot of luck. I didn't get it, but I did notice that the gate creaked open and allowed a small bit of space between the two doors. Thanks to the chain it wasn't enough of a gap for me to slip inside, but if I laid on the ground and peered through the opening I could see inside.

It looked like a normal cemetery. Some of the tombstones were ornate and somewhat garish, but it was merely a cemetery. It was quiet, peaceful and ... huh, is something moving around in there?

I squinted to get a better look, but the hint of movement I swore I saw only seconds before was gone. I edged closer and looked harder, tilting my head to the side. I heard the obvious sounds of groaning.

"What the ... ?"

It seemed like I was asking that exact question every five minutes since landing, but there was a very obvious reason. In fact ... yup, there were people in the cemetery. They were shuffling and moaning. They appeared to be multiplying, too. Where were they coming from?

I jerked back when a gray face appeared in the opening, the creature – which looked humanoid – letting loose an unearthly screech in my face. I scrambled back when a hand snaked through the opening, the moans increasing. I didn't stop until I smacked into something hard, my heart jolting as I leaned my head back and looked up.

There he stood. Galen Blackwood. His hands were on his hips and there was a very obvious scowl on his lips.

"Oh, hey." I found my voice, but just barely. "I got lost on my way home."

"I see that." Galen's tone was firm as he leaned over and grabbed beneath my armpits. He tugged me to a standing position, dusting off my rear end before realizing that probably was a bit invasive. "Sorry."

It was dark, but I swear I could almost see his cheeks flushing with color.

"Don't mention it," I gritted out, flicking my eyes to the cemetery gate when the chain rattled. "Did you know you have zombies in the cemetery?" It was an absolutely stupid question, but I could think of no other word to describe the creatures locked inside.

"I'm well aware," Galen said. "Five years ago the Day of the Dead party got out of hand and someone cast a spell, so they rise every night. There's nothing we can do about it, mostly because we have no idea who cast the spell or why."

"A spell, huh?" Of course it was a spell. "There's been a lot of talk about spells today."

"So I've heard." Galen's expression was hard to read, but I was fairly certain he was trying to be sympathetic. "Lilac called because she was worried about you. She wanted me to check, but you weren't home."

"I decided to take a walk."

"By yourself? No one has seen you since this afternoon."

"I didn't realize I needed a babysitter." I folded my arms over my chest. "By the way, I don't need a babysitter. I'm just … getting used to things."

"It's a lot to get used to."

"Oh, no." I curled my lip into a haughty sneer. "Most communities have zombies locked in their cemeteries."

Galen shrugged. "The zombies aren't a problem. I mean, they were a problem that first night when they were running all over, but we rounded them up and had the problem fixed after that."

"So you just live with zombies wandering around the island?"

"They don't wander around. We locked them in the cemetery. It's fine."

"Why not chop off their heads or shoot them or something so they don't rise again? That's what they do on television and in movies."

"That hardly seems fair," Galen countered. "Why destroy them when incarceration works just as well?"

"I … don't … know." That was a fair question. "I'm guessing you're against the death penalty, huh?"

"Actually I'm for the death penalty under the right circumstances," Galen clarified. "As for this … these aren't the right circumstances. We're still hoping to reverse the spell one day. We don't want to destroy the bodies because they were loved ones of many Moonstone Bay residents."

"I never considered that." I rubbed my chin as the zombie astonishment wore off. "So zombies are real."

"I'm sorry you had to find out this way." Galen was contrite. "We wanted to ease you into things."

"Yeah. You had a meeting and everything. Lilac told me."

"We didn't want to frighten you, but there was a lot you needed to be aware of," Galen supplied. "There still is. You're on the verge of being overwhelmed. But we need to talk."

What could he possibly want to talk about now? "If you tell me mummies are real, too, I'll be on the next flight out of here."

"You only have to worry about mummies in arid climates. They deteriorate in high humidity."

Great. That made things so much better. "I need to go home and ... drink or something."

Galen extended his arm and pointed toward the sidewalk. "I'll walk you back."

"I can find my own way."

"I said we needed to talk."

Well, the hits just keep on coming. "Oh, well, by all means ... you should definitely lead the way."

9

# NINE

"Nice night, huh?"

Galen dropped the bomb about us needing to talk and then immediately zipped his lips as we trudged in the direction of the lighthouse. He seemed to know where we were going – which side streets to take to cut down on our trek – but otherwise he was nothing but a big, uncomfortable presence walking to my right.

"Yes, it's lovely," I drawled. "It's a beautiful night to discover zombies in the cemetery."

"It's always a nice night for that."

I slid a sidelong look in Galen's direction and found him grinning. "You have an odd sense of humor."

"You're not the first person to say so." Galen's smile ebbed as he stared up at the sky. "You've had a busy day. I'm guessing you have some questions."

"I do have questions," I confirmed. "I'm not sure you can answer them. You answered the obvious zombie question, which is nice, but I doubt you have any particular knowledge on shark shifters and witches."

"I'm knowledgeable on both. Which one are you more concerned about?"

"Just a hint, it's not shark shifters."

"That's good. They're like unicorns. The odds of ever seeing one are slim. I keep hoping I will one day because *Jaws* is the best movie ever, but it hasn't happened yet."

I wrinkled my nose. "*Jaws* wasn't a real shark."

"If that's your story."

Wait ... no way. "Are you saying that the *Jaws* shark was really a shifter?"

"Why else do you think it was so strong?"

"It was a movie."

"Some movies are autobiographical."

"I think you're suggesting that Steven Spielberg is a shark shifter. Also, that movie was a book first."

"I have no proof of that, but there are always rumors regarding Hollywood folks."

Oh, now he was just messing with me. "I'm really not obsessed with shark shifters. It's just something that keeps surfacing."

"You brought it up."

I bit back a sigh. "Fine. It's something I accidentally keep bringing up."

"Which means the witch part is what has you walking in unbearable heat for an entire day," Galen noted. "I thought you knew right up until the moment you said you'd never met May and your mother died while giving birth. That's when I realized you didn't know. I didn't know what to say to you."

"So you didn't say anything."

"Would you have preferred that I blurt it out? I'm not great with the soothing."

"You don't seem terrible at it," I countered. "As for the witch stuff ... I don't believe it's true. Or, well, I don't believe it's true for me. If it is a thing – and I'm not saying it is, just for the record – I believe it skipped me."

Galen arched a dubious eyebrow. "I see. Why do you believe that?"

"Witches have magic, right?"

"Yes. If they're born into the craft, they have magic."

"Well, I don't. That means I'm not a witch. My genes must be faulty."

"Uh-huh." Galen didn't sound convinced. "Didn't you explode a glass earlier today using nothing but the power of your mind?"

That was the most ludicrous question I'd ever heard. "No. Lilac caught me off guard when she said something and I squeezed the glass so hard it broke."

"And that's how you got the scratch on your cheek, right?" Galen slid a finger over to swipe at the mark. It didn't hurt and I'd almost forgotten about it. "So, if I'm understanding things correctly, you believe you can turn into the Hulk, but being a witch is out of the question. Am I close?"

The Hulk? He had to be joking. "The Hulk is not real. Wait ... are you going to tell me he's a shifter?"

"It's not out of the realm of possibility, but I don't believe so," Galen replied. "That's not what I'm getting at. You seem to think you suddenly found the strength to break a glass with an errant squeeze, yet being a witch is unbelievable."

"It is."

"I'll bet you thought zombies weren't real until tonight, too."

He wasn't wrong, still ... I couldn't let him win the argument. That's not how I roll. "I believed in zombies before tonight. That's how I always imagined the people who actually take time to watch the Kardashians on television manage to get through the ridiculous nature of the show."

"Speaking of paranormal creatures."

Despite myself, he managed to pique my interest. "I'm sorry, but are you serious?"

Galen kept a straight face for an extended period of time, but finally couldn't stop himself from cracking a smile. "I have no idea. I'm willing to bet they're something – maybe even something evil – but I have no knowledge of that."

"Oh, well, that's a relief. I thought you were going to tell me they were vampires or something."

"Not with how tan they are."

"Good point."

We lapsed into amiable silence again. I was the first to break it when we reached the lighthouse's driveway. "May Potter popped up in my kitchen last night."

"That was quick."

Good grief. He was expecting it, too. What is it with these people? "You knew she would come."

"I had a feeling she would," Galen clarified. "She was a good woman who left before her time. That usually means returning until business is done or the island releases her."

"And what business do you think she has? Is this about finding her killer because she didn't know she was poisoned?"

"No, I don't think it's about finding who killed her. Don't get me wrong, I think that she wants to know who did the deed, but I don't think that's why she's back. I fully expected her to pop up. I thought it might take a few weeks longer. She must've tied her return to your arrival."

"And why would she do that?"

"Because you're her unfinished business." Galen answered without hesitation. "I know that you're dealing with a lot and you don't want to believe that any of this is real. You probably think if you go upstairs right now and climb into bed that you'll be able to sleep until morning and when you wake up this will have been nothing but a dream."

"Nightmare," I corrected. "It will have been a really weird nightmare."

"That's not what's going to happen."

"And yet it's what I'm hoping for." I stopped in front of the main door to dig for my keys. "You said you had something you wanted to talk to me about?"

"Well, for starters, you need to stay out of the cemetery."

"I figured that out myself."

"Other than that, I want you to know that we confirmed that

Bonnie Wakefield died of poisoning. It was the same poison we found in May's system."

"Which means you really do have a serial killer," I mused, part of me surprised he wanted to talk about the mundane when we had so much of the magical hanging over our heads.

"We do." Galen nodded. "You need to be careful."

"You said you had three elderly women who died," I reminded him. "I'm not elderly."

"No, but you still make an appealing target because you don't know what's going on in Moonstone Bay. You're powerful, but you don't realize it yet. You're not ready to embrace it. That's fine, by the way. No one wants to rush you."

"Rush me to do what?"

"Join the community."

"Haven't I already done that?"

"You've taken certain steps, but you're not part of the community yet," Galen replied. "I believe you will eventually do that, but you need to come to grips with your past before you can look to the future."

That sounded like something he dug up from a fortune cookie. I found it grating. "So … is that all?"

Galen looked torn, but he nodded as he took a step back. "Lock your doors. If someone approaches you and you're at all uncomfortable don't hesitate to call me."

"I wish I would've thought to do that when the naked woman climbed out of the ocean this morning," I groused.

"Aurora is not a danger to you. I'm talking about someone else."

"Who?"

"I wish I knew."

I sighed as I pinched the bridge of my nose. It had been a long day and I was exhausted. I wanted to put the revelations and frustrations in the rearview mirror and shut out the world for a full eight hours. Heck, ten would be even better.

"I promise to be careful," I said after a beat. "Just keep me updated on what you find."

"I will." Galen remained where he was as I opened the door. "If you need to talk … ."

I cut him off with a shake of my head. "I need some sleep. That's all I need right now."

"I understand that, but all this stuff isn't going away just because you think it's a dream," Galen said. "Tomorrow, you're still going to be facing the same problems. When that happens and you feel the need to talk, I'll be around."

I didn't know what to say so I went the lamest route available. This was a dream, after all. It didn't matter. "Thank you. Goodnight."

"Sweet dreams, Hadley."

**MY DREAMS WERE** anything but sweet, a hodgepodge of terrifying and confusing images causing me to toss and turn all night. At one point I swear I felt a hand on my forehead and a female voice urging me to settle. I didn't recognize the voice as belonging to May Potter as much as I felt in my heart it did.

It seemed she was there all night, though she didn't wake me, instead watching and whispering as she tried to help me outlast my troubled sleep.

*It will be all right. Don't fret.*

*This is the first day. The others will be better.*

*He's outside watching. You don't have to worry about someone finding you here.*

*You can start learning now. You're behind, but things will get better. I promise.*

*If it's any consolation, I wish I would've done everything differently.*

It wasn't much of a consolation, and by the time I woke I was a sweaty and tense mess, my hair snarled from all the shifting to get comfortable during the overnight hours. I hopped in the shower, opting for lukewarm water in an effort to shake off the nightmare doldrums. Then, after changing into simple knit shorts and a tank top, I took my coffee to the back patio.

It wasn't until I was already settled that I remembered Aurora's naked visit twenty-four hours earlier. She apparently didn't want to visit today – which I was thankful for – so I could enjoy my coffee in peace. I reveled in the sun and the sound of the surf before draining my coffee and heading inside.

I had a lot of work to do. It was time to focus on that rather than … the other stuff.

It was the other stuff that weighed heavily on me as I climbed the spiral staircase to the third floor. I felt a bit daft for not visiting until now. I thought the third floor – the one where the entire level consisted of a room with a light that was mostly for looks and only fired up when I saw fit because it was no longer necessary for boats coming into the bay – wasn't important. Apparently I was wrong.

I'd given the floor a cursory glance the day I moved in, and by that I mean I climbed to the top of the stairs and looked for about thirty seconds before heading back down. All I could see was a huge light and a couple of shelves. It didn't look like much … and yet, when I gave it a second look given all that I knew I couldn't understand how I'd missed the truth behind the room.

The best way to describe the third floor was as an out-of-control library that apparently doubled as a laboratory on special days. The light took up the center of the room, but there was a simple beauty in the light's design and the way the shelves were spread out, the light enhancing rather than detracting.

I wasn't sure what to think when I hit the first shelf, scratching my nose as I perused the leather-bound books that were most certainly considered antiques. I selected a purple tome, pursing my lips as I read the title. *Toads, Snails and Other Spell Ingredients That Can Go Bad.*

I'm not sure what I expected – maybe *Potions for Beginners* or *Spells for Dummies* – but it certainly wasn't something so mundane. The idea that toad remains could go wrong and inadvertently hurt a spell was both odd and hilarious. I heaved a sigh as I returned the book to the shelf, moving toward the next shelf and pulling up short when I found a photograph of my mother and father staring back at me.

I recognized the photograph. It was taken while they were both still in college. They looked fresh-faced and happy. My mother would never have the chance to age to the point where she was anything else, but my father would have time to turn sad and introspective. I ran my fingers over the frame, wistful. Not for the first time I wondered what would've happened if my mother had lived. The thought took on new meaning now given what I'd learned – and, yes, I believed it all to be true. I could no longer push it off as a dream.

If my mother had survived would she have made up with May Potter? Would I have known May as more than my surprising bene-factor? Would I have been able to call her "grandmother" without cringing? Would I not have this sick feeling in the pit of my stomach when I thought about my father because he would've had no reason to "protect" me throughout my life?

If my mother survived, would I have known about Moonstone Bay before this? Would I have visited as a child? I knew my father would never move here, which meant my mother wouldn't have, but would I have known about my potential second home? Would I have been raised with the knowledge of paranormal beings to the point it wouldn't shock me in the least?

Heck, would I have met a shark shifter? I didn't care what anyone said – and I would never admit it to anyone outside of my own head – but that sounded downright cool.

I returned the photograph to the shelf and moved on to the desk in the back corner of the room. I missed it when I first glanced inside because the huge light cut off the angle of examination. This was clearly where May Potter spent a lot of her time. She had recipe cards scattered about, framed photographs of Moonstone Bay friends, and even a journal sitting in the middle of the desk.

I sat in the desk chair and played with the cover of the journal, debating whether or not I should read it. Journals were meant to be private, after all. Sure, May Potter was dead, but she most certainly was not gone. That made it somehow more invasive.

Still, she wanted me to learn, right? That's what she said. She wanted me to know the truth of her life and what living in Moon-stone Bay meant. I couldn't learn that without some help.

I sucked in a breath as I flipped open the cover, widening my eyes at a photograph of myself staring back. It was a snapshot, something someone printed on a home printer. I stood next to my father as we smiled and mugged for the camera at my college graduation. I couldn't remember who took the photograph – I think it was my roommate's mother – but I remembered the day very well.

"How did you get this?" I murmured.

The question would be repeated in my head throughout the day. When I flipped to the next page I found another photograph of me, this one from when I was a baby. Each page had a different photograph of me, and throughout the years May had made notes next to the photographs, her bold and recognizable script describing my age and how much I reminded her of my mother.

My ears and cheeks burned by the time I was done, my feet feeling light and disconnected from my body as I tried to stand. Instead of forcing myself to be strong and accept everything in the journal, I indulged in a moment of weakness and dropped to my knees.

It was too much. It was all too much. Even if I could get past the fact that zombies were real and my grandmother thought she was a witch, the fact that she kept tabs on me since my early childhood – I knew now that my father kept her away even more than he wanted to admit – it was all too much.

I rested the side of my head on my knees, which I drew close to my chest, and did the one thing I hadn't allowed myself to do since any of this started.

I wept.

And I didn't stop until I couldn't squeeze out one more tear.

I wept for the mother I never knew, the grandmother I'd met only after her death and, for some reason, those stupid zombies wandering the cemetery at night. It was all too much and I needed to cry, so that's exactly what I did.

10

TEN

I put a bag of frozen peas over my eyes for ten minutes to reduce the swelling. I had a feeling I might have visitors – that's apparently the Moonstone Bay way, after all – and I was proved right by the knock on the door shortly before noon.

I took a moment to glance at my reflection in the wall mirror, my makeup-free face serving as a stark reminder that I'd fallen apart not long before. I combed my fingers through my hair to order it and then headed toward the door.

I expected to find Lilac or Galen on the other side, maybe even Aurora asking if she could take another naked dip without upsetting me. Instead I found Ned Baxter standing on the front mat, a bright smile on his face.

"Mr. Baxter." I wasn't expecting him, so I wasn't sure what sort of greeting would be proper given the circumstances. "Do you need something?" I felt a bit slow and stupid. "Was I expecting you?"

Ned's smile never wavered. "Not unless you're psychic."

I was fairly certain I wasn't, but I'd come to the realization that ruling out anything in Moonstone Bay was a bad idea. "So this is just a friendly visit?"

"Well ...." Ned broke off and shifted from one foot to the other, his discomfort evident. "I heard that you had a rough day yesterday."

"You heard?" I should've expected that, right? Moonstone Bay was full of gossip and I was the shiniest new gossip generator in town. Of course I was the topic of conversation. Lilac, Aurora and Galen probably used me as a punchline when telling stories at one of the myriad bars. While I was trying to prove to myself that yesterday was a nightmare, they were living in a comedy. That just figured.

"I heard," Ned confirmed, nodding. "Can we sit down and talk for a few minutes?"

It was a simple request, but it rankled me. I gestured toward the front porch, refusing to grant the man entrance into the only place I considered a safe haven. "Let's talk out here."

"Okay." I doubted that Ned realized why I didn't invite him inside – he probably figured I was a poor housekeeper on top of everything else – but he took a seat at the small bistro table located at the far corner of the porch without complaint. I knew I should offer him refreshments, but I was in no mood to play hostess.

"What have you heard about me?" As far as opening gambits go, it wasn't the friendliest, but the knowledge that gossip was being spread about me set my teeth on edge.

"I've heard that our best laid plans have fallen apart," Ned replied, not missing a beat. "I understand that you've been made aware of Moonstone Bay's more ... um ... magical side."

That was an understatement. "Yeah, it's been a busy forty-eight hours," I confirmed, crossing my arms over my chest as I sat in the chair across from him. My stance was aggressive, but I wasn't in the mood to care. "What do you want?"

"I want to make sure you're okay," Ned answered, his eyes clear as they roamed my face. "Did you sleep at all?"

"I slept."

"Well?"

"That wasn't the original question."

Ned chuckled, clearly uncomfortable. "No, it wasn't. I'm sorry this all went sideways so quickly. The plan was to let you settle in and slowly reveal everything over time."

"I'm the sort of person who would rather have all the information from the start rather than to have it arrive in dribs and drabs," I said. "May I ask why you all thought it would be a good idea to keep me in the dark?"

"I wasn't around for that particular decision," Ned clarified. "If you remember, I didn't even know about your existence until a few months before May died. I was surprised when she had me draw up the paperwork leaving the lighthouse to you."

"It sounds as if she was beloved," I noted, allowing myself to relax a bit. "You probably didn't want to consider the fact that she wouldn't survive."

"No, but I didn't even know Emma had a child. You never visited. May never mentioned you."

My mind drifted to the journal upstairs. May Potter might not have mentioned me, but that didn't mean she didn't think of me. The realization hurt – and yet it also soothed my frayed nerves in a way that I didn't think possible only twelve hours earlier. "Yeah, well, I think my father and May didn't exactly see eye to eye on things."

"I see." Ned steepled his fingers as he rested his elbows on the table. "I know this is a lot to take in. You come from a world where paranormal beings and entities are fiction. Moonstone Bay is the exact opposite. If you're normal on the island you're considered odd."

That was an interesting way of looking at it. "Are you paranormal?"

"I have a bit of wendigo in me, but it's nothing to write home about."

I thought about asking the obvious question, but instead made a mental note to Google "wendigo" once I was alone again. That would probably be easier, and make me look like less of an idiot. "Well, that's nice for you." Really, what do you say to something like that?

"My father was full-on wendigo and my mother was a witch," Ned explained. "I never really got a full dose of either, so I'm more of a half-breed with zero power more than anything else."

"You grew up knowing about this stuff. That makes things easier for you."

"Yes, and no. Still, you're clearly dealing with a lot. That's why I stopped by."

"Are you offering to explain things to me?" That seemed to be the offer du jour. "If so, I have to say I'm not in the mood for a lot of explanations right now."

"That's not why I came." Ned leaned back in his chair, extending his short legs in front of him as he fixed me with a friendly smile. He was the only lawyer I could ever remember meeting who wore a suit coat with knee-length shorts. It was an odd ensemble, to say the least.

"Why did you come?"

"I figured this might be too much for you," Ned said. "This isn't your world, and I know you're probably wondering how you'll fit in once the dust settles. My guess is you only came in the first place because of the will's stipulation that you live here to receive your inheritance."

Was that true? I'd like to think I'm bigger than that, but it wasn't untrue. The inheritance motivated me – yes, I feel small because of it – but I was also prodded into action by the thought of learning more about my mother's family. "I moved here for a variety of reasons. I'd be lying if I said the inheritance wasn't part of it."

"And no one blames you for that," Ned supplied. "I think most people would've done the same in your circumstances."

I believed that, too. Strangely enough, though, that didn't make me feel better. "Yeah, well, the entire thing is a bit messed up. I'm still trying to sort it out."

"You look as if you're suffering because of it," Ned noted, scanning my face once more. "The thing is, I don't think May would've done this if she realized how much you'd be hurt in the process. Even though she didn't mention you until shortly before her passing, I think she cared about you. Er, well, I think she at least cared about the idea of you."

"I don't understand what you're saying."

"I'm saying that you don't have to stay here to claim your inheritance," Ned explained. "Well, at least your full inheritance. I've been giving it some thought, and I don't want to see the lighthouse fall into disarray. It's very important to the island's financial longevity."

I had no idea what that meant. "I'm sorry, but ... um ... ."

Ned held up his hands in a placating manner. "I apologize. I'm getting ahead of myself. It's just, well, the lighthouse is a tourist destination and the beach behind it is very important. May was dedicated to keeping up the building and the land."

"I understand that."

"You're in a unique position," Ned explained. "You came for the inheritance, and now you're foundering under the weight of Moonstone Bay's unique brand of truth."

"I wouldn't use the word foundering," I replied.

Ned barreled forward as if he hadn't heard me. "You don't want to stay. Under the terms of May's will, you would have to if you wanted to claim your inheritance. I'm willing to buy the lighthouse from you so that's no longer an issue."

I opened my mouth to say something, though I had no idea what. No sound would come out. The offer was generous and something to consider, but I was nowhere near competent enough to make that decision right now.

I couldn't decide how I wanted to answer without offending Ned. Luckily I didn't have to figure a way out, because Galen popped up on the side of the porch before I had a chance.

"You want to buy the lighthouse?"

I jumped at the sound of his voice, clutching at the spot above my heart as I made a small gasp. "Where did you come from?"

"I was walking the beach to make sure we didn't have another problem," Galen replied, never moving his eyes from Ned's face. "I heard your voice and wanted to check on you. I didn't realize you had company."

Well, that made no sense. If he didn't realize I had company, who did he think I was talking to? Wait, don't answer that.

"I was just discussing a few things with Ms. Hunter." Ned's smile never slipped, but he seemed surprised by Galen's sudden appearance.

It was obvious that he was uncomfortable. "I heard through the grapevine that she had a spot of trouble yesterday and I wanted to make things easier for her."

"By buying the lighthouse?" Galen narrowed his eyes. "I don't think that's a good idea at the present time."

"Well, I didn't ask you," Ned pointed out, something unsaid passing between the two men. "Ms. Hunter owns the property. Last time I checked, your name wasn't on the deed."

"Which means I don't have a shark in this race."

Hmm. I tapped my bottom lip as I ran the sentence through my head. "Do sharks really race or is this about shark shifters again? I know you think I'm constantly bringing it up but that's really not the case."

For the first time since arriving, Galen cracked a smile as he walked around the porch railing and flopped in the open chair separating Ned from me. He looked to be making himself at home, although I could sense the tension coiling in his body.

"I wasn't trying to do anything illegal," Ned stressed. "I'm not trying to scam her. I would pay fair market value for the property. She's afraid of this place. All of your intricate plans to ease her into things failed and she's afraid to be here. I mean … look at her. You could swim in the dark pools under her eyes."

Self-conscious, I touched the heavy spots under my eyes and made a face.

"You look fine," Galen said, giving my knee a friendly pat. "You just need to catch up on some sleep. It's not a big deal."

Apparently it was a very big deal if I didn't want to frighten small children with my looks. I kept that to myself. "He really wasn't doing anything but giving me another option," I offered, recovering. "He was concerned that I was only staying for the inheritance and wanted to give me another option in case I wanted to leave."

Galen shifted his eyebrows so one was higher than the other as he regarded me. "Is that why you're staying? Is it because of the inheritance?"

It was a pointed question and I couldn't help but wonder if I would disappoint him should I answer in a specific way. Of course, I had no idea why I cared about disappointing him.

"I'm staying – at least for the time being – because there are some things I need to know." I looked to my lap, where my fingers gripped together as I tried to get a handle on my emotions. "I don't know what to make of all of this right now, so ... I'm just kind of going with the flow."

"That's fine." Galen moved his hand to my shoulder, the weight warm and calming. "I don't think anyone should ask more than that of you." His gaze was pointed when he focused on Ned. "No one wants you to make a decision before you're ready."

"That's not what I was trying to do," Ned protested, clearly not missing the fact that Galen was trying to slap him back without causing a scene. "I merely wanted Hadley to know that she has options. She doesn't have to stay if she doesn't want to remain."

"And she doesn't have to leave if she wants to stay," Galen fired back.

"Do you think I'm trying to force her off the island?"

Galen and Ned were in their own world where apparently only they could talk. It was almost as if they'd forgotten I was even present.

"I don't know what you're doing," Galen replied. "We all agreed that pushing Hadley before she was ready to make a decision was a bad idea. I don't think you should be here going against that decision."

Wait a second .... "When did you agree to that?"

"Last night after I walked you home," Galen replied. "We had a meeting."

Oh, good, another meeting. "With the Downtown Development Authority?" I couldn't be the only one who found that weird.

"No, just a meeting of concerned residents," Galen replied. "It was at Lilac's bar. She's afraid that if we pile too much information on you all at once that you'll crack. I happen to disagree with her assessment, but we decided on a compromise all the same."

"Uh-huh." He clearly didn't understand that anyone – no matter their intentions – making decisions about what I could and could not handle was insulting. "I'm glad you guys decided everything for me.

Whew!" I swiped a hand across my forehead. "It's so good to know that you're here to make the hard choices so I don't have to."

Instead of having the grace to look abashed, Galen fixed me with an unreadable look. "That's not what we were doing. I'm more than willing to discuss what we were actually doing in a few minutes, if that will make you feel better. For now, I need to have a discussion with Ned."

"That's entirely unnecessary," Ned said, holding up his hands as he stood. "I didn't come here to cause problems. I honestly thought I was doing a nice thing. I wanted to help Hadley because she appears to be so lost. I don't want that for anyone."

"She's not lost," Galen argued. "She's coping. She's doing it a heck of a lot better than I think most other people in her situation would."

"Wow, that was almost a compliment," I muttered under my breath.

Galen ignored the dig. "This is a new situation, and she's doing remarkably well. I think pressuring her to sell when she doesn't yet understand everything fully is the wrong way to go."

"I wasn't pressuring her," Ned snapped. "I was giving her an option that she wasn't aware she had. I was trying to do right by her."

"Why?" Galen knit his eyebrows. "Why do you care about doing right by Hadley?"

"It's not Hadley." Ned's voice was choked. "It's May. I always had a soft spot for May because she took me in when I was younger. She kept me for a whole week when my father was on a bender and forgot I was even alive. Did you know that?"

"No." Galen looked chastised as he leaned back in his chair. "I didn't know that. I'm sorry."

"I wanted to make sure that Hadley was taken care of to the best of my ability," Ned said. "I owe May that. I wasn't trying to pressure her into something she doesn't want to do. I was merely trying to make sure that she could make whatever choice is best for her."

"I guess that's fair." Galen nodded slowly. "But I think it's too soon for her to make a decision that will change the course of her life."

"I happen to agree." Ned shuffled toward the steps that led to the driveway. "That doesn't mean she can't have all the facts before making her decision."

"No, it doesn't. I would never argue otherwise."

"I guess we're agreed then."

"I guess we are."

Ned didn't speak again, instead turning on his heel and fleeing. Galen leaned back in his chair and waited for Ned to climb into his car and leave the driveway. He was quiet until the vehicle disappeared. Then I couldn't shut him up. "I don't care what he says. You're not selling the lighthouse."

And just like that he was apparently ready for round two.

# ELEVEN

"Did I say I was going to sell the lighthouse?"

While part of me was glad Galen took it upon himself to stand up for me, the other part was annoyed that he seemed to fancy himself the alpha dog of my pack. My father raised me to think for myself – okay, I'd just recently found out that he made a few decisions for me without my knowledge, too, but that was hardly important at present – so I didn't need a guy I'd met three days ago telling me what I should and shouldn't do.

Galen didn't break eye contact as he shrugged. "No, but I want to make sure you're not thinking about doing just that."

"Why?"

"You belong here."

His answer was so simple it should've been easy to ignore. Instead, it only infuriated me more. "You don't even know me. How do you know where I belong?"

"I saw it on your face last night," Galen replied, unruffled by my tone. "You were shocked to find out we keep zombies in the cemetery, but you were also excited. You weren't afraid of them. You didn't scream and run. In fact, you wanted to see more. By the way, when you want to get a better look there's a viewing window on the far side of the cemetery. People go there quite often to get a look at their loved ones."

That was so beyond anything I expected. "You have a viewing window?"

"Of course. We can't risk people trying to open the gate and getting infected."

"Oh, well, great." I shook my head as I lifted my eyes to the sky. "This place is just plain weird. You know that, right?"

"Weird is a state of mind," Galen replied, blasé. "I find it weird to live in a city where people are shooting each other across the highway."

"I didn't come from a city like that."

"I thought you lived in Detroit."

"I lived in a suburb of Detroit," I corrected. "It's not the same. Even taking that into consideration, it's not as if you have to wear a bullet-proof vest while walking down Woodward in Detroit. Sure, there's violence, but it's not like a war zone or anything."

"Oh, well ... ." Galen broke off, unsure.

"That would be a stereotype you were laboring under." I decided to take the offensive. "Kind of like when you ordered me not to sell the lighthouse even though it's not currently a consideration."

"It's not?" Galen scratched the back of his neck, his smile rueful. "I guess I did jump the gun a bit."

"You think?"

"It's just ... I don't want anyone taking advantage of you right now." Galen adjusted his tone and tack. "You're vulnerable."

"Because I'm a girl?"

"Because you're dealing with a lot of stuff you didn't know exist-ed," he corrected. "Hadley, I'm not saying you're weak. In fact, from everything I've managed to glean about you, you're the exact opposite. This is still more than any one person should have to deal with."

"Is that why you keep having meetings about me behind my back?"

Galen shrugged, seemingly unbothered. "It wasn't meant as an attack. We're not mean people."

"You have a serial killer."

"Point taken. There are bad apples in every bunch, though. In general, we're a close-knit community that tries to help. That's all I was trying to do."

My eyebrows flew up my forehead. "You called the meeting?"

"No, Lilac called the meeting and then proceeded to get into an argument with Aurora when they disagreed about how to handle things," Galen corrected. "For the record, they pretty much hate each other. Okay, hate might be a strong word. They dislike each other with claws at times."

"Why?"

"Because Aurora likes to get naked and doesn't care who she does it in front of."

Yeah, I'd seen that for myself. It was definitely an uncomfortable situation. That didn't mean I hated her. More that I wished temporary blindness was a real thing. "And what did you argue during this meeting?"

"That you'll be fine and can take whatever we throw at you," Galen replied. "I think you're more open to this stuff than you realize."

"Paranormal stuff?"

"Pretty much."

"I'm not so sure." I licked my lips as I readjusted on my chair. "I went to bed last night convinced that I would wake up and find all this had been a dream. I thought maybe I would even wake up in my old bed and discover that the will never existed."

"Would that have made you happy?"

It was an interesting question. "I don't know. That's what I need to figure out for myself, right?"

"It is."

"I'm not ready to make a decision either way," I supplied. "It's a lot to take in, but I don't want to make a kneejerk decision that I can't ever take back."

"I think that's very pragmatic."

"That's my middle name."

Galen cocked an amused eyebrow. "Hadley Pragmatic Hunter. It has a nice ring to it. What's your real middle name?"

"May."

Galen stilled, his expressive eyes clouding with something I couldn't quite identify. "How did you end up with that for your middle name? Didn't your father name you?"

"Yes, but apparently he and Mom decided on a name before I was born and he didn't want to change it. He said it was her last wish, so ... there you have it."

"I guess." Galen rubbed his hand over his strong jaw. "It's something that ties you to May. That's probably difficult for you, huh?"

I shrugged, noncommittal. "I finally went up to the third floor this morning."

"You hadn't visited before?"

"No. Do you know what's up there?"

"Spell books. A desk. A lot of photographs."

"Do you know what else?"

"Is that a trick question?" Galen had an unerring ability to remain calm whatever the circumstances. I admired that about him. I also found it an irritating trait.

"It's not a trick question. It's just ... there was a journal on the desk. It was right in plain view. I felt guilty about opening it because those were May's private thoughts, but I couldn't seem to stop myself. Even though I know she's apparently hanging around and might not like it, well, I looked anyway."

"And what did you find?"

"Me."

Galen pursed his lips. "Do you want to be more specific?"

"She had hundreds of photographs of me while I was growing up," I replied. "I don't know how she got them. I'd never seen most of them. They weren't from my father's collection or anything. She wrote little messages next to them."

"What did the messages say?" Galen appeared legitimately curious.

"Usually my age and what I was doing in the photo. Sometimes she wrote little comments like she was sorry she missed my high school graduation or she wished I'd done something different with my hair for the prom."

Galen snorted, seemingly amused. "That sounds like May."

"The thing is, seeing all of that made me realize that she wanted contact with me." My stomach twisted as I worked to maintain control of my emotions. The last thing I needed was another crying jag. "I talked to my father last night. He said she only contacted him a few times. He said he shut her down when I was younger because he didn't want to confuse me."

"How do you feel about that?"

"You would make a fabulous therapist. Has anyone ever told you that? That's exactly the question a therapist would ask."

"You can pay me for my services when I'm ready to leave," Galen said. "I honestly want to know how that made you feel."

"Conflicted."

"Because your father never told you?"

"That's part of it," I confirmed, tapping my fingers on the tabletop as a fresh wave of anxiety washed over me. "I always thought of him as a straight shooter. He didn't deny hiding May from me. He didn't seem to think he'd done anything wrong either, even after I was an adult."

"Do you think he did something wrong?"

"I think that he tried to protect himself rather than me," I replied. "That's the part that I'm having the most trouble living with. He's my father and I love him, but I can't help but believe he made the decision he did because it made his life easier.

"He said he didn't want me to be confused or upset, but I don't believe that," I continued. "He didn't want me asking questions or being upset with him. The only reason he told me about May's will is because he was legally obligated to do it. If he didn't and someone made a complaint he could've lost his law license."

"This isn't any of my business …."

"That hasn't stopped you from commenting before."

"No, it really hasn't." Galen's grin was mischievous. "Still, I don't think you should be too hard on him. He came from a world without magic, or at least a world that does a better job of hiding magic. Over the years, no matter what your mother told him before she died, he might've convinced himself that she was making it up. That probably would've been easier for him."

I'd considered that myself. "That doesn't change the fact that I feel as if I've been robbed of something."

"And you have every right to feel that way," Galen said. "You're dealing with so much I don't know how you don't buckle under the weight of it. I think you're doing extremely well under some very difficult circumstances."

He could say that with a straight face only because he didn't witness my crying meltdown on the third floor an hour before. "Thank you."

"Don't mention it." Galen sighed and patted my hand. "You've got a lot of work to do around here. I think you should focus on that today."

"You're not the boss of me." I meant the words to be playful, but they came out a bit harsher than I expected. Still, he was a bossy thing. I couldn't decide how I felt about it. "I think I'm going to tackle some of the heavier lifting this afternoon."

"Don't do that yourself," Galen cautioned. "I've seen some of the furniture on the second and third floors. It's heavy, and I can't help you today because I'm busy looking for a serial killer, as you keep reminding me."

I cocked a challenging eyebrow. "Did I ask for your help?"

"No, but you strike me as the sort of person who never asks for help. You need to get over that," Galen replied. "If you insist on moving the furniture before I can clear some time to help you, I suggest calling Booker. May left you money, and Booker is essentially our odd jobs fellow. He's strong, and he's likely to be able to help on short notice."

I hadn't considered that. In fact, I hadn't seen the oddly-dressed and yet ruggedly handsome taxi driver since he dropped me off that first day. "I'll consider it."

"Do that," Galen said, heaving himself to his feet. "If you need to talk or have questions, I'll be around. I know it will probably seem like a good idea to shut everyone out right now, but don't. That will only delay the inevitable, and I think that's the last thing you want."

"Do you have any news on your killer?"

"No, I'm still trying to figure out what all three of my victims have in common. It's not exactly easy, because Moonstone Bay is an island full of secret keepers."

"I thought everyone knew everyone's business in Moonstone Bay."

"In some ways that's true," Galen said. "In others ... everyone has secrets, Hadley."

"Oh, yeah? What's yours?"

Galen's smile was back. "You're not ready for that one yet. When you are, we'll have another talk."

I couldn't wait for that day. Um ... actually I could.


INSTEAD OF CALLING Booker I spent the day doing busywork, sorting through shelves and dusting books so I could arrange them in what looked to be the proper way. I'm a big fan of alphabetization, but I was afraid that if I screwed with May's organizational system I wouldn't be able to reclaim it.

I made Campbell's tomato soup for dinner and sat on the back patio to watch the sun set before locking myself inside the lighthouse for the night. I double-checked all of the doors and sent a whispered admonishment in May's direction before drawing a bath.

"I know you probably want to talk, but I need a good night's sleep," I said. "You're dead, so it's not exactly as if you're working on a timetable. I need sleep."

She didn't answer, but I was almost positive I felt a feathered hand brush over my hair before I sank beneath the water and let the heat and steam wash away the day. I spent a good thirty minutes in the tub before draining it, debating whether or not I should tie my hair back in a braid because I was sleeping on it wet. Ultimately I figured I would shower before anyone saw me the next morning, so bedhead wasn't nearly as terrifying a prospect as it could've been.

I was determined to put the day – the past several days, really – behind me. I wanted to start fresh in the morning, meet new and exciting people, maybe even call Booker to help me around the house while also digging for information.

The sheets were fresh and clean when I slipped between them, the breeze from the open window serving as a salve to my healing emotional wounds. Everything was going to be okay. I believed that. I had faith that somehow I would get through this and come out the other side better for it. It might've been naïve to think so, but my weariness made it necessary, so that's what I embraced.

I was three-quarters of the way to dreamland when my inner danger alarm pinged. Even though my body screamed in protest, I bolted to a sitting position and narrowed my eyes as I scanned the surrounding darkness. I registered the hint of movement at the same time I managed to make my muscles work, rolling off the bed as something hard and metallic smacked the middle of the mattress.

I widened my eyes when I realized what I was dealing with – an intruder with an ax – and worked overtime to control my ragged breath as I crawled away from the bed. I wasn't sure where to go or what to do to protect myself. I'd never been in this situation before. Sure, I'd lived in a suburb of Detroit, but that didn't mean home invaders were part of my everyday experience.

I felt rather than saw the figure move in behind me, a hand slide through my hair so the anonymous individual could get a good grip. He – and I was sure it was a man because the shoulders were far too broad to belong to a woman – wore a black mask over his features as he hissed something in a language I didn't recognize.

I had no idea what he said, whether it was a spell or curse or even a threat, but I reacted the only way I knew. I lashed out with my arm, slamming my fist into the man's groin and relishing the way he sucked in a hissing breath and groaned.

His obvious anguish allowed me to jerk away from him – leaving a small chunk of hair behind that I was certain I would miss in the morning (should I live to see it, that is) – and crawled closer to the wall. I was several feet from the door, fear causing me to shake, but I knew that even should I manage to gain some footing I didn't think I'd be able to keep it. I was outmuscled and in a precarious position.

My new friend seemed to realize that, because even though he wasn't fully recovered from my blow he gripped the ax with one hand and swung it toward me. The "whoosh" of the metal blade was enough to chill my blood and all I could think was: I'm not ready to die.

I didn't have time to think of a way to escape or scream for help. Fear overtook me, crawling into holes in my mind and heart I didn't even know existed. I was terrified, yet no sound would come out of my mouth.

It was over and I knew it. I would die here without learning anything of my family's history.

I briefly pressed my eyes shut, bracing myself for the inevitable, and then a frigid breeze blew through the room. I heard a loud crash, and even though I waited for the blow to hit, waited for my life to end and the hereafter to begin, it didn't.

I was cold, terrified and certain I would open my eyes to find imminent death. Instead, when I wrenched them open, I found the room empty.

The window was broken and the breeze bounced between walls, the air moving so fast I was convinced it was about to give birth to a monster of some sort. It didn't, but that didn't mean everything was okay.

The wind didn't dissipate, instead increasing until it was a swirling mass of air that felt strong enough to take form.

And then the screaming began.

# 12

## TWELVE

"**H**adley!"

My head pounded as I tried to regain control of my senses. Wait, it wasn't my head pounding. My heart was – that's for sure – but that wasn't the source of the noise. No, the pounding was from my front door, a full floor down, and whoever was trying to get inside was hitting the door with enough force that the entire lighthouse shook.

Oh, wait, no. I'm the one who was shaking.

"Hadley!"

I heard something break on the main floor, the sound slapping me across the face as I raced back to reality. I rolled to my knees, shoving myself to a standing position and grabbed the only thing on the night-stand that could possibly be construed as a weapon.

Galen barreled into the bedroom, his chest heaving and his hands clenched into fists at his side. I moved before I registered his identity, swinging my newly discovered weapon at his head before sanity gained a foothold. It was too late to stop the forward momentum, and all I could do was watch in horror as my hand moved toward Galen's neck.

As if sensing the blow was about to come, Galen reflexively grabbed my wrist and stared at the item clutched in my hand.

"You were going to kill me with a hairbrush?"

It was a fair question. "I thought you were somebody else."

"I can see that." Galen carefully released my wrist, his eyes keen as they scanned the room. "I heard you screaming."

That was impossible ... mostly because I tried to make my vocal cords work during the attack and failed, miserably. "I didn't scream."

"I heard screaming."

"I didn't scream." My voice was barely a whisper. "I heard what you heard, though. It wasn't me."

"Okay." Galen dragged out the last syllable as if he expected me to change my mind. When I didn't, he continued. "What happened?"

"Um ... ." I wasn't sure. How could I explain what happened when I had no idea?

"Honey, look at me," Galen prodded, moving his finger to my chin so he could tilt my head and hold my gaze. "There you are. Take your time, think for a second, and tell me what happened."

He sounded so reasonable. "I worked all day until I was in a sweaty frenzy. I ate canned soup for dinner because I was afraid to go downtown. I would honestly kill someone for a steak, so it was a real effort.

"Then I took a long bath with a clove-scented bath bomb," I continued. "I sat in there until my skin was wrinkled and pruned. Then I went to bed and slept on wet hair, which is why I have bedhead."

I slid a gaze to the mirror and frowned at my medusa-like style. It caused me to burst into tears. Who knew my breaking point would be bedhead? I couldn't wait for the doctor at whatever asylum I would ultimately be locked in to pick apart my bedhead issues.

"Don't do that!" Galen exploded, his expression pained. "Don't you dare cry!"

The more he yelled, the more I blubbered. "I can't stop myself. Someone was in here ... and he had an ax ... and look at my hair." My shoulders shook as the sobs overwhelmed me and I buried my face in my hands.

"Someone came in here with an ax?" Galen was beside himself.

"Have you even looked at my hair?"

"Your hair is cute," Galen snarled. "Talk to me about the guy with the ax."

"My hair isn't cute. It's terrible. I look like a monster. Oh, maybe that's my superpower. I can leap bad hairdos with a single bound." Instead of returning to reality, I sank to the floor at Galen's feet and lowered my face into my hands, rocking back and forth as I tried to calm myself. "I'll never live down the shame."

"Yeah, that's the real tragedy here," Galen muttered, shaking his head as he moved toward the broken window. He leaned over and touched a shard of shattered glass, narrowing his eyes for a moment before turning his attention outside the window. "It looks like whoever was in here went out through the window. How did you manage that?"

"I didn't do it."

Galen's expression was exaggerated as he peered at various corners of the room. "I don't see anyone else."

"Yeah, but … ." I opened my mouth, picturing the ax moving toward my head, and tripped over my tongue.

"Did you say something?"

"I don't know."

"You don't know if you said something?" Galen sounded as if he was at the end of his patience. "Hadley, look at me. I know you're in shock, but I need you to tell me what happened."

"I told you what happened."

"I need the version that doesn't focus on the bedhead."

That sounded reasonable. "I was asleep. Or, well, I was mostly asleep. Then something woke me. I couldn't see who it was, but I'm sure it was a man. The shoulders were too broad to belong to a woman. I rolled out of the bed as kind of a survival instinct and I heard something whizzing through the air. I heard something hard hit the bed, and I could see the moon through the window and it glinted off the ax blade."

"You were lucky." Galen crouched down so we were level. "If he hadn't been klutzy and woken you things might've gone a lot worse."

I didn't exactly feel lucky, but that was hardly worth focusing on right now. "He was right here." I gestured toward the space between the bed and the wall. "I couldn't make it out in time, so I was just sitting here and he was coming and I was out of time and I couldn't help thinking what my father would say when he found out. I heard a lot of 'I told you sos' in my head."

Galen's expression turned sympathetic. "I don't think that's what your father would say if something happened to you. I know you're angry with him right now, but I think it's fair to say that he loves you. He might've made mistakes, but that doesn't mean the love isn't real."

"You're right." That assumption wasn't fair. "He would've only thought that. He never would've said it out loud."

"We'll table that argument for now because there's no point in focusing on it." Galen slid his hand under my elbow and urged me to stand. "Come on. We'll go downstairs and I'll make you some tea. I want you to settle yourself and tell me the entire story without any colorful embellishments."

That sounded like a terrible way to spend an evening. Because my only alternative was kicking him out and dealing with things on my own, I didn't give in to my baser urges and admit to that.

"Sounds good."

"THERE'S NO one outside."

Galen let himself in through the front door, which was conveniently off its hinges, and forced a smile when he saw me drinking the tea he shoved in front of my face twenty minutes before.

"He went through the window, though." I was feeling a bit better, my mind firing again, although it wasn't yet up to my normal speed. "There is no other explanation. How did he fly out the window and not break something going down?"

"Well ... ." Galen didn't answer, instead flicking his eyes to a spot over his shoulder. I couldn't see what he was looking at, but I was a bundle of nerves, so the simple act was enough to cause terror to clutch at my heart.

"He's back, isn't he? He's going to finish the job."

"He's going to finish the job, but not the job you think," Galen said, holding up his hands in a placating manner and stepping away from the door.

The man swinging through the opening carried plywood and a hammer, his dark hair offsetting a pair of irritated eyes. His Hawaiian shirt was like a beacon in the dim light.

"Booker." I exhaled heavily. "I ... what are you doing here?"

"Fixing your door and window," Booker replied, his tone amiable as he glanced around the kitchen. "I'll start upstairs."

He clearly wasn't in the mood for small talk, because he disappeared from the kitchen before I could question him.

"What is he doing here?" My voice was scratchy, and even though I trusted Galen – well, trusted him as much as I could after knowing him for only a few days – I couldn't help being suspicious.

"He's going to fix the window and door," Galen replied. "It's only a temporary fix for tonight. He'll come back and do it right tomorrow. We've already talked about it."

It was a relief, and yet that's not how repairmen worked in Detroit. "Doesn't he have to give me an estimate so we can agree on terms?"

"Not when he's doing a favor for a friend," Galen replied. "Besides, I'm paying for the door. I kicked it down when I thought you were screaming."

I looked at the sagging door. He'd brought up a good point. "Was he the one screaming?"

"I don't know," Galen replied. "I thought it was you."

"I already told you that it wasn't me."

"Then it had to be him." Galen clearly wasn't in the mood to engage in an argument. "It's okay. You're safe. Booker is going to fix the door and window and everything will be okay."

He said it in such a charming way that I immediately knew he was lying. "What aren't you telling me?"

"You survived this mess, so you're the one with the story to tell."

He was being purposely evasive. I recognized the tactic. My father used it when dating women he didn't think I would approve of when I was a teenager. Now that I was an adult he'd given up hiding the fact that his girlfriends were often inappropriately young. That didn't mean I didn't recognize subterfuge when I saw it.

"Why were you here?"

The question caught Galen off guard. "What do you mean?"

"You said you heard me screaming," I replied. "You would've had to have been close to hear that. Why were you here?"

"If you must know, I was doing a loop around town before heading home and getting some sleep," Galen answered. "After our conversation earlier, I simply wanted to make sure you were okay."

That sounded reasonable, and yet it didn't quite fit. Still, I had bigger problems. "What happened in my bedroom? Why did he stop attacking? What was that wind?"

"Wind?" Galen leaned forward. "What wind?"

"There was a wind in the room. I thought he brought it."

"Was it coming from the window?"

"The window was open but not a lot. The screen was closed to keep out bugs. There's no way that the wind came at the exact right moment through that window. Even if it did, do you have magic wind around here or something?"

"Just when the unicorns pass gas," Booker offered, poking his head in the room. "I'm going to put one large piece of plywood over the window for the night. It will be ugly, but I'll have it looking as good as new tomorrow."

I narrowed my eyes. "Unicorns?"

"He's joking," Galen said hurriedly, making a face when Booker smirked. "Don't you think she's been through enough? Now is not the time to mess with her."

"Who said I was messing with her?"

"Just ... fix her window." Galen waited until Booker clomped up the stairs to turn his attention back to me. "Tell me more about the wind."

"No. I think it will just make me look crazy."

"I don't believe you're crazy."

"Really? I'm not sure I'm sane, so you might be in the minority there."

"Hadley ... ." Galen broke off, exhaling heavily as he rubbed his chin. Whatever he was about to say died on his lips as he shifted gears. "May, I know you're listening. I think now would be a good time to show yourself."

The change in his demeanor was stunning. Did he think he could call a ghost to his side? One I very well might've imagined because I was losing my proverbial marbles.

May Potter's ghost popped into view on the other side of the table, making a small puffing sound as I jerked back and spilled the remainder of my tea on the front of my tank top.

"Son of a ... !"

"It's okay." Galen grabbed a towel from the counter and moved to my side, shaking his head as he wiped off my chest – taking special care to avoid commenting on the fact that I wasn't wearing a bra – and grabbed the mug before it could fall off the edge of the table. "You need to learn to make a better entrance, May."

May graced Galen with a winning smile. "I'll work on it."

Even though he was agitated, Galen returned the smile. "It's good to see you. I had a feeling you'd come back. I didn't know it would be this soon, though."

"I had things to tend to." May's eyes drifted to me. "How are you doing, cupcake?"

I narrowed my eyes to dangerous slits. "Don't call me cupcake. I hate cutesy names like that."

"Chill out, firecracker," Galen instructed, grinning when I scorched him with a look. "At least you're getting your feisty nature back. I was a bit worried when you spent ten minutes whining about your bedhead."

Crap. I'd forgotten all about that. My hand instinctively moved to the top of my head, but Galen slapped it down as he moved past me.

"Leave it alone," Galen instructed. "It's fine."

It didn't feel fine. "You're not the boss of me," I reminded him, mostly because I didn't know what else to say and holding a conversation with my dead grandmother seemed too surreal in front of an audience.

"I'm the sheriff," Galen argued. "I'm the boss of everyone."

"Oh, I've missed you." May beamed at Galen. "You're still as handsome as ever, I see. Hadley, you should probably run a brush through your hair next time you're expecting a gentleman caller."

She couldn't be serious. "He is not my gentleman caller!"

"Certainly not," Galen agreed. "That's not why I'm here anyway. I need to know about the wind Hadley saw up in the bedroom when she was attacked. Did you see any of that?"

"Just the tail end," May replied. "Things were already happening when I realized what was going on. I wanted to warn her, but it was too late. In the end, she didn't need the warning. She handled things on her own."

What was that supposed to mean? "How did I do that?"

"Magic, dear." May's smile was so wide it almost swallowed her entire face. "Before you ask, Galen, I have no idea who or what was in that room. I couldn't get close. Things happened so fast that all I could concentrate on was Hadley.

"I was trying to figure out a way to help her – perhaps crack a lamp over his head or something if I could find the strength to lift it – but she cranked open a canister of ghoul-be-gone and he was through the window before I could even blink," she continued. "The spell was so powerful it actually screamed."

That couldn't be right. "I didn't do that."

"You most certainly did."

"I did not."

"You did, too."

There was only so much I could take in one night. "I did not!" I practically exploded as I slammed my hand on the tabletop, a puff of smoke sneaking out from between my fingers.

"Okay, you need to calm down." Galen put his hand on my shoulder and slid a fresh mug of tea in front of me. "You're in shock and freaking out. I get it, but you're not helping matters by flying off the handle."

"Yes, because believing that I created wind out of nowhere is a much better way to go," I deadpanned.

"You've got a snarky mouth," May noted. "You get that from my side of the family."

I flashed her a sarcastic thumbs-up before sipping my tea.

"I had a feeling she used magic," Galen admitted, his eyes never leaving my face. "She didn't understand what was happening, but I heard the scream. It sounded like her."

"It was her soul reacting out of terror to protect herself," May explained. "She didn't do it consciously. Now that she knows she can do it, though ... ."

"Then I'll never do it again," I snapped. "I don't believe you anyway. I did not do that!"

"You've had a long day." Galen kept his hand on my shoulder, the warm and comforting feeling serving to lull me. "Drink your tea, please."

For lack of anything better to do, I did as he asked, gulping down the entirety of the cup even though it scalded my throat. When I was finished, I flashed an obnoxious smile. "Happy?"

Galen took me by surprise when he pushed a hank of my out-of-control hair out of my face. "No, but you need to rest."

"I'm never going to sleep again. Bad things happen when I sleep."

"You're going to sleep now," Galen corrected, his eyes troubled. "You can't stop it from happening."

What the heck was he even saying? "I am not ... ." I barely got three words out before I realized I was tilting to the side and slurring. "What's happening?"

"What did you dose her with?" May asked, curious.

"One of your sleeping draughts," Galen replied, slinging an arm around my waist as I tried to stand. He caught me before I careened to the floor. "I saw it when I made the tea. I thought it might be a good idea, because she's severely sleep deprived and the only way any of this is going to make sense to her is if she calms herself."

"You're the sheriff," I muttered, poking my finger into his cheek. "It's illegal to drug somebody. You're going to have to arrest yourself."

"I'll keep it in mind." Galen swung me up into his arms as my head lolled back and I stared blankly at the ceiling.

"What's going on here?" Booker asked, appearing at the bottom of the steps. "Are you going caveman or something?"

"He drugged her," May supplied.

"Oh, there's my favorite ghost who used to be a witch!" Booker beamed as he mimed high-fiving May. "I heard you were back. I'm excited to catch up with you."

"Likewise."

"Yes, we're all excited about catching up," Galen said. "Is the upstairs window fixed?"

"Yes."

"Then I'm going to put Sleeping Beauty to bed. We have some things to discuss."

"You can't discuss things without me." My words sounded like gibberish, as if I was uttering them out of order. "This is my life."

"Shh." Galen moved toward the stairs. "I'll fill you in on everything over breakfast. I promise that you'll be okay tonight. I won't let anything in this house."

Oh, well, that was convincing. "I'm going to make you pay."

"I have no idea what you just said, but … okay." Galen's smile was bright as he flicked his eyes to mine. "It's okay to sleep. This will all be here in the morning."

I wasn't so sure, but for the first time since finding out the awful truth I hoped this wasn't all a dream. I couldn't kick Galen where it hurt if this was a dream … and he had it coming.

Most definitely.

That was my last thought before the darkness overcame me.

13

# THIRTEEN

I woke to a fuzzy head and eyes that felt as if they were crusted together. I was certain I had a hangover and yet I couldn't remember drinking anything. Surprisingly enough, that wasn't the worst part of my morning, though.

I rolled to my side when I felt a warm presence at my left, widening my eyes to what I'm sure must've been comical proportions as I let them roam over Galen's naked chest. He was in the bed with me, his eyes closed and his chest rising and falling in rhythmic fashion. The sheets were bunched around his waist, making me wonder if he wore anything south of the border.

I blinked rapidly, trying to cast off the remnants of a heavy sleep as I rolled the events of the previous evening through my head. Something had happened. Something bad, in fact. What, though? I couldn't quite remember.

I was inundated with flashes, bits and pieces of things that made no sense. I remembered Galen screaming my name. I remembered Booker showing up with plywood and saying ... something. I remembered a ghost in the kitchen. Wow. There's something I never thought I would be able to say.

I couldn't remember the big things, though. Maybe that was on purpose.

For lack of anything better to do, I lifted the sheets and let loose a relieved sigh when I realized I was still wearing my pajamas. If something had happened, it couldn't have been too bad – or vigorous – because I still had my panties on. That was the most important thing.

Right?

Wait, shouldn't I be figuring out why there was a half-naked man in my bed?

As if on cue, Galen shifted, slowly opening his eyes and focusing on me. He didn't look surprised to be in my bed, but his eyes were dogged by shadows that made me wonder if he'd gotten any sleep at all.

"I can hear your mind working from here," Galen said, his voice gravelly. "Are you about to freak out?"

That was a very good question. I dragged my hand through my hair as a distraction, frowning when my fingers got caught in a bevy of snarls. Crap! I probably had the bedhead to end all bedhead. I vaguely remembered taking a bath and going to sleep with wet hair. "I haven't decided yet."

Galen smirked as he stretched, lifting his arms and flexing one of the most ridiculously cut chests I'd ever seen in real life. Seriously, he looked like a model ... or a fitness trainer. It made me want to punch him. It also kind of made me want to drool, which made me want to punch him again.

"How are you feeling?" Galen asked, sobering. "You had a rough night. If you're going to delay your freak-out, we should get the technicalities out of the way."

"Oh, that's just what a girl wants to hear when she wakes up in a bed with a strange man," I drawled, annoyance getting the better of me.

"I'm not a stranger, and given the circumstances I thought it was best you didn't stay alone."

Circumstances? What circumstances? My memory refused to cooperate. "There's a couch on the main floor."

"Yes, and as much as I like Booker, there's no way I would share the couch with him." Galen's grin was lazy. "I don't roll that way."

Oh, well, that was a relief. Wait … Booker? "Why is Booker here?"

"How much do you remember?"

"Enough to know that I probably have bedhead so bad that I'll want to hide my face under the pillows the entire day."

"So … nothing?"

I opened my mouth to argue and then snapped it shut. "Pretty much," I conceded after a beat. "My mind is full of a bunch of flashes, but … they don't make sense. Why is Booker here?"

"Because we needed to cover up your window and door before going to sleep." Galen was matter-of-fact. "I didn't think you would want us to leave you with gaping holes in both."

What the … ? "I don't understand." My voice was unnaturally squeaky, as if I sensed the conversation was about to take a turn I couldn't quite grasp. It wasn't something I wanted and yet I couldn't quite ignore it either.

"Hadley, I think you're blocking things out." Galen appeared to have infinite patience, but I could hear the annoyance rippling under the surface. "You need to knock that off. We have quite a few things to talk about."

"Like why you're in my bed?"

"I already told you why I'm in your bed. Booker slept on the couch to watch the main floor and the only other place to sleep in this entire lighthouse was this bed. I'm too old to sleep on the floor."

He seemed so pragmatic, calm. He acted as if I was off base. I wanted to slap him for it. "I still don't understand."

"And now you're doing it on purpose." Galen patted my leg as he sat, lifting his arms over his head and stretching again before sliding out of bed. I was relieved to see he wore boxer shorts – although they had lipstick-covered lips on them – and he barely looked in my direction as he shimmied into the shorts and shirt he'd discarded sometime in the night. "I think you should take a shower. That will probably clear your head. While you're doing that, I'll talk with Booker and get breakfast going."

That's it? He thought I'd accept that. He thought ... wait, a shower did sound pretty good. It would solve the bedhead problem. "And you'll be in the kitchen when I come down?"

"I will," Galen said as he buckled his belt. "I don't think you'll be able to focus as long as you're worried about your hair."

Crap. How could he possibly know that? "I hardly think my hair is cause for concern." I put on an air of haughtiness. "If you're that shallow ... ."

"Yeah, say that again with a straight face after your shower," Galen ordered. "I'm guessing you'll start remembering last night – and very soon – and I don't want you to say anything that you'll want to take back."

"I never say anything that I want to take back."

Galen snorted. "Typical woman. I'll meet you downstairs. Try not to take too long. I have a full day and we have a lot to talk about."

And just like that, the uninvited guest I woke up next to in my bed was through the door and heading for the main floor, his demeanor calm, as if he didn't have a care in the world even though his eyes and words said otherwise.

What in the holy heck happened here last night?

GALEN AND BOOKER stood next to the stove, their heads bent together when I descended the stairs. They shifted in my direction at the same time, guilt flitting through their eyes before they masked it and pasted bright smiles on their faces. I wasn't going to fall for that.

"What's going on?"

"Nothing is going on," Booker automatically answered. "I picked up eggs, hash browns, bacon and bread so we can have a proper breakfast. I was merely filling Galen in on some of the town gossip that I managed to glean while out."

"Uh-huh." He was a terrible liar. "What gossip?"

"Well, Deenie Watkins is pregnant with her sixth child and her soon-to-be-ex-husband swears she used magic because he never wanted to have sex with her after the fifth child, but he did one night and now he's on the hook for even more child support. He's not a happy camper."

Maybe I was wrong about him being a terrible liar. That was a pretty intricate story, and he delivered it in a way that made me think it was potentially true. "She should kick him in the nuts so he can never have another child and see if that makes him feel better."

"I'll share that suggestion next time I see her." Booker winked as he moved to the front door, which was missing from its mangled hinges. "I picked up a new door and am painting it to match the old one. The paint is drying right now, so I should have it back on the hinges before lunch."

"That's great." I honestly meant it. "I'm still not going to fall for that Deenie lie. You might've thought of it really quickly, but I know you guys were talking about something. I want to know what it is."

Galen pressed the tip of his tongue to the back of his teeth as he doled hash browns onto three different plates. He was clearly conflicted.

"Tell me."

"I think we're going to have to tell her, bro," Booker said, grinning as he slathered butter on toast. Together they resembled a lean, mean, breakfast-cooking machine, but I couldn't quite shake the fact that something terrible was about to happen.

"You definitely need to tell me," I pressed. "I've been lied to more than enough for one lifetime."

"I didn't lie to you," Galen protested. "I just thought you needed more time to hear the truth. There's a difference."

I folded my arms over my chest. "Not in my book."

"Fine." Galen shook his head as he flipped eggs. He looked ridiculously hot in front of the stove, an apron covering his shirt and shorts, but I didn't care even a little. Okay, I cared a little. That was hardly the most important thing to focus on this morning. "How much do you remember about last night?"

I didn't expect him to go in that direction, but if it meant hearing the truth I was willing to play the game. "I remember it all."

Booker snorted. "She's lying. She doesn't remember anything."

116

I'd show him. "I remember waking up to find someone in my room. I remember crawling out of bed and thinking I was going to die. I remember that whoever it was disappeared and then Galen showed up."

"That's a good start," Galen said. "What do you remember besides that?"

"I ...." I broke off and chewed my bottom lip. "It's difficult."

"Let me help you out," Booker suggested. "You used your witchy powers and blew a guy through the window, bounced him along the ground a bit before he fled into the night, and then your dead grandmother showed up to tell you what you did.

"You melted down because apparently you're prone to it," he continued. "I wouldn't worry about that, by the way, because it's a chick thing. You can't help yourself. It's in your DNA."

"Booker." Galen growled out a warning, his eyes flashing.

Booker ignored him. "You're right. I didn't learn about Deenie while I was in town. I learned about that yesterday. I've been dying to tell someone."

My mouth was dry, but I managed to speak. "I can see that." Now that he'd mentioned everything that happened it came rushing back. How could I have forgotten?

"Hadley, are you okay?" Galen's eyes filled with concern.

I ignored him. "What did you really find out while you were in town?"

Booker didn't risk a glance in Galen's direction, instead increasing the distance between them while pinning me with his gaze. "Mark Santiago was found dead this morning."

The name meant nothing to me. "Why is that important?"

"Because he was wearing all black when the island's refuse department found him curled up in a ditch three blocks from here. They called Galen's office to tell him, but he wasn't there. He was obviously here."

"So ... just because he was wearing black you think it's the same guy who was in my house last night?" In theory, that might make sense, but there were gaping holes in the logic. "Do you think he was working for someone and that person killed him and dumped him in the ditch?"

"No, I don't think that's what happened." Booker was grim. "Ted Ferguson said Mark looked as if he'd been run over with a truck. He was a walking bruise before he died."

"I don't ... understand."

Galen decided now was the time to take over the conversation. He removed the egg pan from the burner and wiped his hands with a towel as he approached. "He's saying that it looks like Mark had the same sort of injuries that one would get from a fall."

"I see." I did. I saw. They were saying I killed Mark Santiago. I used my newfound magic – which I still didn't believe existed – to blow him through a window and bounce him off the ground. "How did he end up in the ditch if I killed him?"

"Honey, I think you're looking at this the wrong way," Galen cautioned.

I ignored him and focused on Booker. He was more likely to tell me the truth, no matter how hard it was to stomach. "How?"

"It's not uncommon," Booker replied. "He would've been running on adrenalin when he hit the ground. That's how he managed to get up and run. Once he calmed a bit, he probably realized that his injuries were catastrophic.

"He was probably bleeding internally, but his energy was high due to the escape," he continued. "Once he slowed down, well, it was too late. He succumbed."

I felt numb, my mind and stomach empty. I wasn't sure how I was supposed to react to the news. "Do you think it hurt?"

Booker shrugged. "No less than he deserved."

Galen elbowed him, delivering a sharp blow to the ribs before shuffling closer to me. "It's not your fault. While I don't agree with Booker's more colorful enhancements, I do agree that Mark deserved what happened to him."

"Because he broke into my house?"

"Because he went after you with an ax."

"Hmm." I rubbed my hand over my cheek, struggling to keep my mind in the here and now rather than what might've been if I'd acted differently the night before. "So I'm officially a murderer. I guess that means you have to take me in."

Galen's expression twisted and he scalded Booker with a dark look. "This is exactly why I didn't want to tell her."

"How was I supposed to know that she'd react like this? I couldn't possibly know she did stuff like this," Booker protested.

I couldn't help being confused. "Stuff like what?"

"Like being dramatic and blaming yourself for things that aren't your fault," Galen automatically replied. "You've got a tendency to fly off the handle in absolutely ridiculous ways – like that whole bedhead thing you were so fixated on last night ... and kind of this morning, too – but I'm also starting to think you have a martyr complex."

The admonishment didn't make me feel better. "I'm sorry, I didn't realize I was supposed to simply brush it off when I murder someone. My bad. I'll know better for next time."

"I like the sarcasm," Booker noted. "But Galen is right about the martyr complex. It has to go."

"Excuse me?"

Booker's expression turned sober. "You fought off an intruder," he argued. "Someone came into your house and attacked you with an ax. A freaking ax! You used the one weapon you had – even though you didn't know you had it at the time – and you saved yourself. That's not murder."

"Then what is it?"

"Self-defense," Galen answered without hesitation. "You didn't do anything wrong ... other than obsess about bedhead. As for the rest ... I don't know what to tell you about Mark. I don't know him well enough to hazard a guess about motive, but I'll do some investigating this afternoon."

"That's it?" I was dumbfounded. "What about me?"

"What about you?"

"What am I supposed to do all day?"

"You just moved to the island and you're missing a door and a window," Galen replied. "I think you have your hands full."

"Yeah, but … ." I broke off, embarrassed to admit I was afraid to stay at the lighthouse alone.

As if reading my mind, Galen offered me a sympathetic smile. "Booker will be here with you for most of the day. If you get afraid you can call me."

Well, that was insulting. As if I needed a man to run to my rescue. "Why would I be afraid? I have my newfangled magic powers and can throw grown men through windows. I don't need a man to save the day."

Galen stared for a long moment, his expression unreadable. "I can already tell you're going to be a lot of work."

"You've got that right," Booker said, grinning. "Is breakfast ready? I'm starving."

"Yeah." Galen handed him a plate, never moving his gaze from me. "Admitting you're afraid is not the end of the world."

"I'm not afraid." In truth, I was terrified. He didn't need to know that. "I can take care of myself."

"I don't doubt that."

I accepted the plate Galen handed me, another flash from the previous night flooding the forefront of my brain. "Did you drug me?"

Booker chuckled as Galen shrank back, amusement evident. "I told you that would come back to bite you, bro. It took her longer to remember than I thought, but you're in trouble now."

"I'm not afraid of her," Galen challenged.

"You should be," I snapped. "I'll make you pay for this. When you least expect it, I will exact my revenge."

"That sounds mildly kinky," Booker offered.

Galen's grin was flirty. "I was just thinking the same thing."

Ugh. Men.

# FOURTEEN

Galen left me with Booker and my anger after finishing breakfast. He had work to do, of course. It was big important man work, and he needed to puff out his chest and do important man things all day.

Did I mention he left me with the dishes? He said he cooked and I needed to clean up. As if that was women's work or something. In theory I didn't have a problem with sharing the workload. But because he drugged me and stripped down to kiss-covered boxers before climbing into bed with me I was in no mood to humor him.

I heard Booker working outside. After Galen left – stopping long enough to whisper something to Booker as he used a power saw in my front yard before lobbing a weighted look in my direction – Booker toiled quietly by himself. I had no idea if Galen warned him to keep his mouth shut, but I figured that was the gist of the closing conversation.

I wasn't about to put up with that.

I unpacked my laptop and carried it to the patio so I could watch Booker work, using my cell phone's hot spot so I could fire up the Wi-Fi. "Do you guys have wireless service out here?"

Booker glanced up from the board he measured, a pencil poking out from behind his ear. "No. Moonstone Bay is actually trapped in the past. Most people don't know it, but it's like that island on *Lost*. It's really 1960. We simply haven't told you yet."

"Ha, ha."

"Yes, I crack myself up regularly," Booker confirmed. "We have Wi-Fi. Just talk to Chip at the deli."

"Why would I talk to Chip at the deli about hooking up Wi-Fi?"

"Because he's the one who does it."

"I should've seen that coming," I muttered, shaking my head. I waited for the computer to sync with my phone and then typed "Mark Santiago Moonstone Bay" into the search engine.

"You seem a little ... ticked off," Booker said after a beat. He clearly wasn't big on uncomfortable silences. "Do you want to talk about what's bugging you?"

"There are so many things bugging me right now that I wouldn't know where to start." I narrowed my eyes as I searched the various sites that popped up. "You guys have a Shakespearean theatre troupe?"

"What are you looking at?"

"Porn."

"Let me know if you find anything good!" Booker had an easy-going nature that I found oddly relaxing. "As for the Shakespeare troupe, they're a bunch of morons. They get drunk and perform sonnets in the park. I wouldn't get too excited."

"Good to know." I clicked on a link.

"So ... was that a no about whether or not you want to talk?" Booker prodded.

"Not necessarily. I just can't decide what we should talk about first. Do you prefer magic or bedhead?"

"Definitely bedhead."

"Me, too." I clicked on a second link. "How bad was my bedhead last night?"

"I didn't think it was so bad," Booker replied, using his pencil to mark something on the board. "I think you looked kind of cute. You were a bit scattered. I can't say I blame you, but I thought your head was going to spin around there at one point."

"Was that before or after your little buddy drugged me?"

"It was before. And I don't think you should hold that against him."

I stilled, slowly lifting my chin and scorching Booker with a look. "And why is that? I mean ... where I come from, if someone drugs you without your knowledge that's considered a big no-no."

"It's not as if he did it for sex or something," Booker argued. "You were about to overload. We all sensed it. He actually helped you by forcing you to get some rest. You were much more settled this morning. It was a good move."

"Settled?" He had to be joking. "I woke up to find a random dude in my bed."

"Oh, let's not play games." Booker wagged a finger. "That can't possibly be the first time that's happened."

"Excuse me?"

"You're a wily witch," Booker pointed out. "Witches like to get frisky."

"I wasn't a witch until I got here," I grumbled, turning back to the screen. "And as for the other part, I haven't done that since college. And at least then I could blame the ill-advised keg stand. I made the mistake and suffered the consequences. That's not what happened last night."

"You were always a witch," Booker countered. "You simply didn't realize it before. There's a difference."

"I think that unless you wield magic you can't be considered a witch, and before last night I never did anything magical. But if you want to know the truth, I'm not convinced I did what May's ghost said I did."

"Oh, really?" Booker arched a dubious eyebrow. "What is it, exactly, that you think happened?"

"I think he jumped."

"Really? Why?"

"Because he was frightened of me." That's totally plausible. I knew it. I felt it. One look at Booker's face told me I was deluding myself. I decided to try again. "Because he was frightened of Galen."

"I guess, in theory, that's a possibility," Booker conceded. "Except my understanding of the situation is that Galen didn't show up until right after Mark went through the window."

My recollection of the event was vague, but that sounded right. "Either way ... I think he jumped."

"I think you're clinging to the past when you should be looking toward the future, but I understand this is hard for you to deal with," Booker said. "Take as long as you want to deal."

"Thank you for permission to feel what I want to feel," I deadpanned.

"You've got quite the mouth on you, missy. You got that from May."

It wasn't the first time I'd heard it. I'd been compared to May Potter a few times now. Each time left me more unsettled than the last. "Did she say anything after your buddy drugged me?"

"Galen is more of an acquaintance than buddy, but you probably don't care about that."

"You think?"

Booker chuckled. "She didn't say much," he replied. "She said that something inside of you escaped and tossed Mark out the window. Of course, she had no idea it was Mark at the time. Next time you see her you might want to ask if she had any goings on with Mark. I can't ever remember them crossing paths."

Speaking of Mark, I glanced back at the computer screen and read two paragraphs before speaking again. "I'll make sure to do that. Are you sure that's all she said?"

"Would I lie to you?"

"I have no idea." I opted for honesty. "You seem fairly trustworthy, but I think Galen is trying to force you into keeping your big trap shut until he can come back and finesse the situation to his liking."

"Finesse, huh?" Booker's face lighted with genuine amusement. "You're a funny little thing. I wondered if there was any finessing going on last night. He acted as if it was a hardship to take one for the team and sleep in the bed with you."

"Not finessing like that." My stomach rolled, and not entirely due to unease. "I think we're getting off point."

"So you don't want to talk about Galen?" Booker's smile was mischievous.

"I don't want to talk about any of it." I closed my laptop – I'd found what I was looking for, after all – and lobbed a bright smile at Booker. "You'll be here fixing the window and the door for the next few hours, right?"

Booker nodded. "That's the plan. You won't be alone so there's nothing to fear."

I was hardly fearful. "Great. I'm going to head out and run an errand. I'll grab food from the market on my way back and we'll grill something for dinner. I've been dying to use that grill out back. How does that sound?"

Booker's smile slipped. "I don't think Galen wants you wandering around."

"I guess it's a good thing that Galen isn't the boss of me, huh?"

Booker opened his mouth to argue but ultimately shook his head. He was beaten and he knew it. "Don't be gone too long. And try not to get in trouble."

"Would I do that?"

"I don't know you that well," Booker answered. "If something happens to you while you're out, Galen will do something truly awful to me. I want you to know that."

"Why?"

"Because that's how he is."

"But why?"

"I'm not getting into that." Booker shook his head and crossed his arms over his chest. "Just keep in mind that you're not only responsible for yourself when you go out to do ... whatever it is you're going to do. You're responsible for my survival, too."

I flashed a faux sugary grin. "I'll consider it."

Booker rolled his eyes to the sky before turning back to his work. "I'm doomed. I just know it."


THE MOONSTONE BAY Construction Company was located in a

small building behind the lone grocery store. It was essentially four walls and a roof, with a huge storage barn sharing space on the lot. I figured the office was basically one secretary with a private line to the big boss, which was all I needed.

What I didn't tell Booker was that I was determined to get more information on Mark Santiago. Galen and Booker talked big about what happened – about what I'd potentially done – but I couldn't shake the idea that I'd killed a man. I wasn't sure how I was supposed to digest that news, but right now I was suffering from a massive case of acid reflux.

Unlike previous days, Moonstone Bay's sidewalks were packed with people, and I did my best to avoid the tourists as I walked to the construction business. One of the tidbits I found while searching the web featured a photograph of Mark Santiago – a normal-looking man with a grim expression on his face. The photograph mentioned new construction by the company and listed Mark as a worker. I figured the construction office was the place to start gathering information.

The small office was plain – consisting of one desk in the middle of the office and a variety of other seating options – but the rush of cold air washing over me from what clearly sounded like an overtaxed central air unit was a welcome blessing. Instead of a secretary sitting behind the desk, I found a man poring over files. He arched an eyebrow when I entered and then offered a bright smile.

"Please tell me you want me to do some work on the lighthouse. I've been dying to get my hands on that place for years."

The statement caught me off guard. "Do I know you?"

"I'm Martin Gullikson." The man stood. "This is my company."

"Oh, I wasn't expecting the main man to be behind the front desk." I stepped forward and extended my hand. "I'm Hadley Hunter."

"I know." Gullikson's grin never faltered. "You're the only new regular in town. We all know who you are and what you look like."

"Right. The Downtown Development Authority meetings."

"That and we like to get drunk on weeknights at one of the main bars and gossip."

Gullikson was in his mid-forties but he had a youthful vibe and his eyes lighted with mirth as he looked me up and down. "Not used to the heat yet, huh?" He briefly turned his back to me and rummaged in the refrigerator behind the desk, returning with a fresh bottle of cold water. "Drink up. You'll learn pretty quickly that the last thing you want to do is get dehydrated."

"Thank you." I was a bit sheepish as I cracked open the bottle and guzzled a third of it. I used the back of my hand to wipe my mouth as I scanned the office. "This wasn't what I expected. The construction offices back in Michigan look nothing like this."

"Most people here know who I am and how to find me," Gullikson explained, resting his hip on the corner of his desk and folding his arms over his chest. He didn't look worried about why I was there, merely curious. "If people need me they call and I go to them. I really don't need the office."

"Then why do you keep it?"

"I have four kids."

"Oh, well, that explains it." I flashed a smile. "So, you're probably wondering why I'm here." I was more nervous than I expected. I wasn't used to asking questions or sticking my nose into other people's business. I never fancied myself a Trixie Belden in training, but that's exactly what I was doing.

"So you're not here for a lighthouse spruce?"

"Do I need one?"

"There are a few things I wouldn't mind suggesting, but you're barely settled. You have time."

"Good to know."

"May wasn't big on changing anything, but I'm hoping you're less resistant to letting go of the past," Gullikson said. "As for why you're here ... does it have something to do with Booker stopping by at the crack of dawn for a new door and window?"

The question threw me for a loop. "How did you know that?"

"It's a small community and word spread at the bar last night that Galen Blackwood called for Booker and he took off in the direction of the lighthouse," Gullikson explained. "Rumor is they both spent the night. You work fast."

If Gullikson's expression wasn't so charming I would've raised a fuss. But I didn't have the energy. "I had a spot of trouble. Booker is working hard, and I owe him for coming so quickly."

"That's what Booker does. If you're not here for Booker, why are you here?"

"Well, I was doing a bit of digging on the internet and I found a photograph that showed a man named Mark Santiago," I replied. "The cutline said that he worked for you. I was hoping to ask a few questions."

Gullikson's eyebrows flew up his forehead. "Mark? That's why you're here?"

"I just ... ."

"Huh." Gullikson cut me off with a shake of his head. "I guess that shouldn't come as a surprise. There's a rumor going around that Mark was found dead in a ditch this morning. I was under the impression he drank himself to death, but now I'm thinking that might not be true."

"Was he a big drinker?"

"Pretty much the biggest."

"And you kept him on staff?"

"Technically I don't have a staff," Gullikson clarified. "I have hourly workers, and when I find someone good I like to keep them on my team. The thing is ... this is an island. We're not always engaged in big construction projects. My workers tend to be temporary and they hop from job to job."

"Oh." I hadn't considered that but it kind of made sense. Very few jobs on an island the size of Moonstone Bay would be of the permanent variety. "Was Mark Santiago working for you?"

Gullikson shook his head. "I had to let him go about six months ago," he replied. "He wasn't fired, for the record. He was a day laborer at best. I couldn't count on him to show up on time, and his work had turned shoddy. I finally got to the point where I couldn't put up with it any longer."

"I see." That was extremely interesting. "Do you think he was an alcoholic?"

"I think that we don't use that word around here because we have a lot of recreational drinkers. It is an island, after all. Still, most people manage to understand that you work first and play second. Mark never understood that."

"Do you know where he was working?"

"No, I honestly don't," Gullikson said. "There comes a point where you want to help, but it's like beating your head against a wall, so you're doing more harm to yourself than help for the other person. That's where I got with Mark."

"At least you tried to help." I mustered a wan smile. "Well, thank you for your time." I turned to leave, but Gullikson stopped me by clearing his throat.

"Do you know how Mark died?"

"There are conflicting reports." That wasn't a lie. I was conflicted and wasn't sure I believed May Potter's report. Still, I felt a bit guilty for saying it.

"It doesn't matter. The truth will spread by the end of the day, and the gossip and innuendo won't be far behind."

That sounded downright terrible. "Thank you for talking to me."

"Don't mention it. If you ever want to change something at the lighthouse, don't hesitate to give me a call. Like I said, I've been dying to get my hands on that place for years."

"I'll definitely do that."

## 15
# FIFTEEN

I hit the grocery store next, cursing myself because I had no way to get a bunch of groceries home. That meant I had to be prudent when choosing, ultimately grabbing fresh fruit, meat for the grill and a pre-made pasta salad. I topped it off with ears of corn, butter and condiments, and then headed for the lighthouse.

Despite my best efforts, my arms felt like mush by the time I hit home. I really thought there was a chance one of my arms would fly out of the socket.

Booker caught sight of me from the second-floor window as I approached and scampered outside to help. At first I thought it was because he was gallant. Ultimately I realized it was because he thought I'd brought snacks.

"No chips?" Booker's expression reflected outright disappointment. "Remind me not to do work here again. This is a very disappointing collection."

I rested my bags on the picnic table close to where Booker worked and murdered him with a dark look. "I can only carry so much."

"Then you should've rented a cart to get your stuff home."

"I didn't know that was an option." Crap. That would've made the past twenty minutes so much easier. "Why didn't anyone tell me that was an option?"

"Probably because you didn't ask," Booker replied, sitting at the picnic table and nosing through another bag. "Ooh. Steaks! I love steak."

"I wanted to get shrimp for the grill, too, but I was afraid I wouldn't be able to carry it." The heat was making me feel pouty and even though it wasn't an attractive quality I couldn't quite shake the urge. "Maybe I should go back."

"I have a better idea." Booker grabbed the grocery bags, heaving them with minimal effort, and turned toward the lighthouse. "Let's put this stuff away so it doesn't spoil and I'll drive you to the market so you can stock up on the basics. Then I'll show you the cart rental corral and maybe even introduce you to a few of the store regulars so you don't look like such a newbie."

I was fairly certain he meant at least half of that as an insult, but I wasn't in a position to turn down his offer. "Thank you."

Booker pursed his lips. "I know that you're still getting used to this, but most people on the island are open to helping. All you have to do is ask."

"If you ask for help in Detroit you end up losing your purse a lot of the time ... and your hubcaps ... and sometimes your entire car."

"You're not in Detroit."

That was starting to sink in.


"OKAY, THE BIG thing to know about the market is that it is best to hit it on Mondays and Tuesdays." Booker took his role as grocery store tour guide very seriously. "It's late in the week, but we lucked out some because it's not all that late. This place will be packed in about an hour."

"I would think that all of the tourists would eat at restaurants. Why do they come here?"

"Everyone loves fresh fruit and liquor. People like to take it to the beach."

Hmm. I hadn't considered that. "Fair enough." I hefted a case of bottled water into the bottom of the cart. "That should be enough of that for now."

"You're cute." Booker grabbed two more cases and transferred them to the lower rack. "This should get you through about a week."

I was appalled. "That's a lot of wasted bottles."

"It is, but the recycling folks on Moonstone Bay are extremely diligent. You have three recycling bins in the garage. I know because I saw them there when I grabbed the saw."

"That's my saw?" I was dumbfounded. "Why do I have a saw?"

"What else are you going to do when you have to dismember a demon?"

He was kidding, right? "No, seriously, why do I have a saw?"

"I am serious." Booker turned down the bread aisle. "I saw you got one loaf, but I'd get some English muffins and bagels. You'll want easy things to grab for breakfast. When the heat really gets going, you'll find you don't have much of an appetite, but it's important to eat."

He sounded so rational, yet I wanted to pound him in the head. "That's why I got the fruit."

"Which is good, but you need more carbs." Booker grabbed a package of blueberry bagels. "These are really good."

"Whatever." I did my best to keep from melting down as I followed him down the aisle. "So I have a saw to dismember demons, huh?"

"That's what I said."

"Don't tell her things like that!" Lilac popped up at the end of the aisle and smacked her hand against Booker's forehead by way of greeting. "She's liable to take it seriously given everything that's going on."

Booker scowled as he ruefully rubbed his forehead. "Don't ever hit me again."

"Don't say stupid things and I won't have to hit you," Lilac countered, grinning as she met my gaze over Booker's shoulder. "Stocking up?"

"She has absolutely nothing to eat in that place and I'm at the point where I'll gnaw off my own arm if I don't get something to snack on,"

Booker replied, his eyes drifting to the salted nuts display. "Here we go. Do you like almonds? Pralines? Walnuts? Ooh, how about some peanuts?"

I stared at him blankly for a beat and then shrugged. "I've never given much thought to my nut needs."

Lilac snorted, her mind clearly drifting to a dirty place. "You should get on that, honey. The whole town is buzzing about the fact that you had two of our most eligible bachelors sleeping in your house at the same time last night. Are you honestly saying you didn't give either of them a test drive?"

My cheeks burned with mortification and I glued my eyes to my flip-flops. "Good grief," I muttered, sucking in a breath.

"Leave her alone," Booker instructed, blasé. "She had a rough night and she went on a secret mission this afternoon. I think if you pile much more on her she'll blow a gasket."

I knew that was an insult. "I didn't go on a secret mission!"

"She went to the construction office and asked about Mark Santiago," Lilac volunteered. "From what I've been able to piece together – and the information is spotty at best because Galen is not in a good mood and he told me to mind my own business – Mark Santiago broke into the lighthouse last night, got hurt in the process and died in the ditch afterward. Do I pretty much have everything down?"

She was good, I had to give her that. "How did you … ?"

"Serafina Caruthers saw you going into the construction office and theorized you were considering getting work done on the light-house," Lilac replied. "I didn't think that made much sense because you've been too busy with other things to give that much thought, so I went to the office and asked Martin."

"And he told you?" Did no one on this island respect privacy? Sure, I went into the office in the first place to get information on a dead man who I may or may not have killed with magical powers I didn't know I had, but I was in a pickle. Lilac was just doing it for show.

Lilac snorted. "Of course he told me. He was curious what I knew about Mark's death and we traded information."

"What do you know about Mark's death?" Booker asked, leading us to the next aisle. He was a good multi-tasker because he kept one ear on the conversation as he filled my cart with stuff I would probably never eat. "I would've thought Galen was trying to keep that secret."

"He was, but Ronnie Sinclair discovered the body while collecting Dolly Winston's garbage," Lilac explained. "You know what a big mouth Ronnie has."

"Yes, it almost rivals your mouth." Booker flicked the end of Lilac's nose, a fond but weary expression on his face. "You shouldn't be passing out information on Mark's death. It's going to turn into a big deal."

"Why not?" Lilac was affronted. "This is the biggest thing to hit Moonstone Bay since Meredith Markham got naked and drove her golf cart down the main drag last month. She even drove it on the sidewalks, which is a direct violation of DDA rules. She owes, like, five grand in fines and refuses to pay. She says menopause made her do it."

I slapped my hand to my forehead, utterly perplexed.

Booker offered me a consoling hand on the shoulder as he grabbed packages of pre-mixed tuna fish and heaped them in the cart. "You'll get used to it. Meredith is actually really funny when she's on her estrogen."

"Oh, well, that makes everything better," I muttered, glaring at the tuna. "I don't even like tuna."

"It's good for you." Booker turned his full attention to Lilac. "I'm not joking about keeping your mouth shut. Galen has his hands full. Between Bonnie's death and Mark's ... whatever it was he was doing last night ... he's got a lot to sort through."

Lilac knit her eyebrows, confusion washing over her face. "I thought Bonnie accidentally drowned."

Booker shot a worried look in my direction, clearly recognizing his mistake, and then squared his shoulders. "It's still a lot of paperwork to fill out. He has to make sure he checks every nook and cranny to make sure a killer clown isn't hiding there."

Huh. What was that supposed to mean? "You guys don't have killer clowns, do you?" I involuntarily shuddered at that thought. I could take murderers, vampires and even witches, but I drew the line at killer clowns.

"Not since last year," Lilac replied, distracted. "We had a brief contagion of them, but the Rocky Beach cult members needed someone for a human sacrifice and the clowns fit the bill."

Wait ... what? "Human sacrifice?"

"She made that up," Booker said, squeezing my shoulder. "Stop being ... well, you, Lilac. She's dealing with way too much truth to sort through your version of lies. I know you think you're being funny, but you're actually being the exact opposite."

"I'm sorry." Lilac was contrite. "I won't do it again." She crossed her finger over her heart, allowing me to exhale. "As long as you tell me what's really going on, that is."

Oh, so close. "Do they carry sleeping pills here?"

"You don't need sleeping pills." Booker snagged the back of my shirt and dragged me back when I moved to wander away. "That's why we have so much liquor on the island."

"Yes, I've heard you guys don't have alcoholics. Just recreational drinkers, right?"

Booker wasn't bothered by the charge. "Pretty much." He kept his attention focused on Lilac. "You need to let this go. What happened to Mark and Bonnie is a lot for Galen and his three-man team to sort through. Don't pressure him."

"Yeah, I hear he folds under pressure," Lilac smirked, winking at me. "You spent the night with him last night, right? Can you verify that?"

I seriously thought I was about to pass out. My feet felt alien, as if they didn't belong to my body, and my brain was doing this weird floating thing. It was kind of nice. "Sleeping pills. Where are they?"

"You're not getting sleeping pills." Booker was adamant. "Let it go, Lilac. You're starting to get really annoying."

Starting? I was pretty sure she passed that days ago. I liked her. She was friendly and had enough personality to fill an entire island. She was also agitating on a level I didn't know existed outside of cheer-leading camp or extreme couponing meetings.

Lilac pasted an innocent expression on her face. "How am I being annoying?"

"The fact that you're even asking that with a straight face tells me that you're in the mood to play games," Booker fired back. "I am not."

"Oh, whatever." Lilac turned her petulant pout toward me. "How did Mark Santiago die?"

"Don't answer that," Booker barked. "She's trying to get around me by asking you."

"Really? I never would've guessed that." I was too tired to put up with much more of this. "So ... does anyone want to head toward the liquor aisle?"

"Be patient, grasshopper." Booker's smirk set my teeth on edge. "We need to talk about the other thing first."

"What's the other thing?" I was truly at a loss.

"Why did you go to the construction office? I knew you were up to something by the way you left, but I'm curious about why you picked that to be your move."

"What do you think my move should've been?"

"Oh, you're not going to distract me." Booker wagged a finger in my face. "Tell me what you were doing talking to Martin."

Crap. I guess there was no way out of this. "I Googled Mark Santiago's name because I was curious and wanted to see what I could find out about him."

"You could've asked me," Booker said.

"Or me," Lilac added.

"I wanted to search for myself," I clarified. "One of the things I found was a photograph of him sitting on a roof. It was a business story about ongoing construction on the island and the caption said Mark worked for Martin Gullikson."

"Oh." Realization dawned on Booker. "You wanted to see if he had any insight on why Mark broke into your house."

"It turns out Martin cut Mark loose months ago because his recreational drinking problem was becoming dire."

"Heck, I could've told you that," Booker said. "You should've asked."

"You're cagey with information," I reminded him. "I think you wanted to tell me, but you came to some manly agreement with Galen this morning and you don't want to break the bro code."

Booker's eyes glinted with amusement. "Bro code?"

"You know exactly what I'm talking about. It's a bunch of hogwash. I have a right to know what's going on."

"I don't disagree," Booker countered. "I think you're like an over-loaded circuit, though. I'm not sure how much more you can take."

"So coddling me is the answer?"

"I thought you said there wasn't any cuddling," Lilac challenged, making a face when I murdered her with the meanest look in my repertoire. "Wow. Your sense of humor is non-existent today, huh?"

She had no idea. "I wanted to know more about Mark Santiago. I think I've earned that."

"I do, too, but you should've asked me about his work history," Booker said. "I could've told you he wasn't doing construction any longer."

"Fine. Then what has he been doing with his time?"

"He's been working on the Durham Farm."

Lilac snapped her head so she could stare down Booker, surprise practically oozing from her pores. "Seriously? I didn't know that. I wondered where he was getting his beer money."

"He's been working there for two months," Booker supplied. "I have no idea how he's been working out, but I know he's been putting in regular appearances."

"Really." I wasn't sure what to make of that. "You have a farm?"

"Of course we do. Where do you think we get the fresh dairy and meat?"

I glanced at the contents of the cart, my stomach twisting. I knew where chicken and beef came from, of course, but the idea that the animals were born and raised on the island simply so they could feed residents and tourists made me feel a bit iffy. "Oh. I guess that makes sense."

"Do you know what we should do?" Lilac was back to being bubbly.

"We should check out and head back to the lighthouse so I can finish my work," Booker answered.

"No, that's boring." Lilac waved off the suggestion. "I think we should go out to the farm and ask Wesley what he knows."

I had no idea who Wesley was, but I was beginning to like this idea. "Can we walk out there?"

Lilac shook her head. "Too far. We need someone to drive us."

I let my eyes drift to Booker, my lips curving as a plan took shape. "I guess it's good we have someone who can drive us out there, huh? A kind and giving soul who wants to help."

"Oh, geez." Booker pinched the bridge of his nose. "Galen is going to beat the crap out of me when he hears about this."

"I'll protect you." I grabbed Booker's arm and directed him down the aisle. "Come on. We'll stop in the liquor aisle and take this stuff home before we head out. Then tonight I'll reward you with grilled steak and whatever else you want."

Lilac brightened. "That sounds promising. I was hoping you would open yourself up to getting some before you risked finding cobwebs down there."

"Not that." I shook my head. "I swear it won't take very long and you won't get in trouble with Galen. Trust me."

# 16

## SIXTEEN

We were on our way out of town when a vehicle pulled onto the road behind us and a set of police lights sprang to life.

"Son of a ... !" Booker looked resigned when he flicked his turn signal to pull to the side of the road.

"What are you doing?" Lilac asked, glancing over her shoulder. She sat in the middle seat, refused to put on her seatbelt no matter how many times Booker ordered her to do just that, and made a face when she realized what was happening. "Why are you stopping?"

Booker was incredulous. "Why do you think?"

"Because you're a weenie."

Booker growled. "I'm going to leave you in a ditch if you don't shut up." He put the bus into park and risked a glance in my direction. "Let me do the talking."

I thought that was an absolutely terrible idea, but I was willing to see how things played out. "Okay."

Booker's gaze held mine for an extended period, almost as if he didn't believe me, and then he turned his attention to the window as he manually rolled it down.

"I didn't even know they still made windows like that," I mused. "I can't remember the last time I saw one of those ... um, handle things."

"I believe it was in an old episode of *MacGyver*," Lilac replied dryly. "Seriously, I can't believe you stopped, Booker. You're like a little old lady. Please don't arrest me, Sheriff Hottiepants."

"Yes, that's clearly what I'm going to say." Booker blew out a sigh as Galen sidled to the driver's side of the bus. The sheriff didn't look to be in a good mood and I didn't miss the way Booker's spine stiffened when Galen leaned his head into the vehicle. "What a pip of a day, sheriff. Is there something I can help you with?"

"I haven't decided yet," Galen replied, his eyes touching on Lilac before landing on me. "What's going on?"

"Did we do something wrong, Sheriff?" Lilac asked, shifting toward the lip of the seat and offering what can only be described as a saccharine smile. "I believe you have to tell us why you pulled us over. It's the law."

"Shut up, Lilac." Galen clearly wasn't in the mood to play games. "Where are you guys going?"

"We're taking a ride," Booker replied, his voice smooth as satin sheets. "Hadley didn't realize that there was more to the island than just the city."

"Really?" Galen cocked a challenging eyebrow. "What did she think was beyond the lights?"

"Empty land."

I don't know why I initially thought Booker was a poor liar. In truth, he was quite masterful. He had the ability to make the obvious seem blasé.

"She thought we built a city and left the rest of the island to collect dust?" Galen queried, dubious.

"I didn't really think about it," I supplied, happy to find my voice strong and my gaze steady. "I want to see some of the stuff that's out here. We've been running errands for a bit, and I wanted a chance to look at something beyond the lighthouse. What's the problem?"

"Did I say there was a problem?"

"No, but you're walking around as if you have a stick shoved up your you-know-what," Lilac muttered.

"Shut up, Lilac," Galen ordered, his eyes never leaving my face. "Tell me about these errands you ran."

I opened my mouth to explain about shopping and then narrowed my eyes. "What business is it of yours?"

"I'm the sheriff."

"Dude, you should really put on one of those ten-gallon hats and spurs if you're going to say things like that," Booker chided. "It makes you sound like a douche."

Instead of being angry, Galen merely shook his head. "I heard it the second I said it. There was no reason to point it out."

"That's why I'm here."

"We'll get to why you're here in a second," Galen countered. "Hadley, what errands did you run?"

He was clearly trying to make a point. I had a feeling I knew what that point was. If Lilac found out about my visit to the construction office it was only a matter of time until Galen did the same. I wasn't ashamed of my actions, but I wasn't in the mood to kowtow to Galen either. He did drug me. He also forced me to sleep next to his naked chest and I couldn't remember any of it. That was so unfair.

"I went to the grocery store, but I didn't realize you could rent carts to walk your groceries home, so I only got a few things," I volunteered. There was no way I was giving him what he wanted without a fight. Wait … that came out wrong. "So I was a complaining mess when I got back to the house and Booker explained about the carts."

"She didn't get any snacks at all," Booker lamented. "It was pitiful."

"I did get steaks," I said. "I knew you'd be coming back to tell me about your day, so I got steaks, corn and pasta salad for dinner."

"And we're both invited as a thank you," Booker said. "Isn't that nice of Hadley?"

"Yes, it's delightful," Galen drawled. "What else did you do?"

"Well, after I found out about the cart, I mentioned that I wanted to add shrimp to the mix and Booker suggested we go back to the grocery store."

"She also needed a better class of snacks," Booker added.

I had to bite the inside of my cheek to keep from laughing at Galen's annoyed expression. "We spent a decent amount of time in the store, and Booker taught me how to shop. Apparently I've been doing it wrong my entire life and didn't even know it. Then we ran into Lilac, and she said something about wanting to show me the countryside and here we are."

"Really?"

I bobbed my head in affirmation. "Really."

Galen took a long, steadying breath as he stared. He didn't believe me. He knew I went to the construction office. He even knew what I asked. He obviously didn't want to call me on my behavior, though. If I had to guess it was because he thought I would be uncomfortable about everyone on the island knowing my business. I already knew that and was definitely uncomfortable, but he wasn't saving me from anything by keeping the information to himself.

"How long do you plan on being out here for your ride?" Galen asked, shifting his eyes to Booker. "Not after dark, right?"

Booker shook his head. "I still have to finish the upstairs window, although it's mostly done. It just needs a few finishing nails and a coat of paint. We'll be back in plenty of time for dinner."

"A dinner that you're expected for because you owe me information," I said.

Galen ran his hand over the back of his neck, his face showing hints of fatigue for a few moments before he caught himself, smoothed his expression, and nodded. "Okay. Dinner sounds nice. I will be there by six."

Really? That was easy. "Great. I'm looking forward to grilling. I can't really cook, but I'm a whiz with the grill."

"And I'm looking forward to eating." Galen's smile was back, although it didn't make it all the way to his eyes. "Keep an eye on Hadley, Booker. She's new to the area and I don't want her getting separated."

Booker mock saluted, causing a muscle to tremble in Galen's jaw. "I'm on it, boss."

"I'm looking forward to dinner, too," Lilac announced before Galen could walk away. "I have a lot of questions about how you guys stayed under the same roof with Hadley and yet she got absolutely zero action."

This time Galen and Booker spoke at the same time.

"Shut up, Lilac!"

**THEY SAID "FARM,"** but I don't know what I was expecting. The sprawling expanse of land featuring cows, pigs, horses and even a full field of chickens certainly wasn't it.

"Holy moly!" I exhaled heavily as I leaned forward to get a better look at the multitude of barns dotting the landscape.

"Nice, huh?" Booker smiled as he navigated the dirt driveway, being careful to avoid ruts. The bus was so old it was probably one good jolt away from completely disintegrating.

"It's so ... big."

"Too bad you couldn't say that last night," Lilac interjected.

"Knock it off!" Booker ordered, his temper fraying. "You're on my last nerve."

"That's so unlike you," Lilac argued. "Usually you love it when I start laying on the sexual innuendo."

"Usually we're not dealing with a dead body in the cove and a local breaking into a house with an ax."

I wasn't sure she was capable, but Lilac instantly changed her expression and looked properly chastised. "I'm sorry. I keep forgetting about that part. To me this is all an adventure."

"And to Hadley she was almost killed in her sleep," Booker said. "We need to focus on the important thing here."

"And what is that?"

"We need to talk to Wesley," Booker replied. "You know how he gets."

Lilac sobered. "Yeah. I didn't think about that part either."

My interest was officially piqued. "What is he like?"

"A grizzly bear with a poor attitude," Lilac supplied. "He's very growly. I'm sure he was handsome and romantically rugged back in the day – he has that look, you know – but he's more rough than romantic these days."

I had no idea what that meant. "Is he going to throw me around or something?"

"Probably not," Lilac answered. "Just in case, though, hide behind Booker."

"Yes, that sounds like a great idea," Booker muttered. "Everyone hide behind me."

Lilac refused to rise to the bait. "That's what I plan to do."

**WESLEY DURHAM WAS** exactly as Lilac described him. He was a big bull of a man, broad shoulders giving way to a solid middle that looked as if he drank a bit of beer during his off hours. Still, he was a muscular man, especially for a guy pushing seventy. I couldn't help being impressed.

"Wesley, how are things?" Booker led the initial approach once we found Wesley oiling a saddle in one of his barns. Despite the size of the farm, as far as I could tell, Wesley was the only inhabitant.

"Well, I had a mare give birth this afternoon and no one wanted to put it on the news because it wasn't a giraffe, and then I had part of the fence in the eastern pasture go down, so that took three hours to fix. I got a big splinter while doing it, and I just found out I'm out of strawberries, so there will be no shortcake for dessert."

"Oh, you should've called," Lilac said. "We just came from the market."

Wesley knit his sparkplug eyebrows and shook his head, barely sparing a glance for me before focusing on Booker. "What are you doing out here? I didn't think you and I were on friendly terms."

Uh-oh. Were they about to fight?

"I didn't realize we were on unfriendly terms," Booker countered. "I simply thought we disliked each other on the surface but deep down we really wanted to bond. You know, go fishing and hunting and stuff. Pump fists. Bump chests. Pee while standing up."

Despite his gruff exterior, Wesley cracked a smile as he shook his head. "You've always had a bit of your mother's charm."

"Thank you."

"I didn't say it was a compliment," Wesley said. "You still haven't answered the question. What are you doing out here?"

"I don't suppose you've heard about what happened at the lighthouse last night?"

"May's lighthouse?" For the first time since we arrived, Wesley registered a full facial expression other than a scowl. "No. What happened?"

"Someone broke in and attacked Hadley." Booker jerked his thumb in my direction and when Wesley looked at me I offered a lame wave because ... well ... I have no idea why. I felt the need to do something with my hands, but I'm sure it came off as spastic.

"Attacked how?"

"With an ax," I answered. "Thankfully I saw movement right before it happened and rolled off the bed."

"I see." Wesley's eyes were thoughtful as he continued massaging the saddle. "I don't understand what that has to do with me."

"We believe the man responsible was Mark Santiago," Booker supplied. "He was found dead in a ditch a few blocks away this morning."

"And you think I killed him?"

"No, we want to know if he was still working for you."

Wesley shifted from one foot to the other, some internal debate going on behind his eyes. "Can I ask how you know it was Mark who broke in?"

"Well ... ." Booker, clearly not anticipating that question, looked to me for help.

"Whoever it was got blown through the upstairs window," I volunteered. "Galen – I mean the sheriff – said that he hit hard, but managed to limp off afterward."

"I see."

"When Mark's body was found, he had multiple injuries," Booker added. "Those injuries looked to have been sustained in a fall. He wasn't very far from the lighthouse, so … we believe it's him. Galen is still doing some investigating on the subject, but that looks to be the case right now."

"Well, I don't know how else you could look at the situation and think otherwise," Wesley said. "I knew that boy was going to get himself into trouble. I tried to put him on the right path, but he refused to walk in that direction. It's sad."

"Was he still working for you?" I asked.

Wesley shook his head. "Several weeks ago I had to cut him loose. It wasn't just that his work was bad. I could've put up with that if I thought it might help him. I have a lot of help that comes in and out of this place, so I wouldn't have had a problem making up for his slack."

"But?" Booker prodded.

"But he wasn't in the barn as I expected one day and I happened to come across him inside the house," Wesley explained. "The men aren't allowed in the house. I have facilities in the barns, including a kitchenette and refrigerator.

"He was going through a chest in my office," he continued. "When I asked him what he was doing, he fumbled through an answer that made absolutely no sense. He said he was looking for toilet paper because they were out in the barn."

"What happened then?"

"I fired him on the spot and told him not to come back," Wesley replied. "I want to help, but my giving spirit only goes so far."

"Was that the last time you saw him?" I asked.

Wesley nodded. "He hasn't been around since. I thought there was a chance he might try to break in, so I made sure the security system was up and running, but he never did. Er, well, at least to my knowledge."

"So he was unemployed at the time of his death," Booker mused. "Maybe he was desperate for money. Just out of curiosity, what was in the chest? What did you find him looking at?"

"It was just some of my ex-wife's stuff," Wesley said. "Some old photographs and a few folders full of divorce documents. There was nothing in there worth stealing."

Mention of an ex-wife stirred my curiosity. "Who is your ex-wife?"

"May Potter."

I stilled, my stomach doing a somersault. I heard him wrong, right? "I'm sorry?"

Booker blinked several times in rapid succession, his face draining of color. "I thought you knew."

"Knew what?" My heart pounded so hard I thought I might pass out. "Is he saying what I think he's saying?"

"He's saying he's your grandfather," Lilac supplied happily. "Congratulations! It's a really crabby bear."

I did my best to ignore the joke and looked to Booker for help. "But ... why didn't you say something?"

Booker held his hands palms up and shrugged. "I thought you knew."

Right. That should be the new Moonstone Bay motto. Crap on a cracker.

## 17

# SEVENTEEN

"**Y**ou're my grandfather?"

The question felt alien coming off my tongue, like I was stuck in a dream and part of the rules included saying the most absurd thing that comes to mind. Sadly, I've had dreams like that.

Wesley didn't look nearly as flummoxed as me. "You're Hadley, aren't you?"

That wasn't much of an answer. "But ... ." I broke off, unsure what to say or feel. This wasn't what I expected. This entire place wasn't what I expected. I needed time to decompress and do ... something, though I had no idea what that something entailed.

Booker leaned in my direction, his eyes unnaturally wide as he waved a hand in front of my face. "You're not overloading are you? If you think you're going to pass out, sit down."

"I think we broke her," Lilac announced. "She couldn't take another surprise, yet you insisted we come out here so she could get one. I blame you, Booker."

"I thought she knew," Booker hissed. "I just assumed she didn't want to talk to Wesley because May and Wesley hated each other."

"I hated May," Wesley corrected. "She deserved it. She was bitter about our breakup and hid her broken heart in mean statements and name-calling. There's a difference."

Lilac snorted. "Okay, if that's what you need to tell yourself. She's the one who dumped you."

"Who told you that?" Wesley challenged. "It happened thirty-five years ago. That was long before your time."

"I know things."

"You don't know jack," Wesley fired back.

Booker ignored their argument and focused on me. "Would you like me to help you sit down?"

"Not in the least." I found my voice and slapped his hand away. Wesley stood with his arms crossed over his chest as he waited for me to get my bearings. "Did you know who I was when I came in here?"

Wesley shook his head. "Not at first. It's not as if I recognized you with my heart and soul or anything. I realized a few minutes in who you were."

"Why didn't you say something?"

"Because I didn't know if you wanted me to do that," Wesley replied. "You were playing it cool."

"I didn't know!" I barked out, frustration bubbling up. "How could I possibly know that?"

"How could you not know that?" Lilac challenged. "I mean … he's your grandfather. My papa is one of my favorite people. He wears black socks and sandals no matter how hot the day is. He also sexually harasses random waitresses when they wear short skirts and actually yells at kids to get off his lawn. He's hilarious."

"I should've realized that you didn't know him," Booker lamented, scratching at his five o'clock shadow. "If you didn't know May, how could you possibly know about Wesley?"

That was a very good question. I locked gazes with Wesley, trying to find a bit of him in me. Other than the shape of his nose, there was nothing. "I'm not going to pretend to understand any of this," I said, keeping my voice low and even. "I didn't know May Potter existed until her will showed up three months ago. I guess I never gave a grandfather much thought because … well … I figured

149

anyone alive who loved my mother would've tried to get in touch with me."

"Do you honestly think I didn't try to see you?" Wesley challenged.

My stomach flipped at the implication. "Are you saying my father kept you away?"

"I'm saying May kept me away," Wesley replied. "We split up before Emma was out of high school. After that I was cut out of every decision. I didn't get a say in where Emma went to college. I didn't get a say in who she married. I was just some guy who provided sperm at the right time."

That was an unsettling image. "But you could've approached me on your own."

"Yeah, well, it's not that simple, dolly." Wesley forced a smile for my benefit. "You look a little pale. Do you need some water?"

"Sure. Thank you."

Wesley shuffled over to a small refrigerator in the corner of the barn and grabbed several bottles, handing one to Booker before donating one to my pitiful emotional breakdown. He ignored Lilac and kept the third for himself.

I mechanically cracked open the bottle and drank, not stopping until it was completely empty. I hoped the water would serve to fill the hole inside of me, but all it left me feeling was cold.

"Are you okay?" Booker asked after a beat.

"Yeah, I'm just groovy."

"Do you want to go home?"

Where was home? I didn't feel as if I belonged anywhere right now. "I want to finish this," I replied, squaring my shoulders. "Did Mark Santiago take anything from the chest?"

"Not that I saw," Wesley said. "He wasn't in there very long. I'm not sure what he was looking for, but at the time I thought maybe he was searching for old jewelry. I even considered that May hired him to infiltrate my house to steal back an old pair of earrings or something, but I didn't have anything like that."

"So what's in the chest?"

"There's a quilt my mother made May when we first got married,"

Wesley replied. "It has all of these interlocking patterns on it. My mother said it was supposed to signify a life spent together. May packed it with my stuff when we split."

"That's all?"

"There are copies of divorce documents and a few things regarding Emma's custody. Those wouldn't come into play now, and it's not as if there was bank information on anything. The divorce documents specified that May got the lighthouse and I got this parcel of land. That was before the farm was here – which I started right after the divorce – but it was basically a property split and we only had two pieces of property."

"You didn't want the lighthouse?" I was naturally curious.

"The lighthouse belongs to May's family," Wesley explained. "I never had a claim to it and no matter how rough things got between us, I never would've made a play for what belonged to her. My grand-father left this land to me.

"For years before the divorce it was used for herd grazing," he continued. "There was another farmer back then, Robert Baxter, and I leased the land to him for grazing. Once the divorce was finalized, I was looking for something to do and realized that farming might be my future. It turns out it was."

"What happened to the other farmer?"

"He stayed in business until the end," Wesley replied. "When he died I bought out his land and doubled my parcel. Farming turned out to be something that was in my blood. Perhaps it's in yours, too."

I doubted that very much. Still, he seemed as if he was trying to be kind and attentive. I couldn't ask for much more than that given the circumstances. "I had an ant farm as a kid."

"Yeah, how did that go?"

"The glass broke and they got out and infested the kitchen. I could never have another pet after that."

Wesley tilted his head to the side, something I did on occasion when trying to figure out how to respond to something ridiculous. "Ants aren't pets," he said finally.

"No. Definitely not." I handed him the empty bottle. "Thank you for your time and the information. I'm sorry we dropped in without calling."

Wesley's expression was hard to read. "You don't have to leave if ... ."

I held up a hand to still him. "I need to do some thinking. It seems that's all I'm doing these days, but I really need a little air and space. I'm not sure what to make of all this."

"Fair enough." Wesley bobbed his head. "If you want to talk in a few days – or even a few weeks – I'll be out here. I'm sure you'll have questions."

"The problem is, I'm not sure you can come up with satisfactory answers."

"Maybe not, but every story has multiple sides."

"I guess." I shook my head to snap myself out of an imminent case of melancholy. "I need to think a bit. I hope that's okay."

"It's fine. Come out when you need to talk."

"What if I never need to talk?"

Wesley took me by surprise when he chuckled. "Dolly, you might not be all me, but you still have a dose of my genes. You'll need to talk."

Oddly enough, I was pretty sure he was right. For today, though, I was talked out. "Thank you for your time. If we have more questions, we'll give you a call."


**DO YOU WANT** to talk with us about it?"

We were back in the minibus before anyone spoke. I would've been happy to make the entire trip in silence, but Lilac had other ideas.

"I don't know what there is to talk about." I focused outside of the passenger window as Booker drove down the winding driveway. "It's just more of the same."

"How can you say that? You have a grandfather you've never met. That must be exciting."

"You'd think so, wouldn't you?" I was anything but excited. "To me it's just another person who knew who I was, knew I existed, yet did nothing to get to know me."

Lilac remained optimistic despite my dour mood. "I'm sure he had good reason."

"Shut up, Lilac," Booker ordered, making a clucking sound with his tongue as he pulled onto the highway that led back to the city. "Can't you see that she needs time to decompress?"

"No."

"Then maybe you need glasses," Booker charged. "Give her some space."

"Yes, sir." I could hear the pout in Lilac's voice but didn't shift to see if her expression matched the tone.

"As for Wesley, he's a difficult and obnoxious man at times – but I'm sure you've figured that out yourself," Booker said. "That doesn't mean he's not a good man. If he volunteered to answer questions for you, spend time with you, that means he really wants it to happen, no matter how gruff he appeared."

"That's true," Lilac said. "He's not a very good conversationalist, but you're not either at times, Hadley, so you probably get that from him."

"I'm totally going to thump you," Booker growled.

Lilac continued talking, unbothered. "What you need is a nice dinner and some friendly conversation. I'll help you cook, and then we can talk about our next plan of action."

That sounded like a completely terrible idea, especially because I wanted to be alone. "Maybe ... ."

"I have to finish your upstairs window, too," Booker added. "Galen said he would stop by. You promised him dinner."

It was as if he knew I was going to beg off and kick everyone out.

"Fine." I blew out a sigh. "We'll have dinner and chat and pretend that I didn't find out about zombies, witches and neglectful grandparents. It sounds like a fabulous evening. What could go wrong?"

"**THE KEY TO** great steak is to marinate it in red wine for a bit before putting it on the grill." Lilac was in full chef mode as I sat at the picnic table an hour later and watched her rub four huge hunks of meat with a mixture of salts before shoving them in a bowl surrounded by ice and using plastic wrap to cover it. "Now we'll let them sit for a bit and they'll be delicious when we grill them."

"I'm glad to know the key to a great steak," I said, reaching for the remainder of the wine Lilac didn't use for her marinating project. I considered pouring it into a glass, but that seemed a waste of manual labor when it came to dishes later. "I always thought the best way to get a good steak was to go to Outback Steakhouse."

"You're cute." Lilac patted my head as if I were a small child who needed comfort. "But I'm starting to think that you're losing your mind. I have tranquilizers if you want them. I think you need a good night's sleep tonight no matter what. They're very mild and go great with wine, so ... ."

"Don't even think about it," Booker ordered, strolling toward the table with two bottles of water in his hand. He set one in front of me, eyed the wine bottle as I drank straight from it for a moment, and then shook his head. "Are you in the mood to get drunk?"

"I'm in the mood to get numb," I corrected. "If I wanted to get drunk I'd be drinking straight from a rum bottle."

"She has a point," Lilac said.

"Nobody asked you." Booker was clearly at the end of his rope and Lilac's chirpy voice wasn't doing much to stop him from metaphorically hanging himself. "Listen, Hadley, you suffered a hard blow today ... ."

"Are you talking about almost dying in the middle of the night, finding out I killed a man, discovering a grandfather I didn't know existed – and who clearly doesn't care that I exist – or realizing I've been cooking steaks wrong my entire adult life?"

Booker blinked several times, his face unreadable. "You're in a really bad place, aren't you?"

"Nope. I have wine." I took another swig, pursing my lips as Lilac and Booker exchanged an obvious look.

"Okay, forget what I said a few seconds ago about suffering a hard blow," Booker suggested. "I have no idea where I was going with that and it obviously wasn't going to help."

"Why do you think I have the wine?"

"So you can forget," Booker replied. "Is that really what you want?"

"For right now or ever?"

"Either."

"For right now the answer would be yes. Forever? I'm still debating."

"Oh, geez." Booker pinched the bridge of his nose. "I am not good at this. I'm so not the guy you want around for an emotional melt-down. I can't believe Galen talked me into staying."

"You don't have to stay." I took another gulp of wine and smiled as my mind began doing that floaty thing I was so fond of. I wasn't drunk ... or even tipsy ... but at this rate it wouldn't take me long, and absolutely nothing sounded better than hiding in a bottle for the next few hours. "I know you don't want to. Leave your bill for the work you did on the counter and I'll pay you tomorrow ... just as soon as I remember where I put my checkbook."

"You're not paying me for anything," Booker argued. "I did the work because that's what neighbors do."

"Not in Detroit."

"Yeah? Well, that sounds like a terrible place to live." Booker's patience wouldn't last much longer. I could feel it. "Galen is paying for the supplies because he kicked in your door, and the labor is free."

"That's so sweet." I reached up and poked his cheek, surprised by my boldness. He didn't look like a guy who enjoyed being touched in a teasing way, but I couldn't seem to stop myself. "You're very sweet."

"Are you already drunk?" Booker jerked the bottle from my hand, perplexed. "How much of this did she drink, Lilac?" His tone was accusatory. "You were supposed to be watching her."

"I was watching her," Lilac protested. "I was also giving a cooking lesson. She couldn't have imbibed all that much, because I used more than half of the bottle to marinate the steaks."

"Oh." Booker furrowed his brow. "If you're not drunk, what are you?"

I held my hands palms up and shrugged. "High on life?"

"You're high on something," Galen announced, appearing at the picnic table and shaking his head. "You guys have a lot of explaining to do. I heard where you went this afternoon, and I'm not happy."

His face was so stern I couldn't help but smile as I snagged the bottle of wine back from Booker and patted the open spot next to me. "Do you want to get high on life with me?" I waved the bottle, teasing.

Galen's eyes darkened, something harsh passing through him. He recovered quickly and grabbed the bottle, taking a long drink before handing it back. "Why not? It's always more fun to yell when you're drunk."

"That's my philosophy."

"Just great!" Booker's eyes bounced between faces. "Apparently we've reached the crazy portion of tonight's festivities."

I beamed at him. "It's going to be so awesome."

## EIGHTEEN

"Tell me about your day."

I found my fingers moving toward Galen's hair before I could stop myself. What the holy heck is up with that?

Galen arched an eyebrow as he watched my hand, but he didn't move to slap it away. He looked tired, as if the world was beating him down. I had sympathy for him, but it was nothing compared to what I was going through.

Yup, I was in full-on "woe is me" mode. I didn't like it, yet I couldn't seem to stop it.

"Well, it started with seeing a terrific case of bedhead and looks to be ending with some steaks and corn." Galen grinned, the expression lighting up his handsome features. "Those are both the highlights, by the way. The lowlights are something else entirely."

"I'm almost afraid to ask," Booker said, grabbing a beer from the cooler Lilac placed on the table and twisting the top. "What did the coroner say about Mark?"

"That he had a lot of internal injuries and it looked as if he was either hit by a vehicle and left to die or fell a great distance and bounced off the ground."

I jerked my hand back from Galen's hair, the reality of the day setting in as I inadvertently sobered. I much preferred the fake drunk feeling I labored under moments before, but even my brain couldn't seem to do what I wanted for the time being. "So I killed him."

"No, you protected yourself." Galen held out a hand and waited for Booker to pass him a beer. He took a long swig before continuing. "You did what you had to do."

"I don't think that's going to go over well with a judge," I argued, swirling the remnants of the wine bottle as I considered my fate. "Gee, your honor, I accidentally threw a man through a window using powers I didn't know I had. Surely you can see it was an accident. Have pity on me."

Galen's lips curved. "You're very dramatic. Has anyone ever told you that?"

Lilac raised her hand. "I have."

"You have not," I shot back, narrowing my eyes. "You've spent the entire afternoon trying to get me to be more dramatic."

"That's because I like drama." Lilac's smile reflected a bit of smarm and a whole lot of charm. It was hard not to like her, even when she was being a total pain in the keister. "Why do you think I took one look at you and knew you were going to be my new BFF?"

"Um … ."

"What's a BFF?" Galen asked. "It's that, like, a … chick thing?"

"That's totally a chick thing," Booker answered. "It means 'best friends forever.'"

"Oh, so it's like a young chick thing." Galen snorted, whatever flitted through his head clearly amusing him. "Okay. I'm caught up. Continue. What were we talking about?"

"The fact that I can't use magic as a defense in a court of law."

Galen tilted his head so he could give me a hard stare. "Says who?"

"Says everyone. You might believe me, but that doesn't mean I won't be arrested, tried and sent to a prison where I have to make license plates for the rest of my days. Oh, geez. Maybe I should call my dad. I'm going to need a lawyer."

"I'm not dissuading you from calling your father if you want to talk to him, but you're not going to be arrested," Galen argued. "I've already sat down with the prosecutor. He knows what happened, and it's being ruled self-defense."

I was understandably dumbfounded. "But ... how?"

"The prosecuting attorney is a shifter and the judge is a mage. Do you think this is the first time we've had a paranormal dust-up on this island that resulted in death?"

Huh. I hadn't even considered that. I drained the rest of the wine, rubbing my chin as I considered the implications. "But ... I killed him. Shouldn't I have to pay for that?"

"He broke into your house and attacked you with an ax!" Galen exploded, causing me to jolt. "Stop being a martyr and look at things realistically. You didn't do anything wrong."

"I ... ." My mouth worked, but no sound came out as I blinked back tears.

"You might want to take it easy on her," Booker advised, his voice soft. "She's dealt with a bevy of stuff today that would've floored just about anyone else. I don't think yelling at her is the way to go."

"I'm sorry." Galen rested a big hand on my shoulder. "I didn't mean to yell and upset you. That wasn't right or fair." He shifted his eyes to Booker. "But I am going to yell at you. I think that's both right and fair."

"Oh, yeah, I saw this coming." Booker tipped his head back and downed half his beer. "Lay it on me."

"What were you thinking taking her to Durham farm?"

A fraction of my senses returned and I poked Galen's side to get his attention. "How did you know we went out there?"

"Because I'm not an idiot, and because people tell me things," Galen replied. "I thought that's where you might be going when I stopped you, but I couldn't be sure so I let you go. Now I wish I hadn't."

"Booker remembered that Mark Santiago was working for Wesley a few months back," Lilac interjected as she bathed the corn ears in butter before wrapping them in foil. "We wanted to ask Wesley if that arrangement was still ongoing."

"Even though … ." Galen broke off, briefly flicking his eyes in my direction.

"See, that's the thing," Booker started, chagrined. "I thought Hadley knew that Wesley was her grandfather. Yeah, that came up while we were visiting. It never occurred to me that she didn't know."

"She didn't know who May was," Galen argued. "How could she possibly know who Wesley was?"

"Her life is like a soap opera," Booker complained. "I can't keep up with all the evil twists and dastardly turns. I didn't put it together, and by the time I realized she didn't know who he was it was too late."

"Wesley told her," Lilac said. "He mentioned that he fired Mark because he caught him going through a chest that was left over from Wesley and May's marriage. He said there was nothing in there of any value, but he had to fire Mark anyway."

"He doesn't know what Mark was looking for," Booker supplied. "At the time he thought Mark was looking to feed his drinking habit and wanted something to sell. There was nothing in the chest to sell, though."

"Huh." Galen pressed the tip of his tongue to his upper lip as he absorbed the new information. "That's extremely interesting. I probably would've thought the same thing. But now that Mark broke into the lighthouse … hmm."

"What do you think it all means?" Lilac asked, shifting the corn to the grill. "Do you think Hadley is still in trouble?"

"I don't think Mark went after her himself," Galen replied. "He was too drunk all the time to have the motivation to do that. Someone recognized that in him and sent him after Hadley. The question is: Why?"

"That's the question?" I sputtered, my heartbeat ratcheting up a notch. "Shouldn't the question be: Who is after me?"

"We'll solve that question, too." Galen seemed too calm for my liking. "I swear we'll figure it out. I don't want you tying yourself in knots over this."

Oh, that was easier said than done. "How are we going to figure it out?"

"The same way we figure anything else out. We'll ask questions and kick over stones until we find the answers."

That sounded awfully simplistic. "And how do we start?"

"With an awesome dinner." Galen squeezed my shoulder before turning to Lilac. "When will dinner be ready? I'm starving."

"That makes two of us," Booker added. "This has been one long and crazy day."

I wanted to argue, tell them we needed to focus on the obvious problem rather than steak and corn. The scent of grilling food was enough to cause my stomach to rumble, though, and I realized I hadn't eaten since breakfast – and I was famished.

"What about you, Hadley? Are you hungry?"

Galen's gaze was expectant, and also filled with concern. He'd already done so much for me – the lip-covered boxer shorts and drugging notwithstanding – that I didn't want to give him further cause to worry. "I could eat."

"Good. Everything will be okay. I promise."


"IS THAT ALL of them?"

Galen helped me load the dishwasher after Lilac and Booker left, both of them conveniently dodging the cleanup as they offered haphazard waves and disappeared down the driveway. I shouldn't have been bitter – Lilac cooked and Booker worked all day for free, after all – but I wasn't in the best frame of mind, so I indulged in the pettiness for a few minutes.

Then I realized I was being a complete and total jerk and put it away.

"That's all of them." I offered up a smile to Galen. He looked as tired as I felt. "You didn't have to help. You've already done enough for one day."

"Yeah? Well, doing a little more never hurt anyone."

I thought Galen would say his goodbyes and beat a hasty retreat, but he crossed his arms over his chest and leaned against the counter.

"Is something wrong?" I self-consciously ran a hand over my hair.

Other than the humidity causing it to increase in diameter, it seemed fine. "Have you changed your mind about arresting me?"

"No, and stop worrying about that," Galen ordered. "I was just thinking."

"About?"

"About you."

My cheeks burned under his steady gaze, and I instinctively averted my eyes. "Why?"

"Because you've really been through the wringer the past few days and you're still standing," Galen replied. "I don't know many other people who would be able to do that. I'm impressed."

"I don't see as I have much choice. I can either fall down – which I've done a few times when no one was looking – or get back up. I'm not big on the former, so I guess I have to stick with the latter."

"That's a very pragmatic outlook."

"Thank you."

"You're still struggling. It's okay."

He kept saying things like that, things were going to be okay and such. I wanted to believe him, but I wasn't sure I could. My life was changing at such a fantastic pace that I couldn't help but wonder if it might never slow down until I crashed into a wall.

"I don't know what to think about all this," I admitted. I didn't know Galen well, yet he was easy to confide in. "I never imagined this stuff being real. I read books about paranormal creatures when I was a kid – I was a big fan of Stephen King – and now I find out I might be one and I don't know what to do with the information."

"What do you want to do with the information?"

"Smack you upside the head for asking dopey questions like that," I replied, wrinkling my nose as Galen chuckled. "I don't know. I didn't know I had it in me to kill a man. It's … terrifying."

"You have a lot more in you than that," Galen countered. "You're a witch. Magic isn't one thing for you."

"I don't know anything about being a witch. Am I supposed to buy one of those conical hats and fly around the island or something?"

Galen snorted, genuine amusement sparking in his eyes. "Witches can't fly."

"Can vampires fly?"

"No."

"Can anything fly?"

"You seem to be obsessed with flying."

"I always wanted to be Wonder Woman when I was a kid. She had an invisible plane. I thought that would be nifty."

"Some things fly, but they're generally shifters," Galen explained. "I don't think now is the time to give you a crash course on paranormal history. We can ease into that eventually."

"Eventually? What are we going to do now?"

Galen extended his hand, taking me by surprise. "I'm going to show you that you can do more than defend yourself against a man who was trying to kill you."

I stared at his outstretched hand a minute, uncertain. "This isn't going to go to a kinky place, is it?"

"Not tonight."

I blew out a sigh and took his hand, letting him lead me out of the house and down to the beach. The night air was warm, the remnants of the day snaking through the air as it kissed my skin and caused me to sigh.

"I don't think I'll ever get used to this heat," I lamented.

"You will. One day you'll wake up and realize you've already grabbed a bottle of water without realizing it."

"Will I ever stop caring about what the humidity does to my hair?"

Galen shrugged. "That's out of my realm of expertise. That would be something that Lilac could help you deal with. Aurora might be a good one on that front, too."

"Great. Do you think she'll be naked when I ask her questions?"

Galen squeezed my hand as he chuckled. "She's always naked, so the odds are good."

"Isn't that against the rules?" I asked, genuinely curious. "Doesn't your Downtown Development Authority have issues with naked women wandering around the island?"

"As long as they stay off the sidewalks and out of the cemetery at night, they're good."

"Oh, well, what a relief." I made a face when Galen stopped in front of the water, his expression expectant. "What are we doing out here? Are you going to throw me in the ocean? I'm not going to lie. If that's your plan, I probably won't like it.

"I know I talked big about wanting to meet a shark shifter and everything, but I'm actually afraid of sharks," I continued. "I think a shark attack is probably the worst way to go, and I've heard stories that sharks lurk closer to the beach after dark."

"You don't have to worry about a shark attack around here."

"Aurora said she saw one the other day when she stopped by for her swim."

"That doesn't mean it will attack you," Galen said. "We've never had a shark attack around these parts."

"Good to know." It actually was. "So what are we doing out here again?"

"I'm going to show you something good about your magic," Galen replied, releasing my hand and grabbing my shoulders so he could position me to face the incoming waves. "I want you to close your eyes."

"I thought you weren't going to do anything kinky."

"I said I wasn't going to do anything kinky *tonight*," Galen clarified. "I stand by that. Close your eyes."

I was reluctant, but did as I was told, breathing through my nose as Galen ran his hands down my shoulders and over my arms, not stopping until he touched my wrists. He drew out my arms as far as they would go and lowered his mouth closer to my ear.

"Think of something happy," he instructed. "Think of something that always makes you smile. Don't open your eyes until I tell you. I want you to clear your mind and think happy thoughts."

"Oh, we are going to fly, aren't we?" I couldn't hold back the snark. "We're going to have some pixie dust sprinkled over us during our happy thoughts and we'll fly away."

"Shh." Galen's mouth was so close to my exposed neck that I

shuddered, and not because I was afraid. "Clear your mind, Hadley. Think of something happy. Think of something that makes you feel lighter."

It was difficult given his proximity, but I did as he asked, exhaling heavily as I leaned back against his chest. I wasn't sure what to choose, ultimately opting for the time I'd won the spelling bee in sixth grade and my father actually showed up to see the show. He wasn't much of a joiner in those days, so for him to go to a school event was a big deal. He told me he was proud of me that day. He told me I reminded him of my mother. That was one of the happiest moments I ever remembered.

"Good," Galen intoned, sliding closer. "Keep thinking your happy thought." He linked the fingers on both hands with his. "Remember what it was like when all you could think about was how happy you were. Can you see it?"

I nodded.

"Good. Now open your eyes."

I wasn't sure I heard him at first, but when I registered the order I did as he asked, gasping when I saw the waterspout lifting from the ocean. The water swirled at the base, climbing higher until it formed the countenance of a young girl – one I recognized from the mirror when I was in middle school.

"What the … ?"

"Calm yourself," Galen ordered when the swirling water looked as if it might break apart. "If you get upset you'll lose the thread."

"What thread?" My heart hammered a bit. "Am I doing that?"

"You have a connection to this place, Hadley." Galen's voice was a soft caress. "You haven't had a chance to explore that for yourself yet – which isn't fair, and I'm sorry – but if you let yourself look beyond the terrible things that are happening right now you'll find an entirely new world waiting for you to enjoy."

The girl in the swirl smiled, sliding her hand over her mouth as she giggled and batted her eyelashes in Galen's direction.

"Hey!" I was offended. "I was nowhere near that flirty when I was her age."

Galen chuckled, genuinely amused. "I wondered if that was you. How old were you?"

"Eleven."

"You were cute." Galen tightened his grip on my hands and pressed his body against mine. "Concentrate."

The only thing I could concentrate on was the masculine warmth wrapping itself around me. My heart pounded as I felt his beat against my back, his heat threatening to set me on fire. My mind spiraled, the waterspout swirling higher and wider before exploding, a torrent of seawater splashing over us.

I sputtered as I wiped my face, the heady feeling from before returning. "That was fun!"

"It was until the end," Galen agreed, shoving his hair away from his face. "Do you feel better?"

"I do." I bobbed my head. "In fact, I feel as if … ." I lost my train of thought as I took a step forward and lost my footing, tumbling head-first toward the sand as things spun and bounced inside my head.

Galen caught me before I hit, swinging me up and cradling me close. "What's wrong?" He looked terrified.

I wanted to ease his pain, but I could feel unconsciousness stalking me. I didn't know what to say, so I went with something stupid.

"Thank you and goodnight."

And it was goodnight, because the darkness found me a split-second later.

# NINETEEN

I woke to the sun beating on my face through the newly restored window, a headache the size of Booker's bus pounding between my temples and a warm spot in the bed right next to me. I rolled to my side, frowning as I ran my fingers over the indentation in the sheets. Someone had clearly been here moments before. The residual body heat remained, which meant … .

Despite my headache panic took over, and I clawed to the side of the bed. My eyes went wide when I saw the pile of male clothes – flamingo-covered boxer shorts and all – discarded in a heap on the floor.

I couldn't remember a lot about the previous night – flashes of water spouts and joined fingers overlapping with giggles and breathy gasps – but I had a feeling something very big happened while I was out of it. Okay, I didn't know how big it was, but if his hands and feet are any indication … wait! That's so not important right now.

I pressed the heel of my hand to my forehead and rolled out of the bed, hitting the floor with a thump. I was in an oversized T-shirt that was inside out, and I didn't remember putting it on. I caught a glimpse of my hair in the wall mirror and cringed because the bedhead was back and clearly ready to throttle me for being such a wanton harlot.

Holy crap! I had sex with someone and I didn't even remember it. There was only one option – Galen had been there for the water sports after all – and we'd clearly done the deed and I had no memory of the hot and sweaty ... whatever. Wait, can something be hot and sweaty if you don't remember it?

I registered the sound of the shower shutting off in the next room and shifted my eyes to the closed door. He was still here! He was in the shower ... naked ... and still here! What the holy hell? How could this be happening? As if I didn't have enough other life-altering things on my plate, now I'd had sex with a guy I barely knew and I couldn't even remember it. That was the worst part.

Okay, being loose and free was probably the worst part, but the fact that I couldn't remember it burned brightest in the empty hole of disgust rolling into a ball in the pit of my stomach. How could I let this happen? How could he let this happen? What kind of guy takes advantage of a woman who clearly doesn't remember what's happening? A pervert, that's what kind!

Galen Blackwood may be sheriff – a sheriff who went out of his way to make sure I wasn't charged with murder – but he was clearly a pervert. I knew it the minute I saw him. He was far too good looking to be anything but a pervert. What? That's a thing. I totally saw it on television once. I think it was the Oxygen network.

I jolted when the bathroom door opened, drawing the T-shirt down over my knees as I lifted my eyes and found Galen standing in the doorway with a quizzical look on his face. His chest was bare, water beaded across it – he must shave or wax, because he was smooth as a menopausal woman's upper lip right after it's been deforested – and he had a towel cinched at his waist.

"What's going on?"

The question struck me as stupid. "You took a shower."

"I needed one after we got so wet and dirty last night."

My cheeks flooded with color. I was mortified. That was the only word I could use to describe the emotions flooding through me. "Um ... okay." I felt as if I was an alien caught in someone else's life. Sure, I created the situation – and he obviously took advantage of me – but this couldn't possibly be my life.

"I have to go to work, but I'm glad you're up." Galen leaned over and scooped up his clothes, the towel shifting so much that I thought there was a legitimate chance it would slip from his hips. I was torn about whether or not I wanted that to happen. On one hand, I didn't want to be caught staring. On the other, I'd been deprived of the memories of our dalliance and felt somehow cheated.

"Hey! Are you listening to me?" Galen snapped his fingers in my face, causing me to jolt out of my reverie.

"I'm listening. I … feel … weird."

"I don't doubt it." Galen hunkered down so he was crouching in front of me, his knees spreading in such a way that I had to force my eyes to remain on his face in case I did something absolutely stupid. Er, well, something more stupid than I'd already done. "You expended a ton of energy last night. You probably have a bit of a hangover."

Oh, well, he obviously had a very high opinion of his abilities, which was ridiculous because I couldn't even remember them. "I need some aspirin."

"There's some in the bathroom." Galen gently reached out and pushed my hair away from my face. "I shouldn't have pushed you to do what you did last night. I don't think you were ready."

"It's fine." It's fine? What is wrong with me? It's not fine. It's not even close to fine. "It happened and it's done. Let's not dwell on it."

"I don't want to dwell on it either, but I think we need to talk about it. The thing is, I have to get to the office. I'm already running late. I didn't want you to wake up alone because I figured you would have questions."

Why would he possibly think that? The only question I had was how much of a slut he took me for. "I don't have any questions right now. I'm just … I feel funny."

"You need to have a big breakfast," Galen ordered. "Eggs, hash browns, maybe some sausage."

Oh, now he was going for double entendres. What a creep. If he thought I would fall for that, well, he had another think coming.

"Sausage sounds good." Oh, good grief! Clearly some unseen force invaded my brain while I was unconscious.

"Eat a lot of protein," Galen ordered, his knee cracking as he stood. "I have some things to check on, but I'll be back after my shift. We need to talk, but you slept much longer than I thought you would."

"Yes, well, I expended a lot of energy." Sexy energy that I couldn't remember. Could this day get any worse?

"You needed the sleep," Galen said. "We'll talk tonight. We have some decisions to make. You should be okay here for the day, but if you go to town make sure you stay on the main drag and don't get lost. I'm not convinced someone still isn't after you."

"Yes, sir." I mock saluted because ... well, because I'm a geek and I have bouts of social awkwardness that I can't possibly explain. "I'll be good and keep to myself all day. I promise."

"You don't need to do that. Just ... be careful."

"I'm on it."

Galen's expression was hard to read, but he left it at that, shaking his head as he moved toward the stairs. "Drink some water, too. I think you might be dehydrated after last night."

Could he be more full of himself? "I'll do that."

"Okay. I'll be in touch."

I SCURRIED INTO the shower as soon as I heard the front door on the main floor shut, whipping my hair back into a loose bun rather than worrying about drying it before fleeing the lighthouse and the huge curtain of sex guilt and shame hanging over it.

I headed toward Main Street, a bottle of water in hand, and ignored every stray glance cast my way. I felt as if I was wearing a huge scarlet "S" on my shirt, so I kept my head down and scampered inside Lilac's tiki bar.

For the first time since I arrived on the island there were actual customers in the bar. Sure, it was only eight people and they were spread out at three different tables, but it was people all the same.

Lilac caught my eye as I breezed through the door, arching an eyebrow as she mixed drinks behind the counter. "Your hair looks cute pulled back like that. You should do it more often."

"I generally prefer wearing it down, but the humidity makes me look like I have a dead animal on top of my head."

"I don't think it's so bad. There's some special shampoo and conditioner to get if it's a problem."

Lilac was sunny and happy as she bopped her head back and forth to music only she could hear. Okay, I could hear it, too. I was going to tire of hearing about piña coladas at a certain point, but I ignored it for now.

"Do you want to hear about my night?"

"Absolutely." Lilac slid two umbrellas into the fruity drinks. "I waxed my legs and eyebrows, so whatever you did has to be better than that. Hold on." Lilac carried the drinks to one of the tables, her hips swishing as she did. She stopped at another table before swinging back. My patience was practically non-existent by the time she locked gazes with me. "Did you magically throw someone else out your window?"

"Why don't you say that a little louder," I hissed. "I don't think the couple in the corner heard you."

Lilac craned her neck to see over my shoulder, not bothering to hide her efforts as she stared at the couple in question. "They're sphinxes. Harmless."

I had no idea what that meant. "Sphinxes?"

"Yeah, they're kind of anal-retentive freaks, but they mostly keep to themselves unless they decide to lust for power. Then you have to kill them," Lilac supplied. "Those two are just here for tans and mixed drinks."

Wow! Every single time I think I have my head wrapped around this place something proves me wrong. I don't even know what to think about that. "Okay, well ... ."

"Hey, can we get two more rum runners?" A guy in a corner booth raised his hand to get Lilac's attention.

"Sure thing." Lilac nodded as she hopped to work. "Keep talking. I'm listening."

I wasn't so sure, and I needed her full attention. "Something weird happened last night."

"Did you and Galen get naked and sweaty? By the way, if you answer that question in a negative manner I'll totally lose all respect for you."

How did she know? "Yes."

"Good." Lilac shoveled ice into a glass. "I've been saying ... wait, what?" She stilled before lifting her head, very slowly and deliberately, and giving me an extended once over. "You had sex with Galen?"

"Yes, only I don't remember it."

Lilac wrinkled her nose. "Was this sex in your head?"

"No."

"Then there's no way you wouldn't remember it," Lilac challenged. "He's the catch of the island. No, I'm not joking. Every woman who grew up here wants a piece of Galen. He dates occasionally, but it's never serious. Talk at the gym says he's ... well ... fabulously gifted in that department. The relationships never last long, but the memories are forever."

Oh, good grief. That was the last thing I wanted to hear. "The sex wasn't in my head," I snapped, my voice carrying enough to cause the men in the corner to smile in my direction. "Why would I make it up?"

Lilac shrugged. "Maybe you're lonely. I don't blame you. I'd be lonely living in that big lighthouse alone."

She was clearly trying to give me an aneurysm. "I'm not lonely. I haven't been alone long enough since I arrived on this island to be lonely."

"That's good." Lilac patted my arm before grabbing the drinks. "I'll be right back."

I bit my tongue to keep from exploding as she carried the drinks to the corner booth, stopping long enough to chat with the sphinxes before returning to the bar. She looked as if she didn't have a care in the world. "What were we talking about again?"

"The fact that I turned into a total slut last night," I barked, causing the sphinxes to giggle.

"Don't worry about her," Lilac offered, waving off the curious stares. "She's high strung. She can't help herself. That's why the sex – even if it's imaginary – is a good thing."

"Do you want me to punch you?" I asked, my temper flaring.

"I'm not much of a fighter, but I get the point. You're at the end of your rope. Okay. Spill. Tell me everything that happened."

That's where I ran into difficulty. "I don't remember everything that happened."

"Well, tell me what you remember."

"We were doing dishes ... ."

"Oh, this is how all good softcore porn stories start." Lilac pressed her hand to the spot above her heart and made an exaggerated face. She was trying to be endearing, but I was torn between punching her and bursting into tears.

"We were doing dishes," I repeated. "Then he said he wanted to show me something."

"Was it in his pants?"

"No, it was on the beach."

"That's promising." Lilac's smile was serene. "Continue."

"The story isn't dirty," I supplied.

"Then get to the good stuff."

I really wanted to punch her ... and maybe kick her a little, too. "He wanted to show me that my magic could do more than kill a man, so we made a water monster ... er, kind of a water girl to be exact."

"Is that like making the beast with two backs?"

"Do you want to hear this story or not?"

"Sorry. Continue."

"The last thing I remember is seeing the water beast thingy and then everything goes funny in my memory. When I woke up this morning, the spot beside me was warm and empty because Galen was in the shower and all of his clothes were on the bedroom floor."

"Huh." Lilac cocked her head. "Did you ask him?"

"I was too stunned. He came into the bedroom, said he was late for work and that we would talk later."

"What did you do?"

"I waited until he left, hopped in the shower and then came to find you." I had trouble catching my breath. "What do you think I should do?"

"Get him naked again and see if you can remember it this time," Lilac suggested. "I can't enjoy the story without more details."

I was incredulous. "That's it?"

"What do you want me to say, Hadley? That was a totally lame story."

"No, you're lame," I challenged.

Lilac smirked. "You're so cute I just want to dress you up like a little doll and carry you around in my pocket." She squeezed my cheek and gave it a good jiggle. "Try really hard to remember next time. That will make the story much more exciting."

"Ugh." I exhaled heavily and dropped my head in my hands, ignoring the way Lilac chirped as she poured me an iced tea and took another round of drinks to her guests. When she returned, she was on to another conversational topic.

"So, Mark Santiago's sister works at the bar down the way and I heard she has the afternoon shift today," Lilac announced. "I was thinking that as soon as my relief comes in we can head down there and question her. You know, act like we're real detectives and stuff. I always thought I wanted to be Nancy Drew when I was younger."

"I preferred Trixie Belden."

"They were both fun," Lilac said. "What do you think?"

I thought it was an absolutely terrible idea. "Sure. What have I got to lose?"

2 0

# TWENTY

I'm a big fan of time travel movies and television shows. The idea that I could possibly go back and forth in time and correct a wrong was incredibly appealing given my irresponsible actions of the previous night. I had no idea if any magical creatures could make it happen, but it was an interesting thought.

"Is time travel real?"

Lilac glanced over her shoulder as she led me down the beach. I was surprised when we left the main drag and headed toward the shore but I figured Lilac knew where we were going better than anyone else, especially me. As long as we didn't run into Galen I didn't care where we ended up.

"Are you talking about time travel in like *Outlander* or *The Butterfly Effect?*"

That was an interesting question. "Are they different?"

Lilac held her hands palms out and shrugged. "I think they're very different. In *The Butterfly Effect* he wanted to go back and alter the past to save someone in the present, but each thread he yanked made things worse or just as bad. Ultimately he had to remove himself entirely from her life if he wanted her to survive and thrive.

"In *Outlander* the main character didn't make a choice to go back –

er, well, at least the first time – but once she got there she wanted to change the past," she continued. "They realized they couldn't change their part of the past and became resigned to their fate. Which outcome do you want?"

Wow! That was an extremely heavy question. "I only want to travel back to yesterday and not make a fool of myself."

Lilac snorted, her amusement drawing attention as we ducked into a beach tiki bar. It was much smaller than Lilac's bar and looked to have a removable floor and bar area. I hadn't seen it on my earlier treks through Moonstone Bay. It was kind of cute ... and also worrisome because it made me wonder if a stiff breeze could pick it up and toss it in the ocean.

"You need to let that go," Lilac chided as she led me through the sparsely-populated bar and toward a booth in the corner. "You bagged the hottest bachelor in town on, like, your fourth day here. You should be thrilled."

"I am thrilled. Can't you tell?"

"You also need to work on your sarcasm." Lilac slid into one side of the booth, leaving the other for me, and scanned the bar. "We're looking for Sarah Santiago."

"What does she look like?"

"Really tiny. Cute. Long dark hair. I don't see her, but I know she's supposed to handle the lunch shift. She's probably not here yet."

"What are we going to ask her?" I couldn't help being nervous. The idea of questioning the sister of the man I killed – however accidental or necessary – made me nervous.

"We'll figure it out as it happens," Lilac replied, forcing a smile as a waitress headed in our direction. I didn't know Lilac well, but I could tell when she was being genuine, and the faux sugary smile she brought out to play now was jarring. "Hello, Cordelia. I didn't know you'd be here today."

I watched the woman delivering glasses of water, understandably curious. I'd never seen Lilac be anything but friendly when it came to other Moonstone Bay residents. Even for those she didn't like she put on a brave face. She barely tried with Cordelia.

"It's my bar." Cordelia, her hair tied back in a loose and messy bun, fixed Lilac with a challenging look. "I figured you'd be at your own bar today."

"Yeah? I'm showing Hadley around."

"Hadley, huh?" Cordelia shifted her eyes to me, causing me to squirm on the vinyl booth seat. "You're the one who took over the lighthouse, right?"

"She's May's granddaughter," Lilac supplied. "She's part of our community now."

"I heard she was thinking about leaving," Cordelia challenged.

"Where did you hear that?" I asked, curiosity getting the better of me.

"Ned Baxter."

I stilled, surprised. "Really? He said I was leaving?"

Lilac absently patted my hand, her eyes never leaving Cordelia's pretty face. "Don't listen to her. She's making it up."

Cordelia sneered. "Why would I make it up?"

"I don't think she's making it up," I supplied. "He showed up at my place the other day to see if I wanted to sell to him. He thought I might want to get off the island."

Lilac jerked her gaze from Cordelia. "And what did you say?"

"I said I wasn't making any decisions right away."

Lilac narrowed her eyes to accusatory slits. "You want to stay, right?"

That was a dangerous question. "I don't know."

"Oh, you know," Lilac gritted out. "You want to stay. You're going to stay."

"Ignore her," Cordelia instructed, clearly enjoying herself as she leaned over the table and handed me a menu. "Lilac can't take it when she's not in the know about island gossip. It's not your fault she's so needy."

"Bite me," Lilac hissed, accepting the menu with a sneer. "If anyone should leave the island, it's you."

I wasn't sure what to make of the conversation, so I merely watched for a moment, dumbfounded.

"I can't leave while you're still here," Cordelia drawled. "I have to make sure someone saves the island men from your slutty powers of persuasion."

"Oh, please," Lilac snorted, her lips curving. "You're the poster child for gonorrhea, for crying out loud. You're the name on the bathroom stalls that all of the men warn each other about."

Cordelia's expression darkened. "And you're the one they say reminds them of a toilet seat when they whisper about things to watch out for."

Ah, well, I'd really stepped in it this time. I wasn't sure exactly what I'd stepped in, but it was obvious that Cordelia and Lilac had a past that would make most warring dictators blush. "Maybe I should head out," I suggested.

"You're staying," Lilac snapped, gripping the menu so hard her knuckles turned white. "Cordelia is just trying to upset you. Don't let her."

"I don't even know her," Cordelia corrected. "Why would I want to upset her?"

"Because you're evil."

"Says the woman who slept with the entire rowing team in one weekend."

Lilac's eyebrows flew up her forehead. "The rowing team consisted of one person at the time. Ben Gordon."

"Did you sleep with him?"

"Yes."

"Then you slept with the entire rowing team." Cordelia was haughty as she crossed her arms over her chest. I couldn't help disliking her. I didn't know Lilac all that well – and there were times she irritated me to no end – but I found her to be friendly and funny most of the time. There was an edge to the way Cordelia approached Lilac that annoyed me.

"Am I missing something?" I asked, uncomfortably shifting on my seat. "Maybe I should go and let you guys … do whatever it is you're about to do."

Cordelia and Lilac stared each other down for a long moment, something unsaid passing between them. Finally Cordelia dragged her eyes from Lilac's face and forced what could pass for a smile.

"Don't be silly," Cordelia clucked, her eyes flashing. "This is simply how Lilac and I get along. It's not personal. It's ... quirky."

That was so not the word I would use. "Well ... okay."

"It's fine," Lilac said, catching my gaze and grinning. This time the light behind her eyes was real. "Don't worry about it. This really is the way we get along."

"I'm surprised you haven't killed each other."

"We are, too," Cordelia agreed. "Are you guys here for lunch or gossip today?"

"Both," Lilac answered, catching me off guard with her fortitude. "We're here because Sarah Santiago is supposed to be working the lunch shift. We want to talk to her."

Cordelia's expression was hard to read, and when she glanced toward the guests at other tables before nudging me over with her hip and forcing me to slide in, I thought things might get ugly. Instead, she merely seemed intrigued as she sat on the booth bench and locked gazes with Lilac. "Does this have something to do with Mark?"

"No, we came all the way down here for our health," Lilac said dryly. "This place really is a health hazard, by the way. When was the last time you cleaned this dump?"

"Last night. I used your toothbrush."

"Ha, ha." Lilac rolled her eyes. "Your wit astounds me."

"And your dippy nature astounds me."

"You both astound me," I interrupted, my temper getting the better of me. "This isn't the Old West. There's no reason to threaten each other to a duel at high noon. We're simply here to get some information."

Cordelia's expression was thoughtful as she turned her full attention to me. "I guess that means the rumors are true, huh?"

My mouth went dry. "What rumors?"

"They're true," Lilac confirmed. "Mark broke into the lighthouse and attacked Hadley with an ax. She protected herself and he ended up dead."

My mouth dropped open and dumbfounded mortification washed over me. "Lilac," I hissed. "Are you supposed to be telling people about that?"

Cordelia patted my shoulder as she leaned back in the booth seat. It wasn't a soothing gesture as much as a "there, there, you're giving me a headache so you need to shut your mouth" gesture. "It's fine. Everyone already knows."

"Define everyone," I prodded.

"Everyone," Lilac and Cordelia said in unison.

Lilac must have read the look on my face, because she took pity and squeezed out a smile. "Don't worry about it. No one blames you."

"What about Sarah?" I challenged.

"She may blame you," Cordelia conceded. "But she's the only one. She never saw her brother for what he really was. She couldn't. It's not personal."

That didn't make me feel better. "What did you see when you looked at her brother?"

"A man who had already lost the battle but didn't realize it," Cordelia replied. "You have to understand that Mark wasn't always a loser. When we were in school, he was a few years ahead of us and he was easy on the eyes and fun to be around."

"She's right," Lilac said. "She's wrong about most things, mind you, but not this."

"Stuff it," Cordelia growled.

"Both of you stuff it," I ordered. I couldn't tolerate another argument. I was finally getting a picture of Mark Santiago, and it wasn't a pretty one. "When did Mark change?"

"That's a good question." Lilac rubbed the back of her neck as she tilted her head to the side. "He was the big man on campus when we were in high school, but within a few years of graduation he was kind of a nobody."

"I'm guessing you guys had a different high school experience than I did," I mused.

"I think high school is the same everywhere," Cordelia corrected.

"Mark was a big athletic star, so he was extremely popular and girls threw themselves at him."

Something occurred to me. "What kind of star?" I looked through the tiki window opening to the rolling water off the beach. "You guys went to high school on an island. I'm guessing there weren't bus rides to neighboring schools for football and basketball games."

"No, we didn't have that," Cordelia agreed. "I guess high school wasn't exactly the same for us. I get what you were saying earlier."

"We had sporting events," Lilac explained. "They were simply solo efforts. We had beach volleyball teams, for example, but everyone competed from the same school. We just broke into groups of twos. I was the island champion with my partner senior year."

Cordelia made a disgusted sound in the back of her throat. "Because you cheated and purposely spiked the ball in my face so I wouldn't be able to compete during the playoffs."

"That was an accident." Lilac looked anything but innocent as she grinned at me. "I didn't do that on purpose."

"Oh, whatever." Cordelia rolled her eyes. "Everyone knows you did it on purpose."

"I think you're the only one who thinks it, because you're crazy," Lilac corrected.

I held up my hands to stop the sniping. "So Mark was popular in high school because he played beach volleyball. That's what you're saying, right?"

Lilac and Cordelia shook their heads in unison.

"Mark was popular because he was great at sailing, kayaking and paddle boarding," Cordelia corrected. "We have different sports here, which you probably don't get, but he was a big deal in high school."

"He was a couple years ahead of us, which Cordelia already mentioned, but there weren't a lot of choices in our age group," Lilac explained. "Everyone had a crush on him."

"Including us," Cordelia interjected. "He was cute and hot, and everyone liked him."

I was lost again. "So what happened?"

"Life happened," Cordelia replied. "The things you find cool in high school aren't necessarily the things you respect as an adult. Do you think exactly like you did in high school?"

"No. I've gotten over letting random dudes feel me up under the bleachers," I muttered.

"Oh, that never goes out of style." Lilac winked as I rolled my eyes. "Mark didn't realize that his high school popularity wouldn't carry over forever. He thought he'd continue to be a hero to the female masses despite the fact that he refused to hold down a job and often slept on the beach because his mother kicked him out of the house for refusing to work."

Things clicked into place. "He developed the drinking problem because he finally realized that he was never going to regain the popularity he lost, didn't he?"

Cordelia nodded. "He kept thinking that things would go back to the way they were, but he didn't want to hold a job and he had a terrible drinking problem."

"I thought drinking was a way of life on an island."

"It is, but there are degrees of drinking," Lilac explained. "What we did at your house was social drinking. Sure, you got completely drunk and slept with the island heartthrob, but that's still normal behavior."

My cheeks burned as I lowered my gaze and stared at my glass of water.

"Mark couldn't quite come to grips with his drinking. Instead of controlling it, the addiction began to control him," Lilac said. "It was sad, and people tried to intervene and help – people like Wesley, Booker and even Galen – but Mark was beyond help."

"It was really sad, but it became something we simply accepted," Cordelia said. "Instead of walking to work in the morning and being sad because I saw Mark passed out on the beach I found I was relieved at a certain point because that meant he wasn't dead."

"It may sound callous, but that's how we all started thinking at some point," Lilac said. "It wasn't a question of *if* the drinking would claim him. It was a question of *when*."

That was unbelievably sad. "So you're basically saying that he would pick up odd jobs for anyone because he was a slave to the bottle."

"Pretty much." Cordelia agreed. "He couldn't break free of the cycle, so eventually the cycle broke him. We tried to get him in rehab. Heck, we tried to come up with a schedule where he would always have a sober buddy for accountability purposes, but he fought every effort."

"Finally we gave up," Lilac added. "It's not nice to say or admit, but we couldn't help. And beating ourselves up over something we couldn't handle was eating away at us."

"We let Mark coast ... and then sink," Cordelia said. "It's on all of us."

"It's not on any of you," I corrected, shaking my head. "He made his own decisions. You couldn't force him to choose a life he didn't want to live. It's not fair to blame yourselves."

"He's still dead," Cordelia pointed out.

"You didn't cause his death."

"I want you to repeat that to yourself," Lilac ordered, drawing my attention to her. "Do you think you can do that?"

The question caught me off guard. "What do you mean?"

"Sarah is walking in the door right now, and you tend to have a martyr complex when it comes to Mark's death," Lilac replied. "Galen was right about you being a big baby. Hopefully your little tryst last night will have loosened you up a bit."

Cordelia narrowed her eyes, an odd expression passing over her face. She opened her mouth to say something, but she didn't get a chance because Sarah spotted our trio in the corner the moment she walked through the door ... and her face twisted into something ugly and grotesque when she recognized me.

"And here we go," Lilac muttered under her breath as Sarah stormed in our direction.

Here we go indeed.

# TWENTY-ONE

Sarah Santiago was all fire and fury as she stalked toward me. Her hands were clenched into fists at her sides, and when she arrived at our table I was understandably thankful that Cordelia sat between us. I didn't want to use Cordelia as a human shield, mind you, but I wasn't above doing it if necessary. Cordelia was her boss, so I was hopeful that Sarah wouldn't physically attack her.

"What is she doing here?" Sarah hissed, her eyes lighting with malice.

"Calm down," Cordelia ordered, glancing around the bar before focusing her full attention on Sarah. "There's no reason to get all worked up."

"No reason to get all worked up?" Sarah was practically apoplectic. "You have got to be kidding. She murdered my brother!"

In my head I knew it was an emotional argument from a grieving sister, but the blow struck hard all the same. "I'm sorry."

"Don't apologize to her," Lilac ordered, shaking her head. "You didn't do anything wrong."

"Didn't do anything wrong?" Sarah shrieked. "She killed Mark. He's dead because of her!"

"After your brother broke into her bedroom with an ax," Lilac shot back. "What was she supposed to do? Do you think she should've laid there and let him kill her?"

Sarah had the grace to look abashed, but only marginally. "I don't believe that story," she sniffed, crossing her arms over her chest. "I think something else happened."

"Like what?" Cordelia challenged. "She's only been on the island for a few days. Apparently she worked fast in those few days – and might have used her magic for more than self-defense – but what motive would she have to kill your brother?"

What was that supposed to mean? How did I work fast?

"What motive would Mark have to go after her?" Sarah challenged.

"Money," Lilac answered without hesitation. "You know as well as anyone that he would do just about anything for money."

"He didn't need money," Sarah protested. "He was working for Wesley Durham."

"No, he wasn't." Lilac shook her head. "We went out there yesterday. Wesley fired him two months ago."

Sarah's eyes widened. "But ... Mark said he was working out there."

"Mark said a lot of things," Cordelia argued. "Very little of which was true. I'm not saying everything Hadley here says is true – and a lot of it is outright nonsense – but she had absolutely no motive to kill your brother. What could she possibly gain from it?"

I was starting to think that Cordelia wasn't happy with my presence in her bar. I wasn't exactly sure when her mood shifted, but it was obvious she and I weren't going to suddenly become best friends.

"Maybe she wanted to steal from him," Sarah suggested.

"Steal what?" Lilac's eyebrows flew up her forehead. "Mark didn't have any money. He broke into her house. He had an ax!"

"But he had no reason to go after her," Sarah protested.

"Someone clearly paid him to do it," Cordelia supplied. "Do you know who he had been in contact with before his death?"

"Just Wesley."

My stomach twisted at what she was insinuating. "Why would Wesley want to go after me?"

"Maybe to get the lighthouse," Sarah suggested, rubbing her hands together as she warmed to the topic. "He lived there with May a long time ago, when they were married. Everyone says she's the one who wanted the divorce. Maybe he found out that she was going to leave the lighthouse to Hadley and he freaked."

"I don't think that's true," I shook my head. "He didn't seem all that interested in the lighthouse when we visited."

"Plus, that theory doesn't free your brother from the specter of any wrongdoing," Cordelia pointed out. "That only makes him look guiltier. It would mean Wesley lied about Mark working for him and that he paid Mark to attack his own granddaughter.

"Now, he might've realized his granddaughter was a total slut and wanted to make sure she didn't do any further damage to the family name, but that doesn't mean Mark wasn't involved," she continued. "No matter how you look at it, Mark was in the wrong in this situation."

Okay, that was definitely weird. I tilted my head to the side and fixed my gaze on Cordelia's profile. "Do you have something you want to say to me?"

Cordelia's expression shifted from pragmatic to innocent. "I have no idea what you're talking about." She slid out of the booth and rested her hands on Sarah's shoulders. "Listen, I understand you're upset. There was a time when you and Mark were really close. But you can't deny what he became over the years. That's not fair to him or yourself."

"I'm not denying that he had difficulties," Sarah argued. "He did. But we were working on them. He was going to beat it."

Cordelia made a sympathetic clucking sound with her tongue. "He couldn't beat it. He was too far gone. You know that."

"But he was going to try." Sarah's eyes filled with tears. "He told me he was going to try. He wouldn't just make that up."

"He made up stuff all the time," Lilac argued. "He told me he was going to buy the hotel and that he buried money in the woods to cover the purchase. Are you saying that was true?"

Sarah looked caught. "No. It's just … why go after her?" She jerked her thumb in my direction. "Why is she so special?"

"We're all trying to figure that out," Cordelia replied, tucking a strand of Sarah's hair behind her ear. "Apparently she has magical powers that will suck every man in the area into her web. It's definitely something to be concerned about."

Okay, that did it. "What is your deal?" I snapped, my temper getting the better of me. "I don't understand why you're attacking me. I don't even know you."

Cordelia was back to looking innocent. "Who said I was attacking you?"

"I do." I raised my hand for emphasis. "You've said three passive-aggressive things in a row. You weren't going out of your way to be friendly at the beginning, but you weren't attacking me either. Now you're attacking me."

"I am not."

"You are, too."

"I am not."

I looked to Lilac for help. "She is, right?"

Lilac nodded without hesitation. "She's totally upset. It's because of something I said, though."

Wait … she knew why Cordelia was upset. When did this happen? "What did you say?"

"What doesn't she say?" Cordelia muttered, turning her eyes to the ceiling. "I'm not angry about anything. Can we give it a rest?"

"Obviously not," I shot back. "You're saying weird things. It's like you have the world's weirdest case of Tourette's."

Cordelia's eyes filled with fire. "Excuse me?"

Sarah grabbed Cordelia's arm in solidarity. "See. She is crazy. She went after my brother. You see it now, right?"

Cordelia offered Sarah a pitying look. "I'm not going to pretend I like her – she's a big slut, after all – but she didn't kill your brother out of malice. There's absolutely no realistic reason she'd do that."

Sarah's lips curved down. "But … ."

"I am not a big a slut," I argued, ignoring the fact that I'd been feeling exactly that way for the past two hours. "Why would you even say that?"

"Oh, I can read between the lines," Cordelia snapped. "You slept with Galen. You'd have to be a big slut to do that."

"Why would she have to be a slut to do that?" Lilac asked, genuinely confused. "You've been trying to do it since we were in high school. Does that make you a big slut, too? Or is it that she actually succeeded when you've done nothing but fail? That's it, isn't it?" Lilac's expression sparked with triumph. "You're a big, jealous hater. That's what you've always been, Cordelia. That's why you went after me when I snagged Jeff Haskins at the clambake senior year."

"You got naked to do it," Cordelia barked. "Only a slut would do that."

"Who cares about who's a slut?" Sarah challenged. "This one is a murderer." She reached around Cordelia, taking me by surprise when she grabbed a handful of my hair. "Why did you kill my brother?"

I instinctively slapped out at her hands. "I didn't mean to do it. He took me by surprise."

"To be fair, she didn't even realize she was a witch until it happened," Lilac offered, raising a finger when Cordelia moved in her direction. "I will slap you silly if you try anything with me."

I had no idea how it happened, but I was in the middle of a girl fight. I couldn't remember being in a girl fight – with actual hair pulling and other stuff – since elementary school.

"This is really undignified." I made a whimpering sound as I tried to pull away, which only made Sarah grip my hair tighter. "Let go!"

"You killed my brother," Sarah bellowed. "I want to make a citizen's arrest."

"You've always been a slut, Lilac," Cordelia charged. "I see you're already turning your new best friend into one. That's so ... tacky."

"You're tacky," Lilac hissed. "You're a tacky and jealous whore, and you've always been bad for the island's reputation."

"That hurts." I grabbed Sarah's wrist, my temper flashing. "Let go or I'll make you let go."

"I'm not afraid of you," Sarah argued. "I'm making a citizen's arrest and there's nothing you can do about it."

"I said let go!" I screeched the words, something ripping free from inside of me at the same moment. After the fact, I would have trouble giving words to the feelings and emotion surrounding the event, but it was as if another being hiding inside of me broke out to wreak havoc on the bar. That was the only way I could describe it.

My anger bubbled up and burst forth, a bright light flashing as Sarah screamed and jerked back her hand. Cordelia's eyes widened to comical proportions as she fixed her full attention on me. Lilac happily clapped.

"That was impressive," Lilac said. "May would be so proud."

I had no idea if that were true, but I teetered to the side a bit as I tried to regain my focus. "What was that?"

"That was you," Cordelia muttered, shaking her head as she flicked a gaze toward a terrified Sarah. "I guess, in addition to being a big slut, you're powerful, too. Well ... this just bites."

"DOES SOMEONE WANT to tell me what's going on?"

Galen arrived ten minutes later, someone calling 911 to alert him to a chick fight at the beach tiki bar. He looked beyond frustrated when he strolled inside, his gaze bouncing between faces before focusing on me.

"What happened to you?" He hurried to my side, tilting my chin so he could stare into my eyes. "She looks drunk. Have you guys been drinking? It's not even noon, for crying out loud."

Lilac and Cordelia shook their heads in unison.

"We haven't been drinking," Lilac replied. "Hadley is wiped out from using magic. She's already feeling weird, so don't make a big deal about it."

Galen was incredulous as he lowered himself so we were at eye level. "You used your magic again? I would've thought you'd be too wiped after last night."

I couldn't believe he was bringing that up – and in front of

Cordelia. She would think I was an even bigger slut than she already did.

"Oh, that's nice." Cordelia made a face. "This really hasn't been my day. In fact, it's been an awful day. I'm sick to death of all you people."

"Right back at you," Lilac shot back. "I'm thinking of forming a club of people who are sick to death of you."

"I'm going to make a citizen's arrest of my own," Cordelia warned. "I'm going to lock you up for being a public nuisance."

"I'm going to lock all of you up for being a nuisance," Galen snapped, squeezing my knee before turning his furious countenance to Cordelia and Lilac. "What's going on? And what happened to Hadley's hair?"

My hair? I instinctively reached up and ran three fingers through the gathered mess. Sarah really did a number on it when she decided to give it a good, hard tug.

"Sarah pulled Hadley's hair," Lilac volunteered.

Galen's eyes widened. "Why?"

"She murdered my brother," Sarah barked, cradling her wrist. "She murdered him, and I want her arrested."

"I see." Galen cast me one more worried look before crossing over to Sarah. He gently tugged at her hand so he could see the area she was trying to protect. "This looks burned."

"She did it!" Sarah looked like a crazy person as she pointed, as if we were in Salem and they were about to start hanging witches. "She burned me."

"Uh-huh." Galen didn't look all that worried. "Why did she do it?"

"Because she's evil," Sarah replied.

"That's not why," Lilac protested. "Sarah was pulling her hair and Hadley warned her to let go and then it was like something just kind of ... I don't know ... whooshed through the room."

Galen cocked a curious eyebrow. "Whooshed?"

"It was a magical wave," Cordelia supplied, offering up a pretty smile for Galen's benefit. "Whatever it was built inside of her and then vented. I can usually sense these things, but it happened quickly."

"Hmm." Galen's expression was thoughtful as he turned to me. "Do you feel sick? Wiped out?"

"More shaky than anything," I replied, staring at my quivering fingers. "It's weird."

"Try this." Galen grabbed an orange from the counter and handed it to me. "This should help even you out."

"An orange?" I accepted the fruit and stared at it. "Are oranges magical and nobody told me?"

"No. They're just good for you and should even out your blood sugar." Galen patted my shoulder before turning back to Sarah. "Why did you pull her hair?"

Sarah still seethed. "She killed my brother."

"Your brother tried to kill her first," Galen argued. "She protected herself. You can't blame her for what happened."

"Well, I do blame her," Sarah sniffed. "I don't believe my brother would go after a woman under any circumstances. He doesn't even know this one. He was a drunk, not a killer."

"He was a drunk who would do anything for a dime," Galen corrected. "As for you not believing he would do it, believe it. I was there right after it happened. I saw her bedroom. He was in the light-house for the express purpose of killing Hadley."

"Why were you near the lighthouse in the middle of the night?" Cordelia queried.

"I was checking the property."

"For what?" Cordelia's expression turned dark. "Were you checking to see if the inhabitant was wearing panties?"

Galen furrowed his brow. "No. I ... what do panties have to do with anything?"

"Nothing," I answered hurriedly, mortified to think our private business would be discussed in public ... again. It was bad enough we would have to discuss it ourselves in a few hours. I so wasn't looking forward to that.

"Cordelia is jealous," Lilac interjected.

"I am not!" Cordelia's hands landed on her narrow hips. "You take that back, you slut!"

Lilac ignored her. "Cordelia was perfectly pleasant – er, well, at least for her – until she found out you and Hadley did the naked dance of our ancestors last night. Then she turned into a monster and got all passive aggressive. It's so annoying."

"I can see that." Galen's expression twisted as he rubbed the back of his neck. "And she turned mean because ... ."

"She knows you and Hadley had sex last night."

"Oh, geez!" I slapped my hand to my forehead. "Did you have to bring it up in public? I told you that in private."

"You may have only known me for only a few days, but you should be well aware by this point that I'm not capable of being quiet," Lilac argued pragmatically. "If you want something kept secret, you can't tell me. It's an island rule."

"She's right," Cordelia said, feigning brightness. "So, do you want to explain yourself, Galen?"

"What I do in my private life is none of your business, Cordelia." Galen's voice was flat, firm even. I could feel his eyes on me, but refused to lock gazes with him. I was too embarrassed. "Hadley, maybe we should talk."

That sounded like the last thing I wanted to do. It was bad enough we'd slept together and I didn't remember it. If I had to listen to him explain to me why it was a mistake I'd be mortified for the rest of my life. I already knew it was a mistake. I didn't need him to refer to it that way.

"Actually, um, I need a little air," I said, struggling to refrain from touching him as I got to my feet and skirted around his muscular frame. "I don't feel well, and I need a few minutes without people staring at me."

"Okay, but ... ." Galen forced my eyes briefly to him by making a small throat-clearing sound. "We need to talk. If you need air, I get it. Don't wander away. I'll be out there in a few minutes."

That sounded absolutely terrible. I didn't let him know what I was thinking, instead faking enthusiasm as I nodded. "Sounds good. I'll be right outside."

I would definitely be outside. Right outside of Cordelia's tiki bar?

Not a chance. I needed to make an escape, and Galen's distraction would give me just enough time to do it.

"Take your time."

2 2

# TWENTY-TWO

I had no intention of waiting outside for Galen. Leaving Lilac behind could be considered rude, but I knew she'd understand. I needed to get away from it all, which was funny because I now lived on an island that people visited to "get away from it all."

I lucked out while walking the beach, spotting Booker's bus in the main parking lot. I hurried in that direction, searching the area before following the sound of pounding and discovering him on top of the visitor center's roof.

"What are you doing?"

Booker shifted so he could stare down at me. The visitor's center was only one story, but he looked very far away when our eyes locked. "What are you doing? I heard you got into a chick fight at Cordelia's place, by the way. Nice job." He flashed a sarcastic thumbs-up that caused my stomach to twist.

"How could you possibly know that?" I didn't bother to hide my frustration. "It happened, like, thirty minutes ago."

"Yeah, but Todd Hamilton was in the bar when it went down. He said there were bras flying everywhere." Booker's smile was mischievous. "Sorry I missed it."

"No bras were flying." I wrinkled my nose, irritation bubbling up. "Speaking of that, I need to borrow your bus."

Whatever Booker expected me to say, it wasn't that. "I'm sorry?" His expression remained neutral for the most part, but I didn't miss the way his eyebrows edged up. "What does my bus have to do with bras?"

"Absolutely nothing, but I was tired of waiting for an appropriate transition," I replied. "I need to get out of here for a little bit and you're the only person I know who has a vehicle."

"Yes, and it's a vehicle I need."

"I'm not going to wreck it."

Booker didn't look convinced. "Do you know how to drive?"

"Of course."

"Sometimes I'm surprised you can walk, so I'm not sure I believe that."

He was either trying to get under my skin or hide the fact that he was a bit sexist. I had no idea which. "Can I borrow your bus or not?"

"Well ... ." Booker broke off, rubbing his chin as he debated. "Why can't you borrow Galen's truck?"

Because I'm hiding from Galen. I couldn't say that, though. It would open the door to questions I was not inclined to answer. "Because I found you first."

"Aren't I lucky." Booker made a face. "Where are you going?"

"Where do you think I'm going? I only know about one place away from this stupid city. I have no intention of going on an adventure, so ... I'm going there."

Booker remained unconvinced. "Maybe you could call him and ask him to come to you. He has a truck."

He did, but since I made the decision to escape on a whim that seemed counterintuitive. "Fine." I threw my hands in the air. "I'm sorry I asked." I moved to stomp away, but Booker stopped me with a whistle before I traveled far.

He was on his feet, and I watched as he dug in his pocket before tossing his key ring in my direction. "I'm not doing this because of your little meltdown. I want you to know that."

"Then why are you doing it?"

"Because I think you and Wesley need to talk alone for both of you to be comfortable with your newfound relationship. I think it will be good for you."

"Thank you."

"You're welcome." Booker winked, his mischievous smile back. "Just for the record, you might want to fix your hair. It looks as if you've taken a hard tumble, and I'm sure the gossip will have made it out to the farm before you get there. I would hate for Wesley to assume Galen did that."

"Ugh." I twisted my features into a hateful scowl. "How do you people know things so fast on this island? Is there a magical gossip trail I know nothing about?"

Booker nodded, catching me off guard.

"There is?"

"It's all the females on the island," Booker explained. "They can't stop yapping."

Now I knew he was being sexist. "We're going to talk about that assumption when I get back." I waved the keys for emphasis. "Thank you for this."

"Don't mention it ... and don't take all day," Booker ordered. "I have things to do, too."

"I won't be long. I just ... I have some questions."

"Of course you do. You wouldn't be human if you didn't."

I wasn't so sure I was human any longer, but that was hardly something to focus on given the time constraints. "I won't be long."

He grinned. "I'll see what gossip I can gather by the time you get back."

"Great. Just what I need, more gossip."


THE FARM LOOKED quiet when I parked in front of the house, struggling with the stick shift to get it in the correct gear four times before killing the engine. I was thankful the driveway wasn't on an incline when I finally finished, because I wasn't one-hundred percent sure I knew what I was doing.

When I climbed out of the bus, I found Wesley sitting on his front porch. He had a pitcher of iced tea sitting on a small table and a pipe in his hand.

"I figured you'd come." Wesley smiled. "You were quicker than I thought."

"I had to get out of town for a few hours," I admitted sheepishly, keeping my head down as I climbed the porch steps. "This is the only place I know that exists outside of the main town."

"There are many other points of interest on Moonstone Bay," Wesley explained, pouring a glass of iced tea and handing it to me. "You'll discover them yourself when the time is right."

"That sounds ominous."

"It's not ominous. It's just … everyone on this island is weird. Did you know there are mud pits out on the far side of the island and people actually pay to sit in them?"

That was news to me. "No, but a mud bath is supposed to be great for your pores."

"There's mud over there." Wesley pointed toward a spot on the other side of the driveway. "Go roll around in that if you're interested. It's free."

I couldn't hide my chuckle as I shook my head, staring at the eave offering us shade. "I need to ask you something," I ventured after a few minutes of silence. "You're probably not going to like it, but I still need to know."

"You want to know why I never contacted you."

"Well, yes, but that's not the question. Sarah Santiago brought up the fact that you might've wanted me dead because you wanted the lighthouse. I just … that's not true, right?"

One of Wesley's sparkplug eyebrows winged up as he regarded me. "I have trouble believing anyone who shares my genes would drive out to a farm in the middle of nowhere to meet with a man she thinks might be a potential killer."

"It's not that," I said hurriedly, pressing the iced tea glass to my forehead to ward off the heat. "It's just ... Sarah seemed certain that you wanted the lighthouse. Everyone seems certain that the lighthouse is some big prize. I'm afraid I'm missing something."

"You're missing a lot, girlie, but it's not your fault." Wesley stretched his long legs in front of him as he reclined in the chair. "For the record, I have no interest in killing you."

"That was only half of the question," I pointed out.

"Are you asking if I want the lighthouse?"

I chewed my bottom lip and nodded, something about the expression causing Wesley to smile.

"Your mother used to make that face when she was younger," Wesley noted, his voice taking on a wistful quality. "You remind me of her."

"I've seen photographs," I argued. "I don't really look like her."

"You're a mixture," Wesley corrected. "You have your mother's bone structure ... and my eyes. You have a few of your mother's mannerisms."

"I never knew her to compare."

"Which is a shame." Wesley took me by surprise when he reached over and patted my hand. It was the first tactile contact we'd managed since meeting. "I should probably start from the beginning for your benefit?"

I held my hands palms up and shrugged. "You can start wherever you want."

"I'll start with May." Wesley pressed the heel of his hand to his forehead, perhaps centering himself, and then launched into his tale. "I fell in love with her the moment I saw her. Your grandmother was a fiery woman. She had a mouth like ... well, back in my day women didn't talk like your grandmother."

"She was bossy?"

"She swore like a drunken trucker after a three-day bender," Wesley corrected. "She was also funny, bright, and beautiful and she had a smile that always made me happy to see her. We dated only a month before getting married."

"Wasn't that kind of the norm back then?"

Wesley's eyes twinkled. "Do you mean back in the olden days?"

"I wouldn't put it in that rude of a manner, but kind of."

"It was normal. We had a blissful two years, a time that included the birth of your mother, and then reality set in. We might've loved each other – heck, we always loved each other – but living together was another story."

"So you divorced because you couldn't live together?" That sounded rough. "You mentioned that you didn't go after the lighthouse when you divorced. If the property is as important as everyone seems to think, why not?"

"Because that lighthouse was part of your grandmother's family history," Wesley replied. "I probably could've gone after it, forced her to sign it over or sell it, but I had no interest in that. Even when we divorced I was trying to find a way to make things work."

"You never did, huh? That's too bad."

"No, I did." Wesley's smirk was playful. "We divorced and only saw each other about once a week. We lived in separate homes, ran separate businesses and fought six days a week. On the seventh day – usually a Sunday – we rested."

I had no idea what that meant. "Are you saying … ?"

"That your grandmother and I pretended to be married on Sundays but no other day of the week?" Wesley nodded. "Yes."

"Holy crap! Did everyone on the island know?"

"Everyone on this island knows everything," Wesley answered. "That's how I know you've already hooked up with Galen. You move a little fast for my taste – I'd hoped to impart some of my wisdom before you got that far – but he's a good choice. The boy has always been strong, and he has an impeccable set of ethics."

My cheeks colored under his studied gaze. "I don't really want to talk about that. No offense, you seem like a nice guy and I'm, like, ninety percent sure you don't want to kill me, but I don't want to talk about that."

"Ah, you're a prude. Good to know."

I balked. "I'm not a prude."

"Only a prude would say that." Wesley chuckled as he tapped his foot on the deck. "You remind me of your mother that way, too."

He seemed happy to reminisce about her, which opened the door for another set of questions. "Didn't you ever want to see me?" It was a difficult question, but I needed to ask it. I wouldn't be able to let it go otherwise.

"We did want to see you," Wesley countered. "In fact, we talked about it quite frequently."

"On your Sunday sex days?"

"Yes."

I briefly covered my eyes. "I think I'm going to have nightmares picturing that."

"Then don't picture it." Wesley was in a pragmatic frame of mind. "Honey, we loved your mother. We raised her to be her own person. We raised her to be strong. We wanted her to be the sort of person who didn't care what others thought. Unfortunately for us, she did exactly what we raised her to do and made her own decisions."

"You mean marrying my father, don't you?"

"We expected her to return to the island," Wesley explained. "We didn't know about your father until she decided to marry him. They'd only been dating a few weeks, and we knew it was a mistake. We tried talking to her about it, but she wouldn't listen."

"You said you married after a few weeks," I pointed out. "Would you have listened if your parents tried to talk you out of it?"

"My mother did try to talk me out of it. Didn't work," Wesley said. "The thing is, marrying a mortal is frowned upon. Paranormal cultures all over the world do it, and even though Moonstone Bay is progressive in some ways, it's not in others."

"So you didn't want her to marry Dad because he wasn't magical?"

"No offense to your father, because he seems to have done a good job raising you, but I wouldn't have picked him for my little girl no matter what," Wesley said. "I thought she deserved more. She felt differently."

"So you didn't talk to her either, huh?"

"That was a mistake." Wesley fixed his eyes on me. "I shouldn't have fought with her and I definitely shouldn't have fallen out of touch. In the back of my mind I had time, you see. I had time to make things right. The thing is, I really didn't."

Wesley broke off, clearing his throat as he fought the emotion storming his face. "We found out about you the same time we heard that our daughter was dead. It was a difficult time, to say the least."

"Did you blame me?"

"No, honey." The look on Wesley's face was firm enough that I believed him. "That doesn't mean we weren't broken hearted. It's just … we didn't know what to do. We didn't have rights where you were concerned. We thought about trying to push your father, but that seemed unfair. He was grieving, after all. We all were."

"So you did nothing," I mused.

"No, we gave your father a few years to get settled and then we went to him regularly with requests to see you," Wesley corrected. "He always turned us down. I can't say I blame him. I probably would've turned us down, too. It was still frustrating.

"You see, we wanted a life with you, but your father worried that we would try to indoctrinate you into this life," he continued. "No matter how much we promised not to do that, he wouldn't budge."

"I'm kind of angry with him right now," I admitted, sipping my iced tea and wiping the cool condensation against my cheek before continuing. "He never told me any of this. He acted surprised when May's will showed up. I believe he told me only because he was legally required to do so."

"I won't make excuses for the man," Wesley said. "Part of me hates him because I'm just now meeting you. But when I put myself in his shoes I can't help but wonder if I wouldn't have done the same."

"Really?" I didn't bother hiding my surprise. "Why?"

"You were safe and you were all he had left of your mother," Wesley replied. "I think he truly loved your mother, and her death leveled him. It takes a strong man to pick up the pieces and raise a child on his own. That's what he did.

"He never remarried as far as I heard," he continued. "That means he did all the work where you're concerned on his own. That's worth some respect in my book."

It was strange – and oddly refreshing – to hear him say that. "He didn't date when I was a kid, but he does now. His most recent girl-friend is younger than I am."

Wesley shrugged. "Is that bad?"

"Um ... yes."

Wesley snorted. "You're cute. I'm glad I'm going to get the chance to spend some time with you."

"I'm glad, too." I flashed a genuine smile. "Why didn't you come to see me as soon as I arrived?"

"I wanted you to get settled," Wesley replied. "I figured May's ghost would pay a visit and explain the big things to you. I'm not a witch, although I have a bit of mage in my blood. Your mother seemed to inherit only witchy abilities from May, which I was fine with. May was always stronger than me. We figured you would inherit only witchy genes from your mother, so it only made sense to let May explain."

"I burned a woman today," I blurted out, worry getting the better of me. "She was pulling my hair and something kind of clawed out and burned her."

"Sarah Santiago?"

I knit my eyebrows. "How did you know?"

"One of my farmhands was in the bar having lunch when it happened," Wesley explained. "I figured you'd make your way out here by the end of the day."

"Why?"

"Because you need answers and I'm the only person alive you think you can get them from," Wesley said. "That's not true. If you have questions you need answered right away, Galen can do it. He's a good guy to have on your side ... although we're going to have a talk about the rest of it."

My furious blush was back. "I said I didn't want to talk about that."

"I'm your grandfather. It's my job to embarrass you."

"You're doing a good job."

"Thank you." Wesley beamed as he watched me shake my head. "Now drink your tea and I'll give you a tour of the farm. This will be yours one day, after all."

I stilled, dumbfounded. "Seriously? I already have a lighthouse that I don't know what to do with."

"It's your lucky day."

"I didn't feel that way this morning, but I do now."

"Then come on." Wesley grunted as he got to his feet. "Let's take a look around, shall we? There's more to this island than beaches and muscle-bound sheriffs playing beach blanket lothario."

It took me a moment to grasp what he was saying. "I really don't want to talk about it."

"That's okay. I can talk for the both of us."

I believed him.

23

# TWENTY-THREE

I stayed longer than I should have, the tour of the farm serving as entertainment and a way for me to bond with a grandfather I didn't even know I had. I didn't have Booker's phone number with me, so Wesley took it upon himself to call the jack-of-all-trades and explain my lateness. Apparently Booker didn't care, and said he'd pick up the bus at the lighthouse in the morning.

By the time I hit the road it was dark. I wasn't particularly nervous about making the trek back to town – it was a straight shot, after all – until I realized there were no streetlights on the highway. I wasn't used to that. In the Detroit area, even in the suburbs, there were lights on every corner. The highway heading back to Moonstone Bay was absolutely desolate and I couldn't shake the creepy feeling that I was about to lose myself in a horror movie if I wasn't careful.

I slowed my pace. The signs said I could go sixty miles an hour, but that seemed too fast given the winding road. I decreased my speed to forty and still felt as if I was flying around a few curves.

I shouldn't have stayed so late, I chastised myself. Next time I'd make sure to leave long before the sun set. The darkness was too much. I kept expecting masked serial killers to leap out of the nearby trees and throw themselves at the dated bus. My imagination ran wild

... and then I saw a flash of something in the road and reacted instinctively.

Whatever it was moved on the left, so I swerved right, dipping into the ditch. I thought I was going fast enough to pop out on the other side, but the old bus didn't have much "get up and go," so it stalled, the wheels spinning helplessly as I tried to navigate back to the road.

I pressed my lips together and peered through the window, looking for a hint of whatever I'd seen in the road. It had been a brief flash of movement, nothing more. For all I knew it could be an animal. I didn't see anything, yet I wasn't in the mood to climb out of the bus and search the area on my own. I'd seen too many horror movies to fall for that.

I forced myself to remain calm and shifted the bus into reverse, slowly pushing on the accelerator. The tires spun helplessly, refusing to gain traction. I was well and truly stuck now, half of the bus's front end hanging in a ditch that I couldn't back out of.

"Well, crap."

Now what?

I reached over to the passenger seat and felt around until I found my cell phone. The battery bar glowed red, which meant that I didn't have much juice left. Worse than that, I had absolutely no service bars showing. I punched in 911 anyway and pressed the phone to my ear. Other than a brief error message, I got nothing.

"Son of a ... !"

I slapped my hands against the steering wheel and debated my options. I was essentially halfway between Wesley's farm and town. That meant at least ten miles of walking in either direction. I hadn't seen another vehicle during my drive out to the farm or my ride back, so the odds of someone else finding me were slim.

I had no idea what to do.

Ultimately, I realized I had no choice. I would have to pick a direction and start walking. It might take me four or five hours to get to a destination, but it obviously made more sense to head toward town. At least that way I could eventually see the lights on the horizon.

I pocketed my phone and grabbed my cross-body purse, slipping it over my head and pocketing the keys before slamming the bus door shut. This was not the way I envisioned my night going. I thought I'd be able to sneak back to the lighthouse, turn off all of the lights and lock the doors before Galen showed up for our serious talk. It wasn't a mature reaction, but I wasn't sure how much more maturity I could muster in one day.

I set a brisk pace that I knew I wouldn't be able to maintain, but fear was a motivator. I heard scuffling in the underbrush occasionally, causing the hair on the back of my neck to stand up. I rationalized that it was probably animals. Islands have animals, right? I pictured fluffy bunnies and slow tortoises.

That wasn't so bad.

Then my mind shifted to the horror movie *Anaconda* and I couldn't help wondering if the island was littered with giant snakes. Then I thought of the movie *Turistas,* when the natives went crazy and wanted to hack people for ... well, I have no idea. I think it was body parts, but I couldn't really remember. Then my mind drifted to a really bad zombie movie in which an entire island was taken over by zombies, which made me realize Moonstone Bay already had zombies.

It took me fifteen minutes to cover a good bit of ground, and I wanted to break into a run. If I thought I could run in flip-flops I probably would've given it a go. I didn't have much time to dwell on it, because the sound of a larger animal crashing in the growth to my right caught my attention, causing me to jerk my head in that direction.

My heart pounded, sweat slicked my palms, and my mind revolted against what I thought I saw. I couldn't be sure. The movement was fleeting, but I swear I caught sight of a pair of yellow eyes flashing to life only nine or ten feet from me.

I ceased all forward momentum and slowly let my eyes drift from one side of the road to the other. I've never been one for believing I can sense the presence of a malevolent force or anything, but I was certain I wasn't alone.

"Who's out there?" My voice cracked as I fought the urge to curl into a ball and hide in the ditch.

The answering sound was enough to make my blood run cold, a low growl emanating from a spot far too close.

"Oh, my ... ." I bit off a whimper when the yellow eyes flashed again, this time only three feet away. I ran, my body reacting even though my head couldn't wrap itself around what I saw.

My breath came in ragged gasps, and footfalls echoed behind me, although they appeared to be punctuated by nails clicking against the asphalt.

I could feel the unseen force closing the distance and exhaling warm air on the back of my neck, and then I saw it.

At first I thought it was my imagination. Perhaps I envisioned someone racing to my rescue while I was really a hundred feet back getting my throat ripped out. My mind couldn't handle that, so it went to a different place. That made sense, right?

The vehicle was almost on top of me before it slowed, the headlights blinding me as someone opened the driver's side door and climbed out. I couldn't help but wonder if I was in even more danger now. I had no idea who was stopping. It could be an evil madman ... or a snake shifter, for all I knew. Hey, if they have shark shifters they probably have snake shifters.

Then I heard a familiar voice and my heart leapt as I threw myself at the figure.

"Hadley?"

"Galen?" I was crying when I buried my face in his chest.

He wrapped his arms around me, holding me close as he ran his hand down the back of my head. "What happened?"

"There's something out there," I whispered, my lower lip trembling.

Galen's body stiffened "What kind of something?"

"I just saw yellow eyes."

Galen licked his lips, taking a moment to decide. "Okay. Get in the truck."

I fought when he tried to push me inside, but he was too strong. "What are you doing? Come with me. Let's leave."

"I just want to look around." Galen forced a tight smile. "You'll be safe in the truck. Now get in." He gave me another shove, hoisting me inside and slamming the door shut before I could mount another argument.

"Don't leave me here," Galen warned, wagging a finger. He flashed what I'm sure he considered a reassuring smile before stepping into the blazing lights in front of the truck.

I watched as he tilted his head to the side and lifted his nose to the air, my heart skipping a beat when I realized his mannerisms reminded me of a very specific animal. It was only then that the obvious question hit me. If all of the residents and workers on Moonstone Bay were paranormal creatures, what did that mean about Galen?

I didn't get a chance to ponder the question for long. Galen clearly heard something in the brush toward the left side of the road. I lowered the window a crack so I could listen, cringing at the unmistakable howl ripping through the night air.

"What was that?" I hissed. "Was that a ... wolf?"

I barely got the question out before Galen's body began to shift. It had to be a trick of the light or something. There could be no other explanation. The transformation happened so quickly, though, that when Galen's wolf form hopped away from the shorts and shirt piled on the ground I was left with nothing but my abject hysteria to comfort me.

I heard snarling ... and snapping jaws ... and an exaggerated whine when some sort of canine was terribly hurt. I couldn't see the fight. I couldn't register what I'd seen when Galen leaned over and planted his hands on the ground, his back contorting higher as his fingers elongated and ... no, thinking about it was too much.

Oh, holy hell! What is going on with this freaking island?


**I COULD HAVE** driven away. Galen left the truck running, and after a few minutes of listening to growling and howling I was more than ready to put some distance between myself and whatever was going on within the shadows.

I wasn't so far gone that I could consider leaving Galen behind, though. He saved me from whatever was out there. If he hadn't shown up ... I don't even want to think about what would've happened.

I was just about to do something infinitely stupid – people everywhere would've been screaming at their screens to stop me if I was trapped in a horror movie – but a dark figure appeared in the headlights before I could.

My heart seized at the sudden movement, and I gripped the steering wheel, debating putting the truck in drive so I could run over the stranger before I recognized Galen's strong shoulders. He barely spared me a glance as he leaned over in front of the truck, shrugging into his shorts and hanging his shirt over his arm before moving to the door.

He stared at me through the glass for a very long time, perhaps ascertaining if I was about to freak out. Finally, he tugged on the door, and when it wouldn't open he merely arched an eyebrow. "Are you going to unlock it?"

The simple question snapped me back to reality. I fumbled with the controls on the panel before finally managing to do what he wanted. Galen was careful when he opened the door, making no sudden moves to close the distance between us. Now that I could see him under the dome light I realized he had a gash across his cheek and another, much deeper slash, across his sculpted abdomen.

I openly gaped at the wound. "Do you need to go to the hospital?" I asked, my voice sounding breathy and unnatural.

"I'll be fine." Galen captured my fingers before they could graze over the wound. "Are you okay?"

I snapped my eyes up to his, the terror and fear from only moments before returning. "You're a shifter."

"I am," Galen confirmed, his lips curving. "How do you feel about that?"

I was struck dumb by the question. "You turned into a wolf. Or, wait, was that some sort of dog? It looked like a wolf. I've lived in Michigan all my life, but the only wolves I saw were in the zoo. I guess you could be a dog."

"I'm a wolf." Galen's smile was kind, his patience apparently never ending. "Do you have questions?"

I pressed my lips together and nodded.

"What are they?" Galen prodded.

"I'm not sure yet," I murmured, my mind threatening to shut down. "I just … what happened? What was out there?"

"It was another wolf shifter, but I couldn't get close enough to figure out who."

"I heard one of you cry out."

"Yes, well, there might've been a bit of chasing and our friend fell down an incline. I'm guessing he hurt himself, but I can't be sure."

"He? How can you be sure it's a man?"

"I can't, but that's my assumption."

"Because only a man would do something like stalk a woman along an abandoned road after dark?" I asked.

"No, because I simply believe it was a man." Galen gestured toward the passenger seat, making small shooing motions with his hands to get me to slide over.

I did as he asked, although I was unable to move my eyes from Galen's battered torso as he climbed into the driver's seat and shut the door. "How did you get hurt?"

"It was during the chase. I fell down a hill and smacked into a rock. It will be fine in the morning. I heal rapidly."

"Because you're a wolf?"

"Yes." Instead of putting the truck into gear, Galen kept his eyes on me. "Are you going to freak out?"

"I haven't decided yet."

"Well, can you fasten your seatbelt before you decide?"

I nodded and did as he asked.

"Thank you." Galen licked his lips, giving the appearance that he was calm. Instead of maintaining his cool, though, he exploded. "What were you thinking getting out of your vehicle and trying to walk back to town after dark? Are you stupid? Are you trying to kill me?"

The yelling was enough to allow me to recover at least a portion of my wits. "Excuse me?" I was beside myself. "The bus got stuck. I thought I saw something in the road. My phone had zero service and the battery was almost dead."

"So you saw something in the road and decided to get out of the vehicle?" Galen was incredulous. "You are stupid, aren't you? That's the only explanation."

"Hey! I'm the victim here," I spat. "I was minding my own business, visiting my grandfather and drinking iced tea, and then my life imploded. Again. Do you know how many times my life has imploded since I landed on this stupid island?"

"If you expect me to feel sorry for you, I won't," Galen argued. "You were supposed to wait outside the tiki bar for me. We had a few things to talk about, if you remember correctly."

Crud. Of course he'd bring that up. "I'm trying to deal with a lot here," I countered. "I burned a woman today and have no idea how I did it. That was after I went all sex crazy and apparently did the dirty with you. I can't even remember it, which totally sucks. It's been a long, freaking day."

Galen worked his jaw as he considered my outburst. "I don't even know where to start."

"If you're going to start by yelling at me, pick another spot."

"Okay. How about this? We didn't have sex," Galen barked, taking me completely by surprise.

"We didn't?" I should've been relieved, but part of me was a bit disappointed. I had no idea why. Okay, I've seen him without his shirt on, so I know why. "But ... you were naked in my bed."

"So what?" Galen challenged. "We got wet when you lost control of the spell last night. I didn't want to sleep in wet clothes. You had nothing for me to wear. I didn't want to leave you alone in case you woke up in a panic so I slept naked. Big whoop."

"But ... ." That couldn't be right. That would mean I misread every sign.

Galen continued to stare. "I'm waiting."

"For what?" I tripped over my tongue. "I … what are you waiting for?"

"An apology," Galen replied, unruffled by my squeak.

"Apology? Why would I apologize? I didn't do anything."

"You thought I would take advantage of a passed-out woman," Galen argued. "You thought I was the kind of guy who would do that."

"I … well … I didn't think that exactly," I hedged.

"Now everyone in town thinks I'm that sort of guy," Galen grumbled, navigating his truck back toward town. "I should be offended that you think I'd do anything of the sort."

Given everything that happened – especially the fact that he drove so far out of his way to look for me – I couldn't help feeling guilty. "I'm sorry."

"You should be."

"I said I was."

Galen growled as he focused on the road. "You're a lot of freaking work, woman. Has anyone ever told you that?"

I shook my head as I chewed my bottom lip. I felt guilty. I also felt confused. "How did you even know where to find me?"

"I expected you to show up at the lighthouse eventually, but when you didn't I got worried," Galen replied. "I called Wesley, and he said you should've been back in town, so I decided to check the road. That bus is old and could break down at any moment."

"It's also a stick, and I wasn't sure I remembered how to drive one," I admitted.

"That's not what you told everyone about last night," Galen groused, causing me to narrow my eyes.

"I said I was sorry."

"You're going to be sorry." Galen's voice was barely audible as he spared me a dark look. "Believe me, honey, when we sleep together you'll darned well remember it."

Oh, well, that was comforting. Wait a second. "Did you say when?"

"Yes. Now, shut up. I want five minutes of peace."

"Fine." I crossed my arms over my chest. "But I think you're being awfully presumptuous that there's going to be a when."

"Didn't I tell you to shut up?"

"Oh, bite me."

"That can be arranged."

I had a feeling that was true.

# TWENTY-FOUR

"We need to talk."

"Ugh." I threw myself on the lighthouse couch with a bit of dramatic flair and stared at a spot on the wall rather than risk meeting Galen's gaze. "Didn't we already do that?"

"We did but I'm not done."

"I'm done," I countered, plucking at the afghan hanging over the back of the couch. It reminded me of one I'd carried around my father's house for years when I was a kid before it accidentally got thrown out on trash day. "I don't want to talk about it again. It makes me look bad."

Galen snorted, taking me by surprise when he sat on the couch next to me. "It's fine. I can see why you jumped to that conclusion."

"That's not what you said twenty minutes ago."

"Twenty minutes ago I was keyed up from a fight," Galen pointed out. "I'm fine now, although I'm not exactly thrilled with the fact that you just assumed I'd do something like that while you were passed out."

I did my best not to appear embarrassed – which wasn't easy given the way my cheeks burned – but ultimately I could do nothing but rub the tender spot between my eyebrows and sigh. "I'm sorry. That was wrong ... and mean. I didn't know what else to think when I woke up. Your clothes were in a heap on the floor, for crying out loud."

"Because they got wet," Galen reminded me. "You lost control of your magic and the water spout hit us. That's the reason I changed your clothes. I didn't want you getting a chill in the middle of the night."

That hadn't even occurred to me. "You changed my clothes?" The idea was horrifying, abhorrent ... and entirely embarrassing. Were my legs freshly shaved last night? I couldn't even remember.

As if reading my mind, Galen chuckled. "I did change your clothes. It was the second most exciting thing that happened to me last evening."

I narrowed my eyes, suspicious. "The second?" He should be so lucky to see me naked. I mean ... does he even understand what a compliment is? They're always necessary after a bout of nakedness, for crying out loud. In fact, now would be a great time for a compliment.

"The first was watching you play with your magic," Galen replied. "You looked as if you were enjoying yourself until things got away from you."

"I don't remember much of it," I admitted, scrubbing the sides of my face with my hands. "It comes back in flashes."

"It will get better."

"Will it?" I was hopeful he was right. "What about you?"

"What about me?"

"How long have you been a wolf?"

"I was born this way," Galen replied. "Do you have anything you want to ask about that?"

Did I? Absolutely! Was now the time? I couldn't be sure. "So it's not like the movies? Wolves are born, not bitten."

"True shifters are born, not bitten," Galen clarified. "However, there are a number of shifter lines that can create half-breeds by biting. Wolves are one of them. Those lines aren't nearly as strong as born lines."

"Ah, I see." I did my best to pretend I was taking it all in and totally fine with the information. "How many born shifters versus bitten shifters are there on the island?"

"Um, I think that most of the shifters on the island are born," Galen replied. "Born shifters and bitten shifters don't generally play nice with one another."

"Why not?"

"Bitten shifters have inferiority complexes."

"Why?"

"Born shifters are superior."

I snorted, rolling my head back so I could stare at the ceiling. "Are you sure you don't have a superiority complex rather than the other way around?"

"Not even remotely," Galen replied. "Bitten wolves are weaker, and they tend to be power hungry. Think about it. What kind of person would purposely let himself get bitten just so he can turn into an animal?"

That was an interesting question. "I don't know. It was another wolf shifter out there tonight, right?"

Galen nodded. "It was a born shifter. I can promise you that."

"How can you tell?"

"Different scents."

I took a moment to picture Galen sniffing another guy's butt and made a face. "Ugh. This conversation just went to a creepy place."

"Really? And I thought the fact that you believed I had sex with you while you were unconscious was the worst it would get."

"You'll never let me live that down, will you?"

"Probably not," Galen answered. "I'm offended that you think you would've been able to forget."

"Oh, geez." I slapped my hand to my forehead. "This night keeps getting worse."

"You would never be able to forget it," Galen said, refusing to be dissuaded from this particular point of conversation. "It would be seared in your brain and give you naughty palpitations whenever you thought about it for years to come."

"Naughty palpitations? You think a lot about yourself, don't you?"

"Yup." He didn't look even remotely ashamed when he flicked his eyes to the door upon hearing it open. Instinctively I moved a bit closer to him, causing him to rest his hand on my knee. "It's fine. It's Booker."

Booker didn't look happy when he strolled into the room, his expression dark. "I don't like either one of you right now," he announced.

"How did you know it was him?" I asked, impressed. "Could you smell him?"

"I heard the bus in the driveway," Galen explained. "That bus has a particular sound. I see you managed to reclaim your property."

"I did," Booker confirmed, bobbing his head. "It was in the ditch right where you said it would be. Thankfully it doesn't look as if it will need any work."

"I'm really sorry," I offered. I meant it. "I don't know what happened."

"I let you drive against my better judgment," Booker barked. "That's what happened."

"Not that I'm keen to exonerate her, but I'm pretty sure whoever was out there purposely tricked her," Galen offered, never moving his hand from my knee. The contact was warm and friendly. It also caused my brain to go haywire. "She saw movement in the road and swerved to avoid it. I think whoever it was picked that exact spot because he knew the road dipped there."

"See. It wasn't my fault." I offered up a grave expression. "I could've died."

"She's feeling sorry for herself," Galen explained. "She also thought we had sex last night and spent the day feeling guilty. She thought she forgot. As if."

Booker snorted, his good humor returning. "I heard you were totally forgettable, dude. That's what all the women say when they upgrade to me."

"You're a funny guy." Galen rolled his eyes and shook his head.

"Yeah? Well, I'm not feeling really funny right now," Booker said. "Whoever was out there ransacked the bus. I didn't have much in there, but it was tossed around."

I felt sick to my stomach. "I'll pay for whatever damage was done."

"I didn't say there was damage," Booker clarified. "I simply said someone was looking for something."

"But what?" Galen asked, squeezing my knee in a reassuring manner. "Don't get all worked up, Hadley. Booker said the bus was fine. Your only mistake was getting out of it in the middle of the night."

"What was I supposed to do?" I challenged. "Should I have sat there and waited until someone stumbled across me? I didn't have any water and I hadn't seen a vehicle in ... well ... forever. I don't think anyone drives on that road."

"People drive it, but it's not a busy highway," Galen corrected. "As for waiting, yes, you should have waited. I would've found you."

"I didn't know you were looking for me," I grumbled, crossing my arms over my chest. "I thought my only options were sitting there all night or heading to town. I was afraid to sit there all night in case something attacked."

"So you got out of the vehicle and made sure something would attack?"

"I'm done talking to you." I held up my hand to cover Galen's face. "It's too much."

"You are definitely a piece of work," Galen muttered, fixing his full attention on Booker. "So whoever it was thought Hadley had something with her in the bus. I can't help but wonder what that was."

"I can't either," Booker agreed. "What did you do before heading out to Wesley's house?"

"I got into a bar fight with Sarah Santiago. I told you about that already."

Booker chuckled. "What did you do before that?"

"I went to Lilac's bar to tell her ... ." I broke off, risking a worried look in Galen's direction before shifting gears. "I wanted some girl time."

"In other words she wanted to tell Lilac that I was so bad in bed she didn't even remember it," Galen teased, his eyes lighted with mirth. "I'll never live this down."

"And you worked so hard to cultivate your kickass sex rep," Booker drawled. "Now that it's gone, I'm the most eligible bachelor on the island. I can't wait to use that title to my advantage. I might even put it on my business cards."

"I can't wait until you do, too," Galen said. "I could use a break from the notoriety."

The testosterone was firing on all cylinders, and I couldn't help being annoyed. "Can we stop talking about your fiery loins and focus on me?"

"I don't understand what you're asking," Galen deadpanned. "Do you want me to stop talking about my fiery loins or focus on you? I can't do one without the other."

I was mortified. "I hate you," I muttered, covering my face with my hand. "I'll never live this down."

"I have no idea, but it's going to be a lot of fun for me regardless," Galen said. "As for whatever this individual was looking for, I think it must be tied to the lighthouse." He shifted from teasing to serious without missing a beat. "Someone wants something that they believe originated in this lighthouse."

"You think that's why Mark broke in the other night," Booker mused, sitting in the chair across the room and thoughtfully tapping his chin. "You think he was really here to steal something rather than hurt Hadley."

"No, I think he was here to hurt Hadley," Galen said. "You don't bring an ax to a burglary unless you plan on doing some damage."

"Maybe he brought a weapon for protection in case he got caught."

"Then why an ax," Galen argued. "Why not bring a knife? It's easier to wield and hide in your clothing. Plus, he didn't search the house as far as I can tell. He went straight to the bedroom."

"Maybe he thought whatever he was looking for was there."

"Or maybe he knew Hadley would be there and went for her first," Galen said. "Maybe he wanted to kill her and then search for whatever he wanted without risking her waking up and notifying the police."

Booker asked, legitimately curious. "Did you bring anything with you of value when you moved here, Hadley?"

I was so used to Booker and Galen talking to each other I didn't bother to hide my surprise when they finally addressed me. "I thought maybe you forgot I was here."

"That's not possible," Galen said. "Did you bring any family heirlooms or anything valuable when you moved?"

"I don't own any family heirlooms. I brought clothes, shoes and a few photographs of my mother and father. That's it. Everything else is in storage at my father's house in Michigan."

"I don't think it's her that's drawing the attention," Galen said after a beat. "I think it's the lighthouse. Someone must believe that May had something of value stowed here."

"But what?" Booker prodded. "May had some antiques and jewelry, but most people would recognize it, so stealing it would be a waste of time. No one would allow them to fence it without calling you."

"What about the books?" Galen suggested, lifting his eyes to the ceiling. "Maybe there's something of importance in the books."

"Why don't we just ask May?" I suggested. "She seems to pop in whenever the mood strikes. Wouldn't she know?"

"That's a good question." Galen cleared his throat. "May, are you here?"

Everyone waited, expectant. Nothing happened.

Booker tried. "May, if you're here, we really need to talk to you." Again, nothing.

"Do you think she's playing coy?" I couldn't help being suspicious. "Maybe she's trying to avoid answering questions. Wesley told me some really odd things when we were together this afternoon."

Galen's eyes sparked with interest. "Like what?"

"He told me that they loved each other, but couldn't live together. They spent one day a week after their divorce pretending they were married." I lowered my voice to make sure only Galen and Booker could hear me. "I think they spent that entire day having sex."

Instead of being appalled – or even surprised – Booker and Galen dissolved into twin fits of laughter.

"It's not funny." I made a petulant face. "I'm scarred for life knowing that."

"I think you're kind of a prude," Galen countered, pressing the palm of his hand to his forehead and grinning. "I think we're going to have to fix that."

"Is this more of that 'I'll remember when I have sex with you' crap? If so, I'm not convinced I'm going to have sex with you."

Galen moved his hand to my shoulder and patted. "You'll get used to the idea. Trust me."

"Oh, so cute." Booker made a disgusted sound in the back of his throat. "Do you need me here for the verbal foreplay or can I go?"

"You can go for now," Galen replied. "I'll need you back here to hang out tomorrow."

Now it was Booker's turn to balk. "You want me to babysit?"

"I don't need a babysitter," I argued.

"Yes, you do," Booker and Galen said, locking gazes like angry bulls would lock horns.

"You definitely need a babysitter," Booker said. "I just don't have time to be your babysitter. I have a job tomorrow."

"Postpone it," Galen instructed. "Hadley's safety is more important."

"I can take care of myself," I said.

"Of course you can." Galen's hand was placating as he continued patting my shoulder. His tone, however, was dismissive. "Booker, we can't leave her here alone. It's late and she'll need help going through all the books and stuff on the third floor tomorrow."

"Why can't you help her?" Booker challenged. "That will give you a chance to enjoy all of the verbal foreplay you can possibly shake a stick at." His smirk was impish. "Do you see what I did there? I helped you with the foreplay."

"We don't need help with the foreplay."

I couldn't decide if that was a good or bad thing. "I don't need a babysitter," I repeated.

"You can't stay alone," Galen shot back. "Someone has tried to go after you twice now ... and that's just that we know of. There might've been other times you were watched or stalked that we're unaware of."

"I think you're being a bit overbearing," I argued.

"Get used to that." Galen kept his eyes on Booker. "She cannot be alone tomorrow."

"Then we'll have to find a way to cover shifts." Booker refused to back down. "I really have a job that I can't flake out on."

Galen pursed his lips, his mind busy as he debated pushing Booker further. Finally he must have realized that it was a lost cause. "Fine. I'll call Lilac in the morning to see if she can stop by. If she's busy, I'm sure Aurora can make a cameo."

That sounded absolutely terrible. "Will she be naked?"

"Only if you're lucky." Booker winked as he stood. "I'll see if I can carve some time out in the afternoon, but I can't make any promises."

"You can only do what you can do." Galen said the words with an easy tone, but his expression reflected something else. "I'll figure a way to keep her covered myself if I have to. Don't put yourself out or anything."

"Hey! I've done nothing but put out since she landed on this island."

I wrinkled my nose. "That makes me look as bad as when I thought I couldn't remember having sex with this one." I jerked my thumb in Galen's direction. "I'm really sick of looking like a sex maniac."

"That's the only reason we like you so much," Booker teased. "As for tomorrow ... I said I would do my best, Galen. I meant it."

"Fine." Galen blew out a sigh. "I'll figure it out myself. I don't need you to do my job."

## 2 5
## TWENTY-FIVE

"**W**hat are you doing?"

I expected Galen to leave, perhaps tease me a bit more about the misunderstanding before admonishing me to keep the door locked overnight. Instead he locked the door once Booker left and gestured toward the stairs.

"It's time for sleep," Galen said. "It's been a long day."

"I agree. It's just … what are you doing?"

Galen smiled, perhaps sensing my discomfort. "I'm going to bed."

"Upstairs?"

"That's the plan."

"There's only one bed upstairs."

"Yes, and I've slept in it twice now." Galen climbed two steps. "You really do move fast. You're a forward woman. I like that about you."

He was messing with me. There could be no other explanation. "I didn't invite you to sleep in the same bed with me either time."

"How would you know? You were out of it both times."

"Yes, but I know myself."

"And yet you were extremely upset this morning because you thought you'd slept with me, which I'm guessing goes against that prudish streak I'm becoming so fond of," Galen pointed out.

"Yes, but … ." Crap!

"Do you want to know what I think?" Galen's stance was haughty, his expression smug. "I think you assumed we'd had sex because you want to have sex with me."

"That is ridiculous!" Well, it is. I don't find him attractive in the least.

"I don't think so." Galen climbed a bit higher, his eyes never leaving mine even as he hit a bend in the circular staircase. "I think you believed it because you wanted it to happen. Quite frankly, I'm flattered. We can't discuss that until I'm sure you're safe, though. Mixing business with pleasure is a bad idea."

I found myself trailing him for lack of anything better to do. "And yet you seem to think you're sleeping in my bed."

"I am. I'm too tall for that couch."

"It was good enough for Booker."

"Booker is a … unique … individual."

The way he phrased it was odd. "What is he?"

"What do you mean?"

"You're a wolf shifter. Everyone here is some sort of paranormal creature. What is Booker?"

"You'll have to ask him that." Galen disappeared from view when he hit the second floor. By the time I caught up with him he was already shoeless and shirtless.

"Don't you dare get naked," I hissed, extending a finger. "I draw the line at you getting naked."

"I just told you that I don't mix business with pleasure." Galen dropped his shorts but left his boxers – which featured colorful margaritas – in place. "You're going to have to stop begging. I find you adorable and sexy, but I can't focus on that until we solve the case."

His sense of humor was grating on a level I didn't know existed. "I am not begging."

"If that's your story." Galen lifted the covers and slid underneath. "Can you kill the lights? I really need a good night's sleep."

I was flabbergasted and briefly wondered if he would keep up the charade if I melted down. In the end, I was too keyed up to sleep alone and exhaustion stalked me to the point where I thought I legitimately might fall down ... and soon.

"Fine." I blew out a sigh and killed the lights, grabbing a T-shirt from the open dresser drawer and changing my clothes in the dark to make sure he couldn't see anything. Sure, he'd already seen more than enough, but I had no intention of adding to the madness.

Galen lifted the covers for me when I approached the bed and I rolled in next to him, making sure to keep a bit of distance between us.

"Goodnight." Galen surprised me when he pressed a kiss to my cheek.

"Knock that off!" I smacked his shoulder. "Stay on your side of the bed. I'm not kidding."

"Okay."

"And I don't beg." I turned my back to him. "I never beg."

"That's too bad." Galen sounded as if he was about to lose the battle for consciousness. "Just for the record, when I dream about you tonight, you're totally going to beg."

"Stop it," I ordered. "I mean it!"

"Shh. I'm trying to sleep. Must you be so unprofessional? This is a job, not playtime."

Galen was clearly enjoying himself, which only served to further infuriate me. "I'm starting to really dislike you."

"Well, at least I'll be guaranteed the knowledge that you won't forget me when we actually get to engage in some real playtime."

"You're infuriating."

"Shh. It's quiet time."

With nothing better to do than focus on my anger I dropped off within five minutes.

**I WOKE TO A WARM** body draped over mine from behind. It took me a moment to gather my thoughts, and when I realized someone was exhaling against my ear I was overwhelmed with the urge to start some vigorous smacking. Of course, Galen was so warm and comfortable that the feeling was only fleeting.

"This is un-freaking believable," I muttered, with a frustrated groan.

Galen stirred, although he didn't move to pull away. "Shh. It's not time to get up yet."

I flicked my eyes to the window, where the sun filtered through the blinds. I saw the waves rolling toward the beach. It was a beautiful setting, calm and relaxing. Of course, the fact that I was in bed with a man who could shift into a wolf – one who thought an awful lot about himself – was utterly frustrating and ruined the moment.

"You're drooling on my cheek."

Galen didn't shift his weight away from me. "That's a compliment. You're so cute, with your bedhead and red cheeks, I can't help but drool."

"Oh, geez." I elbowed him in the stomach. He was expecting the move, so he managed to evade most of the blow. I didn't miss the way his body shook with laughter. "You're so full of yourself."

"I can't help it." Galen sobered as he rolled to his back and ran a hand through his dark hair. "You're so easy to tease that I can't seem to stop myself."

I shifted to face him, taking a moment to tame the wild mass of hair that had clumped together over the course of the night. He, of course, looked ridiculously fresh and handsome. The morning stubble only served to enhance his features. It was so unfair.

"You should have some sympathy for me after what I've been through."

"I do. That's why I enjoy the teasing. You need to lighten up."

"Believe it or not, before I came here and discovered a grandfather I never knew, tripped over a body on the beach, saw a naked woman swimming for ... who knows what reason, got attacked by a wolf and almost got taken out with an ax, I was a pretty easygoing person."

Galen pursed his lips, considering. "Fair point," he said after a beat. "You're basically saying once this is solved you'll be easy to deal with, right?"

"Absolutely. I'll be easy. Wait ... that came out wrong."

Galen barked out a laugh. "Don't worry about it." He stretched his arms before folding them behind his head. The new position served to make him look buffer than before, which should've been against the law. "We need to talk about what you're going to do with your day."

"I've decided to hide in bed all day," I said. "I figure if no one sees me there won't be an attempt on my life for an entire twenty-four hours."

"That's a reasonable assumption."

"So that's what I'll do."

"No." Galen was so sure of himself I wanted to punch him all over again. "I need you to go through everything on the third floor to see if May hid anything of note up there."

That didn't sound terrible, but I was in no mood to do what Galen wanted, given his actions over the past nine hours. "Why should I do that?"

"Because I told you to."

"Try again."

"Because I asked you to?" Galen looked hopeful. He was cute enough I almost gave in. Almost.

"Try again."

"Because I'm willing to let go of the fact that you erroneously thought I would have sex with an unconscious woman?"

I extended my finger in his direction. "Sold."

Galen chuckled. "You're very funny, especially when you're crabby before your morning dose of caffeine. I'm going to try to get someone over here to work with you because I'm nervous about leaving you alone. But for the start of the day you need to be careful and lock all your doors."

"I'd planned to do that."

"Good."

We lapsed into amiable silence for a moment, something niggling at the back of my brain and forcing me to ask a question that I'd managed to bury for most of the night. "How well do you know Wesley Durham?"

"Well enough to know that he's pretty straight forward," Galen replied. "He's a cantankerous guy who says what's on his mind. I wouldn't want to spend an extended amount of time with him because he's kind of bossy, but I would never worry about him stabbing me in the back."

That was kind of what I was getting at, yet … . "Sarah Santiago mentioned that she thought her brother was still working for Wesley. She thought it made sense for Wesley to want to lay claim to the lighthouse."

Galen turned on his side and faced me. "Are you asking if I think Wesley is the type to hire someone to murder you?"

"I want to believe he's not, because … because … ."

"Because he's your grandfather and you never got to know your grandmother," Galen finished, his fingers finding a strand of my hair and idly playing with the ends. "I'm torn on this one."

"You're torn because you think he's dangerous?"

"I'm torn because I don't think he'd hurt you," Galen clarified. "When I called him last night he seemed as worried as I was when I realized you should've already been home. He volunteered to go out and look for you."

"That doesn't mean he's innocent," I pointed out. "He could very easily have purposely kept me busy on his property for longer than I wanted, ensuring I had no choice but to drive home after dark. Maybe he even called someone to alert them when I would be on the highway so he or she could intercept me."

"All of that is possible."

I pressed the heel of my hand to my forehead. "I don't know what to think. That makes me feel … guilty."

"Because he's your grandfather?"

I nodded.

"Hadley, the thing is, you're right." Galen adopted a pragmatic tone. "He is your grandfather, and on paper it would seem that maybe you owe him the benefit of the doubt. In truth, you don't owe the man anything.

"He never went out of his way to see you," he continued. "As much as I loved May – and I did love her – I don't think she did enough to be part of your life either. You're so thrown by this life that it's almost painful to watch you at times. What they did wasn't fair to you."

"We talked about that," I admitted. "He said that they tried to see me several times, but my father shut them down."

"Then perhaps they should've tried harder."

"I think it's because my father wasn't magical."

"That's not fair to you," Galen argued. "You're clearly magical. Even if you weren't, you're their granddaughter. They had one child and she had one child. You're all they had left of your mother. I don't think they treated you fairly."

"I think maybe you're just saying that because you want to get naked together." I offered up a rueful smile. "You even said you want to do it when you can claim I remember everything."

"I definitely want to do it," Galen agreed, refusing to show any trace of shame. "I still think they treated you unfairly. We can't go back in time and change that, though, so we can only go forward.

"The thing is, I want to tell you to trust Wesley because I think you need it," he continued. "You're looking for a family tie that you can hold onto for a bit. He could give you that. From what Booker said, he seemed genuinely interested in you."

"You and Booker talk about me behind my back, huh?"

"Booker and I have a unique relationship that is better left unexplained for the next little bit," Galen replied. "As for Wesley, I've never known him to be anything less than honest. He's a fiery guy who has gone after trespassers with a shotgun a time or two, but I've never looked at him and seen a killer."

"But?"

"But we have a killer on this island," Galen said. "Someone is killing older residents. Do you know much about serial killers?"

"I know that they're usually men who hunt in their own ethnic groups."

Galen arched a surprised eyebrow. "How do you know that?"

"*Criminal Minds.* Shemar Moore is all kinds of hot."

Galen's smile slipped into a frown. "I'm way hotter than him."

"You keep telling yourself that."

Galen poked his finger into my stomach to get me to laugh. "I will keep telling myself that," he said. "It's the truth. I constantly tell myself the truth."

"Whatever."

"You're right about serial killers hunting in their own ethnic groups," Galen said, sobering. "We've never really had a normal serial killer on this island – if normal is a word you can use for that – but I've done a decent amount of research.

"Serial killers tend to pick an age that means something to them," he continued. "If some blonde did him wrong in high school, for example, he might go after blonde teenagers to get even."

"Like Ted Bundy going after girls who looked like a girlfriend who dumped him," I offered.

Galen nodded. "Exactly. You know more about this than I expected."

"I watch a lot of television."

"That makes me feel a bit worse, but okay." He forced a smile. "Most serial killers go for younger women. They don't go for older women."

"Maybe you're missing something," I suggested. "Maybe the age isn't what is important."

Galen looked intrigued. "What do you mean?"

"Maybe they have something else in common."

Galen hummed as he ran his finger up and down my arm, the movement so intimate – something I don't think he realized – that it sent chills up my spine. "The only thing I can think of is that they were property owners."

"Isn't everyone who lives on the island a property owner?"

"Yes and no," Galen hedged. "They're all business owners, but property is a different thing altogether on this island. Property generally passes from family to family, like it did from May to you or to Wesley from his father. Property is at a premium here."

That was both interesting and confusing. "But there are so many businesses. Even if it's not residential property, the people here own the businesses, so that's property ownership."

"No, the downtown property is owned by the DDA, which controls leases and placement."

"What is it with this DDA? They sound like megalomaniacs."

Galen's chuckle was warm. "They are simply interested in the economic health of the island. They own the property and structures. The business owners rent the buildings from them."

"So they don't own the property."

"No."

"But May, Bonnie and the other dead woman you mentioned did own their property," I mused, my mind busy. "That seems like an important tie, don't you think?"

"It's definitely worth pursuing." Galen cupped the back of my head and forced my eyes to him, moving his face close and causing my breath to catch in my chest. "Promise me you'll stick close to the lighthouse until I can get someone out here to hang with you this afternoon."

"I can take care of myself."

Galen tightened his grip. "Promise me."

"Okay. I promise."

Galen stared into my eyes for a long time before releasing me and rolling back a bit. "I'm going to go into the office, but I'm hopeful I will be able to work from here this afternoon. I'm still going to see if I can get someone to come hang out with you."

"I'm going to lock myself in the lighthouse and go through everything on the third floor like you asked. And, yes, I promise I'll be good."

"I trust you." Galen's eyes were clear. "That doesn't mean I trust whoever is trying to hurt you. Just ... be really careful. I will call you if I send over someone you don't know."

"I would really rather you didn't do that."

"You'll have to live with it if I have no choice. Now ... come here." Galen wrapped his arm around my waist and tugged me so I was pressed against his chest. I considered fighting the effort, but ultimately rested my cheek against his beating heart and remained still. "We have exactly five minutes before we have to get up."

"And what do you want to do with that time?" I was both excited and terrified of his answer.

"I'm doing it."

I almost melted. "Has anyone ever told you that you have enough charm to build an entire island all your own?"

"No one as cute as you."

"Well ... you do."

"I know." Galen stroked the back of my head, the movement soothing. "Now, let's talk about the fact that you thought I would have sex with you while you were passed out."

"You said you wouldn't bring it up again," I protested.

"I said I would consider not bringing it up again. I've considered it ... and then I discarded the notion. What kind of guy do you take me for?"

"Oh, geez. I'm going to have to choke you to shut you up, aren't I?"

"Who told you I'm into that?"

"Ugh. I knew I should've ignored what you said and stayed in bed all day," I complained. "This day is already starting to suck."

# TWENTY-SIX

"What are you doing here?"

I was beyond annoyed when I found Lilac on the front porch after I'd finished breakfast. She had a bright smile on her face, a pair of short shorts that looked as if they were in danger of falling into a crevice and never returning showing off her toned legs, and a tiny bra top (complete with fringe) that revealed enough cleavage that I momentarily thought I might've stepped into an alternative world that only allowed strippers to inhabit the island.

"I'm happy to see you, too," Lilac said dryly, smirking as she pushed past me. "I don't think I've ever had such a warm welcome in my entire life."

Part of me felt guilty. The other part – the bigger part – was certain I was about to be overwhelmed with agitation. "I'm sorry."

"Are you really?"

"Not even a little," I admitted. "I'm tired. It's been a long two days."

"I heard all about your adventure last night," Lilac said, taking me by surprise when she shut and locked the door, testing the handle a few times before pointing toward the stairs. "Why do you think I'm here?"

I already knew the answer. "Galen."

"Yup."

"He said he would call if he sent anyone over," I argued. "He didn't call. I've had my phone with me all day. I think that's against the rules."

"He said you would say that." Lilac didn't appear bothered by my tone. "He said to tell you to suck it up or he'll explain how he can see in the dark so even though you thought he didn't see you change your clothes last night ... he did."

I tightened my jaw. "He told you that?"

Lilac held her hands palms up and shrugged. "Men are pigs. What can I say?"

"I'm going to kill him."

"That would be a shame given the fact that he's openly flirting with you. Every woman on the island wants to claim him for herself." Lilac headed toward the stairs. "I can't remember the last time he showed this much interest in a woman."

"I suppose you think that makes me lucky," I groused, frowning as I followed Lilac. "What are you doing?"

"It definitely makes you lucky," Lilac confirmed. "You're too tense to realize that right now – and I get that – but it definitely makes you lucky."

"It doesn't make me feel lucky."

"Have you seen him shirtless?"

"Yes."

"Without his pants on?"

"Yes."

"Without his boxers on?"

Lilac was relentless, but I refused to meet her gaze. "Technically ... um ... yes."

"Then you're definitely lucky." Lilac's grin widened. "And you need to give me every detail while we're going through the stuff on the third floor."

"Ugh." I covered my eyes with my hand. Lilac's enthusiasm would prove contagious. I could already sense it. The last thing I wanted was to admit my attraction to Galen and then have it parroted back to me when Galen returned in time for dinner. "I'm guessing you still believe you're incapable of keeping a secret, right?"

"Pretty much," Lilac confirmed, climbing the stairs. "I can promise to try to keep what you say to myself, but I think my record is eight hours if it's a good secret. There's nothing I can do about it."

"You could force yourself to keep a secret."

"What fun is that?"

She had a point, but still .... "Let's just see what we can find on the third floor, shall we? We'll keep the gossip to a minimum."

"Oh, sure," Lilac said dryly. "That sounds like a great way to spend a morning."


**SO WHEN DO** you think you're going to sleep with him?"

Lilac promised to refrain from asking too many questions if I agreed to focus my full attention on searching the shelves and crates. She lasted five minutes before cracking.

"I've already slept with him three times," I pointed out. "Granted, I was extremely out of it for two of those times, but I remember the third very well. He snores ... and drools."

"Honey, I've seen him at the beach," Lilac said. "If snoring and drooling is the worst that you have to put up with, you're coming out way ahead."

I wanted to argue the point, but I'd seen him without a shirt numerous times now and I couldn't find a single thing to bolster a contrary position. Instead I turned my attention to the search. "Do you really think there's something up here that's worth killing me over?"

"I don't know," Lilac replied, sitting on the floor next to one of the crates and sifting through its contents. "I knew May to say hello to her and even hang out at some of the music events on the beach. She was always friendly and fun, but she never struck me as the sort of person who was hiding expensive things."

The statement struck me as odd. "How exactly would one act if they were hiding expensive things?"

"I don't know." Lilac's shoulders hopped. "Perhaps they would carry around a shovel or something. Maybe wear an eye patch. Oh!" She jutted out her finger. "I bet that sort of person would walk with a limp."

"Why a limp?"

"Because half the demented people I've seen in horror movies have limps."

I really couldn't argue with her logic. "I just wish I had an idea of what we were looking for," I said, grabbing a huge book from the bottom of a shelf and flipping it open. I widened my eyes as I read the first page. "What's a *Book of Shadows*?"

Instead of answering right away, Lilac made a face. "Seriously? You're like the worst witch ever. How can you not know what a *Book of Shadows* is?"

"I must've missed that day at witch school."

Lilac snorted. "I know you meant that in a sarcastic way, but I'll bet that your mind just flashed to Hogwarts, didn't it?"

Sadly, she was right. "They didn't have a *Book of Shadows* at Hogwarts."

"They had wands. Real witches don't have wands. Harry Potter was not realistic."

"And yet real witches are somehow realistic," I grumbled, turning a page in the book. "Holy eye of newt! This is a book of spells."

"Of course it's a book of spells." Lilac made an exaggerated face. "What did you think you would find in there?"

"I don't know. I don't know what to do about any of this. In some ways it's been easier to pretend it's not happening. I have plenty of other things to focus on, after all."

"Naked sheriffs?"

"I was going to say a new grandfather I didn't know existed."

"That's a big deal, too," Lilac conceded. "This is all going to settle eventually. Once it does, you'll be able to think about the rest of it.

You'll be able to enjoy the anticipation of seeing Galen naked. You'll be able to dabble with magic and have fun. You'll be able to sit on the beach and have a drink and absorb the fun of a single day instead of fear the next morning."

"Oh, wow, that was almost poetic."

"Thank you." Lilac beamed. "I wanted to be a poet when I was a kid."

"Really? I wanted to be an intergalactic space warrior."

"Princess Leia?"

"You know it."

"Everyone wanted to be her." Lilac shifted her eyes back to the crate. "A lot of this stuff looks interesting in an abstract way, but I have no idea what we're looking for so I don't know if it's really interesting."

"It's all interesting," May announced, popping into view in the middle of the room. She forced a smile when she caught me staring. "Hello, dear."

"Don't 'hello, dear' me," I snapped. "Where have you been? A lot has been going on and we need answers."

"It's not easy to control my movements yet," May complained. "I'm doing the best that I can. If it was easy everyone would do it."

"Oh, whatever." I rolled my eyes.

"You just reminded me of your mother when you did that." May heaved a sigh, a whimsical expression crossing her face. "I really wish I could talk to you about her – that's why I came today, after all – but we have another problem."

"My whole life is problems," I shot back. "What specific problem are you talking about?"

"The big one," May answered. "He's here."

"Who is here?"

"The man who killed me. I remember. I remember everything."

Oh, well, crap.


**"WHAT DO YOU MEAN** he's here?"

I didn't know May very well, but I got the feeling she was something of a drama queen. There was always a chance I misheard her.

"He's here," May hissed, mimicking gripping her hands together. "He'll be at the door in a second."

"Who?" Lilac asked, hopping to her feet and dusting off the seat of her pants. She didn't look particularly worried. "Why are you so worked up, May? It's good to see you, by the way."

Instead of reacting with kindness, May made an exaggerated face and opened her mouth. Whatever she said died on her lips, though, when she blinked out of existence.

"What was that?" I asked, confused.

"I have no idea." Lilac shuffled to the window and looked out. "I don't see anyone. Do you have any idea what she was talking about?"

"I don't even know the woman," I grumbled. "I would love to be able to sit down and have a long conversation with her about a few things."

"I'm sure you would." Lilac knit her eyebrows. "She said that the man who killed her was here, but I don't see a car in the driveway or a shadow in the yard. Maybe she's confused."

"Maybe," I conceded. "Maybe she had dementia before she died and no one noticed. Can ghosts have dementia? You know, carry it over from life to death?"

"I have no idea, but May didn't have dementia before she died," Lilac replied. "I saw her the day before and ... her mind was still as sharp as ever."

I tilted my head to the side as I regarded Lilac. She looked a bit misty as she swiped at her eyes. "You really liked her, didn't you?"

"She was a dear lady," Lilac said. "I know it's hard for you because you never got to know her, and I'm sure you can't help but wonder how things would've been different if she tried to see you when you were a kid, but ... she really was a great lady. I hope you get to know her some now that she's back from the dead."

"Can you please not say it that way?" I asked, my mind wandering to the cemetery. "I picture zombies when you say that, and now that I know how the cemetery works it freaks me out."

"They're mostly harmless," Lilac argued. "They've gotten out once or twice, but we think we have all the gaps plugged now."

"That's ... comforting."

"Yeah." Lilac enthusiastically nodded. "Well, I don't know what May was talking about, but there's clearly no one down there. Maybe she simply got confused and remembered who killed her and the memories jumbled in her mind."

"I guess that's possible." I looked at the shelf. "Maybe she thought it was the past rather than the present."

"Maybe. It will be much better when she has control of when and how long she can pop up," Lilac said. "Then you'll be able to have an actual conversation."

"Yeah, I can't wait for that," I admitted. "I want to ask her why she divorced Wesley Durham and then proceeded to pretend they were married one day a week for several decades. I still can't wrap my head around that one."

"Some people love each other but can't live with each other," Lilac explained. "Wesley and May were like that. They fought like lions and bears some days ... and they did it publicly, not caring who witnessed the fights. I think, if times were different, they would've been able to make the marriage work full time."

I wasn't sure what she was getting at. "Meaning?"

"Meaning that Moonstone Bay is ahead in some respects when it comes to social issues, but it's behind in others," Lilac answered. "Back when Wesley and May got married it was expected that the man would work and the woman would stay home and raise a family.

"Now, granted, those things have shifted over the years and it's not as prevalent to believe that," she continued. "My understanding is that Wesley was getting it from all sides because May liked to boss people around."

Hmm. That was mildly interesting. "He could've taken the lighthouse from her, right? He could've made a fuss."

"He could have," Lilac agreed. "I don't think that's Wesley's way. Even though he couldn't save the marriage he sent a strong message when he refused to go after the lighthouse. A lot of people teased him about that over the years – the lighthouse is one of the biggest draws on the island, after all – but Wesley held firm. The lighthouse belonged to May."

"He seems pretty straightforward," I said. "Still, what Sarah said has me a bit …unsettled."

"The part about Wesley hiring her brother to kill you because he wants the lighthouse?"

I nodded.

"The thing is, I'll wager that May would've given Wesley the lighthouse if he wanted it," Lilac argued. "Wesley knew she was sick. He'd taken to coming into town to spend more time with her. If he wanted the lighthouse, all he had to do was ask. I think May would've given it to him."

"And he didn't ask?"

"That's not Wesley's way," Lilac replied. "Wesley would want you to have the lighthouse."

I really wanted to believe that, but I couldn't shake the niggling worry in the back of my brain. "I just wish this was over. I have so much going on and people I would like to get to know better. But I can't because we're spending an entire day searching for something we can't identify."

I turned my frustration to the shelf. "There're tons of magic stuff in here, but I haven't found anything else of interest," I said. "Could someone have wanted to kill her over the magic?"

"Doubtful." Lilac's attention drifted toward the window. "The magic stuff is readily available at the bookstore and library. There's no reason to kill for it."

"Right." That made sense. "So what would someone want from this lighthouse?"

"Whatever it is, it has to be small enough that someone believes you're carrying it around with you," Lilac noted. "They had to be watching you when you visited Wesley yesterday. You clearly didn't have a box or anything with you. I think that means whatever it is fits in your pocket."

"That's some good reasoning." I extended a finger and looked to the file cabinet in the corner of the room. "Maybe it's a document or something."

"That's a good idea." Lilac said the words, but never moved from her spot next to the window.

"What are you looking at?"

"I'm not sure. I thought … I thought I saw something."

For some reason, the simple admission caused dread to pool in the pit of my stomach. I abandoned my trip to the file cabinet and joined Lilac by the window. "What did you see?"

Lilac pointed at the corner of the front porch. From our angle, we could see far and wide when it came to the yard. We faced inland, toward the main road. We couldn't see close to the house. The design of the lighthouse allowed us to see only bits and pieces of the ground near the front door.

"What am I looking at?" I squinted and stared. "I don't see anything."

"Right there." Lilac gripped the back of my neck and directed my attention to the spot at the corner of the front porch. "Don't you see that shadow?"

I focused on the spot she indicated, widening my eyes when I caught sight of a hint of movement. She was right. Someone was out there. "Who … ?" I didn't get a chance to finish the question, because the shadow shifted to the open expanse of yard and our visitor was revealed. "Booker?"

Lilac visibly relaxed even as my heart clenched. "Galen must have sent him."

"Why would Galen send him?" I challenged, my suspicion getting the better of me. "He sent you. I don't need two babysitters."

"I don't know." Lilac either didn't pick up on my tone or outright discarded it. "We can ask him."

I grabbed her wrist before she could head toward the stairs. "I have a better idea."

"You do?"

I nodded. "You're going to stay up here and call Galen. I'm going down there to see what Booker wants."

Lilac's expression was unreadable. "It's Booker. He's here because he wants to help."

I desperately wanted to believe that. I liked him, after all, but he spent much of the previous night explaining why he couldn't be the one to serve as babysitter. Now he suddenly pops up?

"He probably is here to help," I conceded, hope washing over me. "I want you to call Galen and check, though."

"Why not stay up here while I do that?"

"Because if he is up to something I don't think we should be together," I replied. "I don't want Booker to know you're here until we have confirmation Galen sent him."

"You don't have to worry about Booker," Lilac argued. "He's a good guy."

"I'm sure he is." I headed toward the stairs. "Call Galen. Make sure he sent Booker. I'll distract Booker for a few minutes, and … I'm sure it will be all right."

"Booker isn't our enemy." Lilac appeared to be irritated, but she dug in her purse for her phone. "I guarantee Galen sent him."

"I certainly hope so."

I managed to remain calm for the duration of the descent to the main floor. Even though the palms of my hands were sweaty, I reined in my fear as I headed toward the front door. I figured I'd greet Booker before he had a chance to come up with a story – not that I thought he would be coming up with a story, mind you, but it was smart to go on the offensive all the same. I simply wanted to make sure.

I heard the light rapping of knuckles against the back door instead. It wasn't a loud knock, but it forced me to jerk my head in that direction as my heart skipped a beat. "What the … ?"

I changed course and headed for the back door. Lilac would've confirmed Booker's intentions by this time. If he wasn't supposed to be here, she would've screamed bloody murder to get my attention.

At least I hoped that was true.

I pasted a fake smile on my face, took a deep breath and opened the door. I expected to find Booker standing there with a harried look on his face. Instead I found someone else waiting on the other side of the threshold – someone I didn't even remotely expect.

"What are you doing here?"

# 27

## TWENTY-SEVEN

**N**ed Baxter raised his eyebrows at my rather rude opening.
"Good morning, dear."

His greeting was amiable, yet I didn't know what to make of it. "What are you doing here?" I repeated, casting a worried glance over my shoulder in hope of seeing Lilac at the bottom of the stairs. The main floor remained empty, though.

"I came to see you."

"Why?"

"So we could talk."

"About what?"

"The lighthouse, of course." Ned's smile never wavered, but there was something about his demeanor that set my teeth on edge. "I wanted to see if you'd thought better about my generous offer to buy the property."

"Why would I do that?"

"I heard you had a spot of trouble last night."

Of course he did. Moonstone Bay was nothing if not overflowing with gossip. "Oh, well, it was a difficult night, but everything turned out okay."

"That wasn't really an answer to my question."

His tone grated. "I told you before that I'm not considering selling the lighthouse at this time. What happened last night didn't change that."

"Really?"

I shook my head. "Sorry."

"That is most disappointing." Ned made a clucking sound in the back of his throat as he turned to survey the vast expanse of ocean. "I had hoped you would see reason." When he turned back to face me, his expression reflected a mixture of sadness and resignation. "Ah, well. I guess you've made up your mind."

"I have," I confirmed. "I want to make this work."

"Well then ... ." Ned extended his hand. "No harm done, right?"

I forced a smile even though his presence irritated me. "Right." I couldn't focus on him. I needed to find out what Booker was doing. I mean ... why was he hanging around the front of the lighthouse without knocking or calling attention to himself to alert us to his presence?

Ned's hand wrapped around mine, holding it tight for what seemed an abnormally long time. He leaned forward, his eyes keen, and lifted his free hand toward my shoulder. I thought he was going to pat me or something, offer a friendly goodbye and then be on his way. Instead I felt something pierce my skin, like a bee stinging my neck and agitating the tender flesh there.

I jerked my hand away from Ned and slapped it to my neck, confused. "What was that?"

"Don't worry about it," Ned said, his eyes shifting to the side of the lighthouse. "There's nothing to worry about."

Even though he appeared calm, I couldn't stop the panic from rising as I realized my fingers were going numb. "What did you do to me?" I stumbled against the doorframe as I struggled to remain upright. "What the ... ?" My tongue felt thick as my mind clouded with muffled thoughts.

Ned didn't bother keeping his attention on me, instead flicking his eyes to the side of the lighthouse as a shadow approached. "There you are. I was just looking for you."

Booker's expression was quizzical as he glanced between us. "You were looking for me?"

Even though my mind wasn't working at full capacity, I couldn't stop myself from grinding my teeth as realization dawned. They were working together. Ned and Booker were a team. That was the only thing that made sense.

"I was," Ned confirmed. "I figured you were close."

"And why is that?" Booker briefly darted a look in my direction and his eyebrows flew up his forehead. "Hadley, why are you standing like that?"

I opened my mouth to answer, but all that came out was gibberish as I leaned against the doorframe to keep my balance. My head felt as if it was floating, somehow detached from my body.

"What in the hell!" Booker took a step toward me, anger splashing across his face. "Why haven't you called for help, Ned? There's clearly something wrong with her."

"Why would I call for help?" Ned asked dryly. "I did this."

Booker's eyes flashed as he extended his fingers – and for a moment I was certain I saw something akin to claws extending from his fingernails – but he didn't get a chance to complete his turn before Ned slammed a knife into his back.

Booker growled and scrambled, doing his best to remain on his feet. "You son of a bitch," he hissed. "It was you all along."

"The fact that you're just figuring that out – and after I stabbed you, for crying out loud – speaks to your intellect in an unflattering way." Ned was freakily bland. "Of course, you've never been one of the great thinkers of your time, have you, Booker?"

Booker made a sound like a wounded animal as he swiped at Ned. The attorney easily sidestepped the attack and used his foot to push Booker off the deck. Even as I struggled to keep my eyes open – and it truly was a losing battle – I couldn't help but feel guilty for suspecting Booker.

"Come along, dear." Ned grabbed the back of my shirt and dragged me down the steps, pointing me in the direction of the water. "I have a special day planned for you. I think you're really going to enjoy it."

I cast a desperate look at Booker and found him prone on the ground, his chest heaving to pull oxygen into his lungs.

I wanted to apologize, call out and tell him I was sorry for doubting him. I couldn't form the words. I couldn't make my mouth work, and my brain was threatening to implode.

The last thing I saw before the darkness completely claimed me was the fear in Booker's eyes. He worried he would die on the back lawn, alone and forgotten. Lilac would find him. I had no doubt about that. Hopefully she would get help and save him. He still had a bit of time.

Me? I was pretty sure I was out of time.

**"WELCOME BACK."**

I clawed my way out of unconsciousness, whimpering when I opened my eyes and the bright sunshine caused a flash of pain to cascade through me. I felt hungover, as if I drank an entire fifth by myself and lived to tell the tale. I wanted to fight the condition, curl up and go back to sleep until the pounding headache receded. I wasn't given that option.

"I'm talking to you!" Ned barked, throwing a cup of water in my face. "Don't be rude."

I sputtered as I struggled to a sitting position, murdering my kidnapper with a harsh glare as I gripped the side of the boat. I hadn't realized we were on the ocean, only a small strip of land in sight, until the rocking motion threatened to throw my stomach into rebellion.

"What's going on?" I gritted out, rubbing my hand over my forehead. "Is this a dream?"

"Oh, my dear, I hope you have better dreams than this." Ned remained calm as he leaned back in his seat and pinned me with a dark look. "Well, you've made a real mess of things, haven't you?"

That was rich coming from him. "I'm pretty sure I'm not the one who has been going around killing old women."

Ned narrowed his eyes. "What do you mean?"

It didn't occur to me until exactly that moment that Ned had no idea Galen was onto him. Or, well, on to his plan. I figured I could play with that information, use it to my advantage. "The women you've been killing," I supplied, my voice raspy. I was desperate for a drink of water, but uncomfortable asking Ned for it given his propensity to poison people. "You've been poisoning them in the hopes of getting their property, although I have no idea how you thought that would work over the long haul."

"Who told you that?"

I saw no reason to lie. "Galen. He's tied all three deaths together."

"I haven't heard anything about that."

"I don't think murder discussions are the same as random gossip, even on an island as weird as Moonstone Bay."

"I see." Ned's eyes drifted to the water, his fingers lightly tracing over his chin as he debated something. "How long has he known?"

I shrugged. "He didn't say. I believe he had his suspicions after May. He was certain after Bonnie. You should've arranged for her to wash up in a different spot."

"She wasn't supposed to wash up at all," Ned barked, his frustration evident. "I drove miles away from the island. I looked at the tide maps before heading out. She was supposed to disappear, not die."

Huh. That was interesting. "Why?"

"Because I was worried that Galen – even though he's terminally stupid most days – might eventually tie things together," Ned replied. "I won't have the funds to buy Bonnie's property for a bit. I figured they would eventually declare her dead and put her property up for auction. But that could take months. Hell, it could take years. It would give me the time I needed."

I felt sick to my stomach. "And all of this is because you wanted property?"

"You make it sound so simple," Ned sneered. "It's not that simple. I've been trying to buy property on this island for twenty years. No one ever sells. The property always passes on to some relative ... even ones I've never considered, like you."

I pursed my lips. "Bummer for you, huh?"

"Yes, indeed."

"I still don't understand why the property is so important to you," I prodded. "You live on the island. You run a business here. Why do you need to own property? Is it a status symbol or something?"

"I would like to say that it's that easy, but there's a variety of reasons," Ned replied. "Moonstone Bay is unique. I think you've already ascertained that."

"I have."

"Owning property here is more than status. The island itself is magical. If you own property, you can apply to become a member of the DDA. With that position comes real power."

"What in the heck is up with this DDA?" I asked, dumbfounded. "I've heard nothing but terrifying things about the group since I landed."

"That's because they're powerful and they want to operate in a way that instills fear. I can respect that."

"So you decided to kill three helpless little old ladies because you wanted a spot on the DDA? That's just ... so much worse than I was expecting."

Ned snorted, disdainful. "May was hardly helpless."

"I guess that's why you waited until she was sick to put your plan into action, huh?" I wanted to yank out his hair, slam my fist in his face and shove his head below the surface of the water until he stopped kicking. I didn't have the strength. My body was slowly recovering, but I was nowhere near full strength. "She knew. She knew it was you who wanted her dead."

"No, she didn't."

My mind flitted to May's panicked reaction on the third floor. "She knew. I don't think she remembered that she knew, but she warned us right before you knocked. She told us the man who killed her was at the lighthouse."

"She told you?" Ned arched a dubious eyebrow. "She's dead."

"That doesn't mean her spirit isn't around," I argued. "She's been popping in for visits."

"I guess I should've expected that," Ned said, shaking his head. "She was too stubborn to just float into an afterlife."

"She'll tell Galen what you did to her."

"Yes, but Galen can't use a ghost's words as testimony," Ned pointed out. "Even on Moonstone Bay the words of the dead can't be used as evidence."

That was disappointing. It was hardly my only weapon, though. "You stabbed Booker. Galen will be out looking for you. He'll make you pay for what you've done."

"Booker will be dead before anyone gets to him," Ned said. "Galen may very well return to the lighthouse – you guys have gotten extremely close in a short amount of time – but Booker won't survive until the end of Galen's shift.

"In fact, the more that I think about it, the happier I am that it happened this way," he continued. "Your disappearance will be talked about for weeks to come. People will tie Booker's death to it, but they won't quite know how he played into the scenario. Eventually it will become an urban legend of sorts, and when I buy the lighthouse and open it to tourists they will ask about the story and wonder if it's haunted."

He seemed awfully sure of himself. "How do you figure that Booker's death will be tied to my disappearance in a way that benefits you?"

"Because you're gone and he's dead. What other suspects does Galen have?"

"I don't know about suspects, but he has another witness."

"I already told you that May doesn't count."

"She might not be able to testify, but she can tell Galen what she saw," I said. "She was on the third floor when you arrived. She told us about you." That was a bit of an overstatement, but Ned didn't need to know that. "She can tell Galen what you did. He might not be able to use the information in court, but that won't stop him from going after you."

Ned shifted on his seat. The boat wasn't large – a mid-sized speed-boat – but it was expensive. It was clear that Ned Baxter was a man of means. Even though I wasn't sure how much credence he'd give my threat, for the first time since I woke in the middle of the ocean Ned looked a bit worried.

"He won't be able to prove it."

"What if there's another witness? A live witness, mind you."

Ned stilled, his hands gripping the arms of his chair. "And who would that be?"

"The person who was upstairs with me at the time of your visit." I let my tone cross into haughty territory. "I wasn't the only one on the third floor when May arrived."

"Booker is dead."

"I'm not talking about Booker."

Ned was grim as he leaned forward, the thin veneer of pleasantness he managed to maintain at the start of the conversation completely eroding. "And who was that?"

"Oh, I can't tell you that." I was in an untenable position, but that didn't stop me from taunting my would-be killer. "That's not playing fair, is it?"

"You bitch!" Ned lashed out, striking me across the face. I wanted to be strong and pretend the blow didn't hurt, but I couldn't stop myself from crying out. "I will rip your heart out!"

I cradled my cheek as I shrank back, pressing my back to the side of the boat as I glared at him. "That won't stop you from going to jail for the rest of your life. Heck, I wouldn't be surprised if Galen decided to kill you rather than arrest you."

"Galen is an idiot!"

"He stopped you last night, didn't he?" I played a hunch. I had no idea if Ned was a wolf shifter, but it seemed to make sense. "How did you know I went out to Wesley's place? Did you follow me?"

"I've been watching you for days," Ned seethed. "I was hoping you would be reasonable and sell me the lighthouse, but you decided to be an idiot instead."

"That's a woman's prerogative, isn't it?"

Ned ignored my attempt at sarcasm. "I hoped you would frighten easily, but that wasn't really an option since Galen decided to attach himself to you. I've never seen him show so much attention to a woman he barely knows. He became your shadow almost from the moment you met."

"That's probably because you sent a drunk to go after me with an ax."

"I didn't send Mark to kill you," Ned clarified. "I sent him to frighten you. He was only supposed to mess up the bedroom, but apparently he took it a step too far. That's not on me."

"The fact that you can say that with a straight face is dumbfounding," I muttered, shaking my head. "What would you have done if he'd killed me?"

"Cut his pay in half and then wait to see what happened next."

"And what do you think would've happened?"

"I think the lighthouse would've gone up for auction, and I would've made sure I was the highest bidder."

Ned's ego was apparently so big it needed its own ZIP code. "Except the lighthouse wouldn't have gone up for auction. My father is a lawyer. I filed a new will before I even flew out of Detroit. I already have an heir in place."

Ned stilled. "Excuse me?"

"My father. He would inherit."

"You didn't mention that," Ned raged. "Why would you do something like that?"

"Because I'm not an idiot and my father is an attorney," I replied, not missing a beat. "Even without a will, my father would inherit. I wanted to make sure that everything was legal and he wouldn't have to jump through a lot of hoops if something happened. If there's one thing my father knows, it's the law."

"But … ." Ned was flabbergasted. "He hasn't even visited this island."

"That doesn't mean he's not my heir."

"You stupid … son of a … !" Ned's face turned red as he grabbed the front of my shirt and shook me. "Are you trying to ruin my life?"

I fought to control my breathing as he bobbed in front of my face. "That's only a bonus as far as I'm concerned."

"I am going to kill you!"

## 28

# TWENTY-EIGHT

I instinctively lurched to the side to avoid Ned's outstretched hands, lashing out with my foot and catching him at the knee. He howled, doubling over in pain, and I did the only thing I could think to do.

It took all of my strength to struggle to my knees and lean over the side of the boat. The shore was a long way off – it seemed miles – but I had no other choice. If I remained in the boat Ned would surely kill me. If I jumped into the water I'd have a chance, however minimal.

My arms and legs didn't want to move as fast as I hoped, so I ended up flopping over the side of the boat rather than jumping. I hit the water face first. Initially I sank, the water threatening to devour me, but my reflexes kicked in and I managed to break the surface with a few kicks, and gulp in a huge mouthful of oxygen before panic overtook me.

"What do you think you're doing?" Ned asked, as if annoyed by a small child.

I didn't bother glancing in his direction, instead stroking away from the boat and pointing myself toward Moonstone Bay. I had no idea how to gauge distance – especially at sea – but I figured it would take me a long time to swim back to shore.

"Do you really think you can swim away from me?" Ned was incredulous. "It's two miles back to the island."

Two miles? That was actually better than I'd initially thought. "I guess it will take me a little bit then, huh?" I kept my eyes focused on the small strip of land so I had something to work toward.

"Get in the boat."

"No."

"Get back in the boat."

"No way."

"Get back in the boat or I'll kill you," Ned threatened.

"I hate to break it to you, but that threat has absolutely zero clout with me," I shot back. "You're going to kill me if I get on the boat. At least this way I have a chance at escape."

"How do you figure that?"

Was that a trick question? "I'm going to swim to shore."

"Do you really think I'm going to let you do that?"

Ned's voice got harder to hear with every stroke. I was determined to put distance between us, and the water lapping around my ears served to drown his voice. "I don't see as you have much choice."

"I could kill you."

"You have a knife and would have to jump in the water to kill me."

"Do you think I won't do that?"

"Probably not, because that would mean a lack of control for you."

Ned was quiet for a long moment. "I have more than the knife."

His voice was chilling, but I refused to glance over my shoulder and confirm the evil expression I was certain I'd find on his face. "I don't care."

"I have something else below deck."

"Good for you."

"It's a gun."

My heart skipped a beat, but I remained facing toward the island. "How great for you."

"I will get it, Hadley."

"I guess you have to do what you have to do."

"Son of a … !" The waves drowned out the rest of his words. I heard him stomping on the boat deck. "I'm going to get the gun. You're making this harder on yourself than you have to."

"Whatever." I increased my speed when I was certain Ned had gone below deck. I couldn't outrun a gun, but perhaps I could get far enough away while he searched for his weapon that he would choose to flee rather than pursue. It was probably a vain hope, but it was all I had.

I counted in my head as I stroked, rationalizing that each number brought me closer to shore even though the island still seemed so small. I thought I caught a hint of movement in the water, but refused to divert my gaze from the island. It was a distraction, and given my fuzzy head the last thing I needed was a distraction.

The physical exertion and cool water helped with the brain mush. I was even thirstier than before, but all I had around me was saltwater.

I saw the flash of movement a second time and gritted my teeth. This time I was certain something was in the water with me. The first thing that popped into my head was a shark. I knew shark shifters weren't a thing on the island, so that meant it was probably a real shark and I was about to become lunch.

I pressed my eyes shut, forcing myself to focus on steady stroking. I'd lost track of Ned and didn't hear anything from the boat – which I'd managed to leave behind thanks to my determination – but that didn't mean he wouldn't pursue me.

I jolted when something surfaced in the water next to me, instinctively lashing out. My fingers brushed against something slimy – something I was certain was a fin of some sort – but my hand ultimately contacted skin when it landed.

"What the … ?"

I thought my heart would burst out of my chest when I opened my eyes and found Aurora keeping pace with me.

"Good morning." Aurora's smile was quick and bright. "Nice day for a swim, huh?"

"Yeah," I choked out, my eyes going wide as I scanned the water and realized the fin I felt belonged to Aurora. Her entire bottom half, in fact, was a fin. "You're a mermaid!"

"I'm a siren," Aurora corrected, moving a bit closer. "Do you know how far out you are?"

"I have no idea. What's a siren?"

"It's basically a mermaid, but I don't like that term. It's far too … Disney. Sirens are stronger than mermaids. They're cooler, too."

"But you have a fin."

"I do," Aurora confirmed, her auburn-highlighted hair streaming in the water as she moved alongside me. "We have a problem. You realize that, right?"

"You mean other than the fact that you have a fin?"

Aurora leaned in closer and stared into my eyes. "Have you been drugged?"

"He stuck me with something. I can't make my head work. I'm not even sure how I'm managing to swim."

"Ned?"

"How did you know?"

"Galen sent me looking for you when he realized what happened at the lighthouse," Aurora replied. "He's not in a good mood. I would hate to be Ned when he gets his hands on him."

"How did Galen know to look for me in the water?"

"Booker told him that Ned had a boat and was leading you toward water last time he saw you."

Hope clawed through me. "Is Booker alive?"

"He's injured, but he's alive," Aurora replied. "Don't worry about that." She risked a glance over her shoulder when she heard a boat engine roar, as if coming to life, and then immediately die. "I know you're confused and you don't know what to make of this, but we don't have much time.

"I would like to let you get to a place of acceptance on your own but I honestly don't think that's possible," she continued. "I need you to trust me."

"All I know about you is that you like to swim naked," I admitted, my eyes going to her fin again. "I guess that makes sense."

"There's no sense wearing a bathing suit, because I would rip it when shifting," Aurora explained. "We can talk about that later. We need to deal with the here and now."

The boat engine roared again but didn't catch.

"How do you suggest we do that?" Now that Aurora had found me and I had more hope of escaping this mess than when I hit the water, the thought of dying in the ocean, of Ned winning, was completely unpalatable. "I can't swim any faster. I can barely swim this fast."

"I know, and you're fading." Aurora's expression was kind. "I need you to hold onto me, wrap your arms around my neck and hold on. I can get us back to shore faster by myself."

"You can?"

"Of course. I'm a siren. I can do anything."

She said it in such a matter-of-fact manner that I could do nothing but nod. "Okay. I ... won't I choke you?"

"It will be fine. Just hold on."

I did as instructed, pushing the odd feeling of Aurora's fin against my thighs out of my mind as I squeezed my eyes shut. "Will we make it?"

"We should. No more talking, though."

As if on cue, the boat's engine roared to life and remained running. Ned was mobile again, which meant he was heading in this direction.

"Let's go!"


THE SWIM BACK to the island was quick. I had no idea a sea creature could move as fast as Aurora, but she was sleek and quick as she glided through the water. Before I even realized what was happening I found my toes touching sand, and I fell forward as I dropped to my knees.

The waves crashed into me, driving me forward, and I discovered I couldn't readily open my eyes because the seawater caused them to burn. I heard footsteps rushing toward me in the water but I couldn't make myself look, terror that Ned overtook us threatening to overwhelm me.

Then I felt strong hands on my arms and I had no choice. I had to look. I wrenched open my eyes, determined to find the magic that evaded me when my mind collapsed thanks to the drugs, and gasped when Galen's handsome face swam into view. "You found me."

"Aurora found you," Galen gritted out, grabbing me around the waist and pulling me to my feet. "Are you okay?"

"I'm thirsty."

"Other than that?"

"I'm really thirsty."

Galen flicked a worried look to Aurora. "She seems out of it. What happened?"

"I found her with Ned, just like you figured," Aurora explained. "He was ranting and raving about wanting property so he could join the DDA. What a putz."

"What else?"

"He drugged her." Aurora wrung out her hair, paying no heed to the fact that she was naked and standing in front of the sheriff. "She's a bit spacey. I think some water will do her good."

"I've got it." Galen took me by surprise when he hauled me into his arms and carried me away from the water. "Where is Ned?"

"He's giving chase, but he's had a few boat problems," Aurora replied. "He should be here soon."

"Good." Galen was grim as he sat me down in the shade and grabbed a bottle of water from a cooler he had lodged in the sand. "Drink this." He twisted the top off the bottle and shoved it in my hand. "Drink all of it."

I wanted to argue, tell him that he wasn't the boss of me and then ask about Booker, but I was so thirsty all I could do was guzzle. It tasted better than any gourmet dinner or expensive glass of wine I'd ever come across.

"Thank you," I gasped, water leaking from the corners of my mouth as I wiped my forehead. "I thought I was going to die out there."

Galen gripped the sides of my face and forced me to lock gazes with him. "I will never let that happen. You should've known I would come for you."

"How was I supposed to know that?"

"Because I said so." Galen handed me a second bottle of water. "Drink that. I'll get you to the hospital as soon as possible."

"What about Booker?"

"He's alive."

That wasn't nearly enough reassurance. "Is he going to stay alive?"

Galen didn't immediately answer. Aurora, who was slipping into a tank top and knit shorts, took it upon herself to do it for him.

"He's Booker," Aurora supplied. "He'll survive."

I had no idea what to make of that, so I opted to let it go for the time being. "What happens now?"

"Now I handle Ned," Galen replied, his fingers gentle as they rubbed my shoulders. "I'll take care of Ned and then we'll get you to the hospital. Everything will be fine after that."

"Ned said he had a gun," I offered.

"He did say that," Aurora added. "He was under the deck for a long time. That's what allowed us to get away."

"Did Ned see you?" Galen asked Aurora.

"Yeah. He didn't look happy about it."

"That's because he knows it's over," Galen said. "He's figured out that there's no way for him to get out of this alive."

Alive? Wait .... "Are you going to kill him?"

Galen quirked an eyebrow as he shifted his gaze to me. "Should I let him live after what he's done?"

"No. Yes. I ... aren't you supposed to arrest him?"

"Island justice," Galen replied. "Ned's about to get a heaping dose of it."

"So you'll kill him?"

"He killed May," Galen argued. "He tried to kill you. He left Booker for dead. That's on top of what he did to Bonnie. Why would I let him live?"

"What about a trial?"

"A trial?" Galen challenged. "He's clearly guilty. It's not as if there's any question about it."

I'd never heard a sheriff talk like that before and was understandably thrown. "Still ... shouldn't you at least try?"

Galen's expression softened as he held my gaze. "I understand that this is new for you, but I'm definitely going to kill him. He's earned it. I don't see why we have to waste money on a trial for a guy like him."

"He's right, Hadley," Aurora interjected. "Ned has proved himself to be an abysmal man. He shouldn't live. He can't offer anything to society."

I couldn't argue with that, yet I couldn't allow Galen to become a murderer because of me. "Galen ... ."

"Hadley, don't get worked up about this," Galen ordered, shifting his eyes to the water as the roaring sounds of the boat engine grew closer. "I've got this. I promise."

He stole my breath when he pressed a quick kiss to my mouth. It was barely a touching of lips, something more friendly than passionate, yet he managed to convey a mountain of emotions with the simple act.

"What did you just do?" I exploded. "You can't kiss me in the middle of a life-or-death situation."

Despite the circumstances, Galen smirked. "I believe I just did."

"Yeah, but ... no!"

"Why not?"

"Because that's not how a first kiss is supposed to go," I complained. "There's supposed to be mood music ... and flowers ... and a pretty dress."

"I didn't realize that." Galen shifted so he was in front of me and could watch the water. "I'll know better for next time."

"There is no next time for a first kiss."

"Ah. Well, I'll have to figure out something else then." Galen grabbed Aurora's arm and directed her to the spot next to me. "Stay over here please."

I opened my mouth, another complaint about Galen's timing on my lips, but I realized Ned was climbing out of the boat and my relationship annoyance would have to wait. He clutched something in his hand. I couldn't be sure at this distance, but it looked to be a gun. Fear returned swiftly ... and with a vengeance.

"I changed my mind," I whispered. "You can kill him."

"Shh." Galen patted my shoulder. "It's going to be okay. I promise. Just ... stay here."

I wanted to believe him, so I did as he asked.

Galen drew his weapon from the holster on his hip and fixed Ned with a dark look as the older man struggled up the beach. "That's far enough, Ned."

Ned jolted at the voice. He clearly hadn't realized Galen had joined the party. He must have missed him as Galen crouched next to me in the shade. "What are you doing here?"

"I believe it's called providing law and order."

Ned snorted. "Whatever she told you ... well ... it's a lie. The girl is clearly delusional."

"What about what Booker told me?" Galen challenged.

"I have no idea what Booker could've possibly told you."

"That you stabbed him and kidnapped Hadley."

"Then he's deranged."

"He left the knife on the boat," I offered, waving in that direction. "He had it the entire time we were talking."

"I've got this, Hadley." Galen's tone was cool, dangerous. "Ned, you don't have a lot of options here. Hadley keeps waffling on whether or not she wants me to kill you. I'm leaning toward doing it, quite frankly, but I think she's been through enough for one day.

"If you drop the gun and surrender, I'll take you into custody and make sure you get a trial," he continued. "If you don't, I'll shoot you dead where you stand."

"You have no evidence to take me into custody," Ned scoffed.

"I have enough evidence to charge you with Booker's attempted murder, Hadley's kidnapping and May's murder," Galen argued. "I'll fill in the rest after you're in custody. I doubt it will be difficult."

"And you think I'll just allow that?" Ned's eyes flashed with derangement. "I have a plan. I'm sticking to the plan. I won't allow you to derail the plan."

"You did that yourself when you took Hadley from her home," Galen snapped. "You should've known I would come after you, that I would rip you apart simply for touching her. Now drop that weapon or . . . ."

A gunshot echoed, causing me to jerk my shoulders. I knew Galen didn't fire his weapon because his hand never moved. Galen was moving fast toward the beach, though, and it was evident he was fine.

When I shifted my eyes to the right, to a stand of trees that I hadn't been paying close attention to, I found Wesley stepping through the dense underbrush. He dropped the gun he was carrying at his feet and held up his hands as Galen knelt next to Ned and felt for a pulse.

"He's dead," Galen announced.

"I'm not sorry," Wesley said. "He killed my wife."

Galen stared at him a moment. "I know. I'll still have to take you in for questioning."

"I don't care." Wesley shifted his eyes to me. "Is she okay?"

"Go see for yourself," Galen said. "Leave the gun behind, if you don't mind. I need to confiscate it for evidence."

"I'm fine with that." Wesley forced a smile as he moved in my direction. "You've had a busy few days, huh?" He didn't look upset in the least about ending Ned's life. I guess I couldn't blame him.

"I've had better weeks."

2 9

# TWENTY-NINE

I was just settling down with May's *Book of Shadows* and a glass of iced tea when someone knocked on the door. I'd spent the better part of the previous day answering questions, filling out paperwork and promising Wesley that I didn't hold his vengeful ways against him. In truth, I understood why he did what he did. He might not have been married to May any longer, but that didn't mean she wasn't the love of his life.

I sighed as I shifted the book to the couch and shuffled to the door, widening my eyes when I found Galen waiting on the other side. I hadn't seen him all day – not that I was bitter or anything – and I wasn't sure when our paths would cross again.

"What's up?"

As far as greetings go, it wasn't my best. Still, I didn't want to appear too pleased or eager to see him.

"It's a nice night for a walk, huh?" Galen smiled as I pursed my lips, extending a colorful flower that I couldn't quite put a name to. "I brought you this."

I accepted the flower, unsure what to make of the gesture. "Why?"

"Because I screwed up the other thing and I didn't want you to think I wasn't listening to you."

That was a good answer. Still ... . "So you dropped by to give me a flower?"

"I dropped by to give you a flower and take you on a walk," Galen clarified, gesturing to the front porch. "I'm multi-tasking."

"Oh, well, hmm." I ran a hand through my hair to smooth it. The humidity had done a number on it – again – but there wasn't much I could do to fix it. "Are you sure you want to take a walk? You can come in and have some iced tea if you want to get out of the heat."

"I think that's a nice option for another night, but I definitely think we should take a walk tonight," Galen replied. "I think it will be good for you to get out of the house and enjoy the fresh air ... and we have a few things to talk about."

I didn't bother hiding my groan. "Oh, geez. I hate it when you say stuff like that."

"I know. Why do you think I do it?"

"Just let me put the flower in some water." I was buying time, hoping to slap a bit of makeup on when Galen wasn't looking, but he didn't give me the option.

"Don't worry about the flower." Galen plucked it from my hand and rested it on the small table to my right. "There's more where that came from."

"But ... ."

Galen shook his head, cutting me off. "Come on." He extended his hand. "Let's walk."

I stared at his outstretched hand for a moment, very aware that I was making an important decision if I took it. I'd managed to live a life in limbo for a full week, but now the real world beckoned and things were about to change.

I blew out a sigh as I slipped my hand in his, grabbing my keys from the table and closing the door behind me as I followed. I didn't really have a choice. I knew that. I couldn't walk away, so it was necessary to look ahead.

I fell into step with Galen as he led me down the driveway. He seemed to have a clear destination in mind, so I let him choose the way. I was relieved when he turned away from the busy downtown area, the bar lights twinkling in the night sky, and instead headed down a residential street.

"Where are we going?"

"It's a surprise."

We lapsed into silence, a few shared moments that should've been comfortable. I couldn't bear the long stretches of quiet, though, so I ruined the moment. "How is Booker? I stopped by the hospital to see him this morning, but the intake nurse said he was already gone, and I don't know where he lives."

"I saw him this afternoon," Galen replied. "He's moving a bit slow, but he'll be okay."

"How can he be out of the hospital so fast after what happened?" I challenged. "Shouldn't he be under observation or something?"

"He is under observation."

"Who is observing him?"

"Someone he trusts." Galen flashed me a warning look before turning down another street. "I didn't plan this walk so we could spend the evening talking about Booker. I promise you he's okay. In a few days he'll be as good as new. I'm sure he'll be around to see you then."

I didn't fail to notice that he was leaving out the most important thing, like how Booker could be okay so quickly, but I decided to leave that for another time. "What about Wesley? Are you going to charge him?"

"No."

"Not with anything?"

"He thought you were in danger," Galen said. "He was trying to protect the last member of his family."

I ran the previous day through my head. I was quite a distance from Ned when Wesley fired, and Galen stood between us at the time. "I wasn't in imminent danger."

"Close enough." Galen squeezed my hand. "Do you want Wesley to go to jail?"

"No."

"Then let it go."

"Fine." I blew out a sigh. "So that's it? Everything is done and closed up?"

"We went through Ned's house," Galen said. "We found some of his plans in his office. He's apparently been trying to buy up island property for years."

"To get on the DDA?"

"So it seems."

"I clearly need to know more about this DDA," I muttered.

"We can talk about that another night," Galen said. "It's a boring story."

Somehow I had my doubts. "Okay, but … I'm going to hold you to that. I have a lot of questions."

"Oh, I have no doubt."

"One of them revolves around the shifter on the road the other night. Do you know who that is?"

"No, and with Ned dead, I'm not sure I'll ever find out. I'm willing to hazard a guess that Ned hired whoever it was to either frighten or kill you. I'm searching through Ned's financial records, but I can't find a payment. He probably used cash. I seem to be at a dead end on that one."

"So … it's done."

"It's done," Galen confirmed as he opted for another turn. It was only then that I realized he was leading me toward the cemetery.

"Wait." I slowed my pace. "You're not going to feed me to the zombies, are you?"

Galen's expression was a picture of patience even as his lips curved. "Why would I want to do that?"

"You said I'm a pain in the butt."

"You are."

"So maybe you don't want to deal with me," I suggested. "Maybe you think it will be easier if I'm a zombie and you can lock me in the cemetery."

"It might be easier, but I doubt very much it will be as entertaining." Galen tugged on my hand. "Come on. There's something I want to show you."

He didn't sound angry or even frustrated. Still, I scuffed my flip-flops against the concrete as I followed. "I really don't want to be zombie food."

"You're not going to be zombie food," Galen promised. "In fact, once we're done here, I have every intention of taking you to a nice dinner on the beach."

That was news to me. "You do? I'm not really dressed for the occasion."

"This is an island. You don't need to dress for an occasion."

"Okay, but ... what if I want seafood or something?" I challenged. "Can we go to a restaurant that serves good seafood if I'm dressed like a bum?"

Galen took a moment to look over my outfit. I wore simple cut-offs and a T-shirt – although both were clean – and I was clearly underdressed for a night out. "You look cute."

Instead of taking me to the cemetery's front gate, he led me along the long wall and toward the back of the plot. I followed, understandably curious, and when we rounded the final corner I found he'd set up a blanket and picnic basket on the ground.

"What's this?" I was absurdly touched and a bit suspicious. "Are you going to feed me before they eat me?"

"Ha, ha." Galen released my hand and flicked my ear. "You're definitely a lot of work."

I leaned over and picked through the picnic basket. "Sandwiches and potato salad. I was hoping for seafood ... and you said we were having dinner on the beach."

"We live on an island. There's always seafood available. Also, this entire island is a beach, but I get what you're saying. We'll do that tomorrow, make a big deal out of it and everything."

I cocked an eyebrow. "What makes you think I'm going out with you again tomorrow?"

Galen smirked. "Call it a hunch."

I considered arguing with him, putting up a token fight for form's sake, but I didn't have the energy, and we both knew he was going to get his way. Still, that didn't mean I wasn't curious. "Why did you bring me here?"

"Because you keep stumbling across information in a manner that hurts you and I want to fix that," Galen replied. "The thing is, I can't protect you from all of that. It's going to happen, and I can't possibly keep up with what you know."

"But?"

"But there's something here I know you don't know about and I need you to see it before someone else accidentally tells you or you stumble across the truth yourself." Galen wrapped his hands around my wrist and directed me toward a slot in the wall. "Come on."

For some reason, the shift in his demeanor made me a bit nervous. He still seemed happy and full of life, but there was a darkness flitting around his eyes. I was almost afraid to see what he wanted to show me.

"Look through here." Galen pulled back a sliding cover and revealed a window in the wall.

I balked. "What am I going to see?"

"Something you probably don't want to see, but you need to know, so I'm making sure it happens under the right circumstances." Galen leaned over and plucked a flower from the vase next to the wall. It was the same sort of flower he'd given me twenty minutes before. "Here."

I took the flower, confused. "So these are stolen flowers, huh?"

Galen smirked. "They're pretty, and they remind me of you." He slipped his arm around my waist and positioned me so I was in front of him. "Look."

I gave up fighting the effort and looked through the glass, taking a moment to let my eyes adjust and grimacing when I saw the lumbering zombies moving on the other side of the wall. "I've seen them before."

"Yes, but you haven't really looked." Galen leaned down so his chin rested on my shoulder, his eyes busily scanning faces. Finally he found what he was looking for and pointed to the left. "There."

I followed his finger, unsure what I was supposed to be looking at. My heart skipped a beat when a familiar face popped into view. At first I was sure I was mistaken. I shook my head to clear my vision and stared harder.

After a long time – what felt like forever – I remembered to breathe and let loose a horrified gasp. "That's my mother!"

"I know." Galen stroked the back of my head. "I'm so sorry."

"But … ." I searched my memory. "She was cremated. My father spread her ashes in the Grand Canyon when we visited. I was ten. I remember."

"I don't know about that," Galen said. "You'll have to ask your father. I do know that your mother's body was transported here. It was about seven years ago, not right after she died. That's one of the reasons I always assumed she raised you. I thought she died at that time."

"I don't understand."

"I don't either." Galen's arms were strong as they came around me. "I knew she was in here, and I also knew it was only a matter of time before you found out. I wanted to be the one to tell you, because … well, because it felt as if it should be my job."

I didn't know what to say. My tongue was tied and there was a very good possibility my mind was about to seize.

Galen pressed a kiss to my cheek, drawing me out of my stupor. "I'm really sorry."

I let loose a shaky breath, my eyes never leaving my mother's face. "It's not your fault. You didn't do it."

"No, but I can't help but wonder if I should've told you sooner."

"You told me now." I patted the hand that rested on my midriff. "It's okay." I said the words, but I wasn't sure I meant them. How could any of this be okay?

"You can ask Wesley about it," Galen prodded. "He's bound to know."

"I will." My voice was unnaturally squeaky.

"I'm so sorry." Galen kissed my cheek a second time. "This was a bad idea, wasn't it?"

I opened my mouth to agree, but found myself shaking my head instead. When I turned, the smile I graced him with was small but heartfelt. "No. It was a good idea."

"How can you say that? I saw the look on your face when you saw your mother. That wasn't a happy look."

"You told me the truth." I gripped his hand. "I'm not going to pretend this island doesn't freak me out … that this witch thing isn't going to give me nightmares … and that these zombies aren't unbelievably weird. But this is my home now, and you told me the truth."

Galen relaxed a bit, but his eyes remained guarded. "So now what?"

"Now?" I flicked my eyes to the incredibly odd and yet romantic picnic. "Now we eat the dinner you put together and get to know one another outside of a catastrophe. After that … it's anyone's guess."

Galen's lips curved. "Seriously?"

I nodded.

"That sounds like a great plan." Galen led me toward the blanket. "I brought pie, too."

"Oh, who doesn't love pie?"

"No one I would ever trust with my life … or my heart."

At least we had that in common.

Made in the USA
Middletown, DE
10 January 2023

21854495R00163